A COUNTRY OF ETERNAL LIGHT

A NOTE ON THE AUTHOR

Paul Dalgarno is an author and journalist. He was deputy editor of *The Conversation* (Australia) and a senior writer and features editor at *The Herald* newspaper group (UK). He has written for *The Guardian*, *The Big Issue* and *Australian Book Review*. Born and raised in Scotland, he has lived in Australia since 2010.

A Country of Eternal Light

Paul Dalgarno

First published in Australia by HarperCollins in 2023.
This edition first published in Great Britain in 2023
by Polygon, an imprint of Birlinn Ltd.

Birlinn Ltd
West Newington House
10 Newington Road
Edinburgh
EH9 1QS

www.polygonbooks.co.uk

1

ISBN 978 1 84697 643 8
eBook ISBN 978 1 78885 604 1

British Library Cataloguing-in-Publication Data
A catalogue record for this book is available on request
from the British Library.

Typeset by 3btype.com

For June

What may not be expected in a country of eternal light?
—Mary Shelley, *Frankenstein*

I lie back (have no back) in the bathtub, can almost feel my scarred pink elbows against the sticky white ceramic, the water taking my head.

Excuse me, where are you taking my head?

Just . . . under.

My face submerging, dark hair fanning into filaments.

Open your mouth (I have none), *I'll flood your body* (what body?).

I used to like the hum of being underwater, the pressure it exerted on my eardrums, how it softened other noises, tickled my skin, wrapped like reeds around my midriff. It sounded like a hoover, the frequency, just a little.

As kids, the girls would sit together in their wardrobe with the door shut while I vacuumed their room – said the purr and blackness made them feel safe. Maybe it reminded them of the womb, legs touching through their amniotic sacs, their hands reaching out for each other in my dark wet body.

I drop further under, breathing out (no bubbles), the oblong light of the bathtub way up above, a meconium murk all around. Sirens singing . . . there are none. Mermaids . . . there are none. A heartbeat marking time in the gloom – no heart.

If someone pulls the plug – who would do that? I'd . . . where would I even go? A sewerage plant or straight into the North Sea?

The water wants me but if I kick (no legs), really kick, head pointing up, palms against my thighs, elbows by my side, I'll make it back to the land of, land of –

Keep going, love, that's it, you're doing so well

– the living. I kick, don't know how, but I kick, keep kicking.

Chapter 1

1984

The girls are eight, I think, which puts me at about thirty-four, although I could say thirty-three, even thirty-two – how would you know? And, even if you knew, why would you care? I look good, though. That headband – I loved that orange headband – my T-shirt, that body. My arms, the tops of them, the shoulders, scapulae, the biceps, skin, the vaccine scar and freckles. Would you say they're big, the tops of my arms, or normal? My body looks better than I gave it credit for at the time. As does everyone else's. Big, small, able or with disabilities, those biological bindings are worth their weight in Wagyu beef. Rachel and Eva – they're only eight, so of course they look divine, even with cold sores and those terrible – my fault – haircuts.

I'm not vain. Or I am, but don't want to be, because vanity working on a weak head produces mischief and inadvertently leads to familial catastrophe. Did Jane Austen write that? Or something similar? I used to read a lot, when I had eyes, my weak head trained on the page. I'm less self-regarding now, maybe. *The surest cure for vanity is loneliness* – I read that too, I think. I don't know who wrote it, forget things these days, there are no days. I feel lonely constantly.

I took a night class in literature while Eva was doing her English degree. She was at the proper university, in Glasgow, but we ... we didn't work to the same level, of course not, but we read some good books and looked at exam papers from the big universities, saw what kind of things the students were asked about. Gobbledygook, mostly.

There's an assumption, more prevalent in the past, that working-class people's brains are inferior, making higher education – the mere thought of it – pointless. The pressure comes from your so-called betters, but also from peers, parents and siblings, as if certain words are too big for our mouths and playing with them is an affront. Where did you get those? Return them to the dictionary at once!

My father read me mobile library editions of *Paradise Lost* and *A Scots Quair* when I was barely into double digits, but still, it lingers, the stigma of having airs and graces. By a couple of weeks into my night class, I knew for sure what I'd suspected all along: brains are classless entities and ideas are everyone's for the taking.

It's May, from memory, and I'm joining the girls on their school trip to Slains Castle, just north of Aberdeen. It's a sunny day and relatively warm judging by everybody's attire, and that's just as well because the castle has no roof. Its new owners had it removed in the 1920s to avoid paying land taxes, cutting off their tiles to spite their facias. Sixty years later – and sooner, I'm sure – there's no glass in the windows, no interior beyond exposed staircases and stone walls perched on the edge of a cliff above the North Sea.

For many years, the Irish novelist Bram Stoker took month-long writing retreats in nearby Cruden Bay. He set two of his novels in the village – *The Watter's Mou'* and *The Mystery of the Sea* ... I'd not read those, but I'd read *Dracula*. Hasn't everyone?

Or seen the films, at least? Or the Count in *Sesame Street*? Slains has an unusual octagonal interior hall, a windowless room at the centre of the ruin that must have looked impressive to Stoker and the other celebrities the owners liked to invite to their roofed and decorated baronial lair. *Welcome to my house. Enter freely and of your own will.* In Castle Dracula, the Count leads Jonathan – what's his name, Harkness, Harker? – to a windowless octagonal room. As he says, 'There is a reason why all things are as they are.'

Vampires batted their folkloric wings long before Dracula, of course – some say they morphed from the affliction of porphyria and its symptoms of light sensitivity and pale skin, the gums receding to make teeth look bigger, its sufferers drinking animal blood to stave off anaemia. But there are plenty of midges in Cruden Bay, minuscule gnats with sharp little teeth for chewing through dermis to reach the blood – is that where Stoker's Dracula came from?

Lauren, the girls' teacher, is happy I'm here. She's holding the platter of egg sandwiches I've made, smiling and saying hello to the children as they get on the bus. Sam, our King Charles spaniel, wags his tail at my feet.

'He looks excited,' Lauren says.

'Yes,' I say, 'he's a good boy.'

'OK, you take these, girls,' I say to Eva and Rachel, handing them their bags. Eva's looks like it weighs more, always does. Even at this age, she's the reader of the two, takes books everywhere. Has she read *Dracula*? At eight? Maybe not. But she can quote from books already, has been doing so since she was five. *The Water-Babies* – I didn't like that one, but she could practically recite it from start to finish. Rachel's bag feels virtually empty – I'm guessing a cagoule in case it rains, her pencil case, a banana. Is it fair to call Rachel the feeler of the two? She's sensitive to conflict, but so are Eva and me. In any case, her still, even choppy, waters run deep.

'Can we go on the bus now?' she asks.

'Yep, hop on,' I say. 'I'll be with you in a minute.'

'Will you sit next to me?' Eva asks, her green eyes glinting with just a hint of cold silver.

'Maybe,' I say. 'Just hop on, I'll be there in a second.'

'Would you like me to store these somewhere safe?' Lauren asks, nodding at the platter.

'That'd be lovely, thank you,' I say in my posh voice. I don't call her Lauren in front of the kids because they all call her Mrs Robertson.

The bus is filling, the children sitting in what look like over-sized seats. The sea at Slains, they'd not survive falling in. My two, any time they were near an edge, even without a huge drop … it gave me vertigo just thinking about it, my dizygotic darlings falling to their deaths, plunging into water – help, Mum, help!

Lauren gets onto the coach and I follow, or try to.

'Woah, wait,' the driver says, his hand up, turning in his seat. 'No animals in the vehicle.'

'I'm sorry, I'm not sure I understand,' I say. 'Sam's very well behaved. He can sit on my knee.'

I climb onto the second step, Sam at my heel, see Rachel sitting with her best friend, Barry, Eva across the aisle from them with a space beside her for me and Sam. Keiron, the boy who will pull Eva's hair later that year and get his rib cracked by Rachel, is blowing bubbles with his gum a couple of seats behind. Lauren is doing a headcount, walking down the aisle from the back.

'He just can't come,' the driver says, shooing, actually shooing, Sam and me from the steps with nail-bitten fingers. 'No problem with you coming, but the rules is the rules. No pets on the bus. No dogs, cats, gerbils, piranha fish, full stop.'

Who would take a piranha on a coach? I reverse down the steps, stand with Sam on the street. Rachel peers through the window, looking more concerned for me than embarrassed. Or maybe it's a bit of both.

'I can just sit him on my knee,' I say again from the street. 'He's a good dog, aren't you, Sam?' He was a present from Henry for my thirty-second birthday – so mild-mannered, hardly cast any hair.

'Yeah, I'm sorry,' the driver says. 'As I said, it's . . .'

Lauren's head appears in the doorway, craning from the first row of seats. 'Is there a problem?' She looks at me, at the driver, back at me. She made a prediction once, or said she would. She told the girls – and they later told me – that she could put everyone's names in an envelope with a forecast about where they'd end up in life and she'd be right, because you could tell everything you needed to know about a person by the time they were eight or nine. I don't know if she ever did it or, if she did, whether she ever opened the envelope – I don't know how long she lived, if she's still alive, although she was only in her twenties so she probably is – but I wonder what she would have said about the girls. Eva, that she would go on to live in Spain, become a teacher, that Rachel would flip out, flop in again, make a success of herself in the antipodes. Was that the kind of thing Lauren predicted? Or was it just a figure of speech?

'He's not letting me on with Sam,' I say. 'I don't know what to do.'

I look down at Sam, his tail wagging, his smiling – that's how it looks – face, give Lauren and the driver time to confer, watch her disembark.

'I'm sorry, Margaret,' she whispers. 'He won't budge. Bit of a jobsworth, this one.'

'Oh right, I see,' I say. 'Could you hold Sam for a second?'

'Of course.' She takes the lead from me, shoulders slumping sympathetically.

I get onto the bus, avoiding eye contact with the driver, make my way to the girls.

'They won't let me on with Sam,' I say.

'Oh no. Can you leave him behind?' Rachel asks. 'Maybe tie him to the school gate?'

'We've got a poodle,' her friend Barry says unhelpfully.

'How can I?' I say to Rachel, ignoring Barry. 'That bloody driver . . .'

Eva winces at the swearword – bloody, it wasn't the worst – winces again as I blow her a kiss, worrying more about that than the fact they could fall from the cliff and it'll be the driver's fault. If they tumble into the water – my girls, anyone else's children . . . If Lauren can't keep her eye on everybody and one or two tykes wander off with their yoghurt pots and slip – the grass is waxy there – their broken bodies on the rocks, arms twisted, legs at strange angles . . . It will be the driver's fault, nobody else's. They'll look after each other, the girls, all the children, that's what will happen, they'll have to.

I'm clearly, can see it now, holding in the tears as I wave at them from the street, the bus pulling away.

I walk quickly homewards with Sam, my eyes on the ground – then, I mean, not now. I quite like seeing it all again, even without eyes. The sycamore trees, the park with its big slides, the little shop where you can get four gummy sweets for a penny. It's all so green, much more than I remembered. Less built-up. It's a poor part of the city, one of the most disadvantaged neighbourhoods in Europe apparently, but it doesn't look that way, not really. There's far less graffiti than there will be a few years later, some white dog poo on the ground – you never see that anymore.

I keep my eyes down all the way home, Sam hurrying alongside me, get the keys in the front door, push it open, slam it behind me.

I feed Sam some dog biscuits – 'You eat those, good boy' – and bite into one too, why not? It's red and tastes like, I don't know. I can't remember. It probably tastes of nothing, they never did.

The girls will have to look after each other, keep each other safe, but the house, I can see what I'm thinking – it needs attention. Right now. We've been saying that since we bought it from the council. We would be homeowners when we repaid the bank, thanks to Maggie Thatcher's Right to Buy, a malevolent masterstroke masquerading as opportunity. Give people mortgages and their moral fortitude starts to fade. Win by giving them something to lose. But we felt like winners buying our house – that's how we saw it then and I still do now.

I go out to the shed, grab the stripper from Henry's rusty toolbox – can't quite believe he has a poster in there of a woman tennis player scratching her bum – march back into the house. I could wait for him. He'll be home at lunchtime, always is unless he's under someone's car or in their loft fixing pipes, but I don't want to wait. Why would I wait? It needs to be done post-haste. That bloody bus driver.

I kneel on the living-room carpet, adjust my orange headband, get the blade under a bottom lip of wallpaper, drive it upwards with both hands, cleaving paper and plasterboard. It strips unevenly to shoulder height, and that's clearly fine for now. I move over slightly, still on my knees, do the next bit, and then the next. I pull at the flayed edges like strips of sunburnt skin, get a chair from the kitchen, start shoving and pulling at the higher-up sections. It's a mess. I don't care.

Sam wanders in and looks at me, his tail wagging, sniffs at the tendrils of green paper on the floor, sneezes. Is there asbestos in these walls? Probably. The ironing board is made of it. The swirly Artex ceiling is full of it. The snow decorations we use at Christmas time – asbestos makes them flame resistant.

After the living room, I do the hallway – or the lobby, as we called it back then: the square space at the front door. Strip, scratch, tear, pull. Under the carpet, there was asbestos there too, that's what Maggie sold us – chronic lung conditions disguised as consumer confidence.

Next, I do the stairwell, as high as I can reach. I'm sweating, the apocrine glands drawing navy half-moons on my T-shirt. Sam follows me, sits on the stairs watching, doesn't look uncomfortable, but those back legs, they'll be the death of him. He'll be young still, just eight, and we'll be offered wheels – but wheels, for a dog? Henry will say no and I'll agree. I'll stroke Sam on a table, watch as the vet shaves his leg and injects him with seizure medication. Good boy. I'll be smiling, I'll be trying to, the last face he'll see, his gammy back legs twitching before settling.

The bathroom. I strip that, as much as I can. Henry can help me later. Our bedroom, his and mine, I do that – a petri dish yielding twins and some love ... or lots of love, there was lots ... and certainly lots of snoring, his not mine. The girls' shared room, its curtains mouldy from condensation. Maggie, we'll also take a couple of compromised immune systems – how much would you like for those? It's too babyish, the girls' wallpaper, has to come off. Post. Haste.

The bastard. If anything happens to my kids, I won't be held ... The stupid bloody bastard.

I'm younger now – I'm not saying that to push your Benjamin Buttons. I really am. I must be seventeen or eighteen, one leg crossed neatly over the other on a stool with wheels, wearing a headset and poking a plug into a switchboard. It's the Aberdeen Telephone Exchange, where we sound posher than most Aberdonians. For some of the 'hello girls' – that's what they called us – it's a professional necessity. They'll say, *Good afternoon – long-distance operator, how may I help you?* as if they have marbles in their mouths. As soon as the call's connected, they'll slip effortlessly back into Doric, the local language. I don't do that because I was taught by my parents to speak properly.

It wasn't until I was in my forties that I properly questioned this, and by then it was hard to kick the haughty habit. I understood Doric, of course I did. It's what nearly everyone spoke, and I also spoke it sometimes, just not very often. Boys were *loons*, girls were *quines*. 'How are you?' was *Fit like*? Or *Foos yer doos*? *Far ye gan*? was 'Where are you going?' and Far'v ye bin? was 'Where have you been?' A nice dusk was a *bonny gloamin* and bumblebees were *foggy bummers*. It was called Doric after the Doric dialect of Ancient Greek, a rustic and unrefined variant of the language that was used in prestige settings, if at all, by the chiding chorus in Greek tragedies. And that's how my parents and other parents viewed it, a tragic, unrefined tic to be tweezed or skelped out of their children's heads. But it was political, that's what I eventually learnt. The Queen's English mattered more on account of it being the Queen's English. James VI of Scotland commissioned the King James Bible in English not Scots because he was also James I of England.

It was all about boosting Englishness by devaluing every-thing and everyone else. That's why I never wrote or said *an historic* after the age of forty-five. In Aberdeen we pronounced the 'h', but they didn't in south-east England, the seat of cultural and political power. That's why they said *an*. I said and wrote *a historic* for perfectly valid sociopolitical reasons – even though no one gave a flying monkey's.

Not that any of this is on my mind as a late-teens telephonist with a blouse that must have been fashionable at the time but now looks too flouncy. My legs. I won't go on about them, or maybe I will – I'm just saying they look good, my legs.

It's my job to connect people with other people they want to speak to, long distance, mainly, overseas.

Am I in a position to listen to their conversations after creating the circuit through which they commune? Yes. Do I ever do it? Yes, all the telephonists do. But we have to be careful as we've all signed the Official Secrets Act and will be sacked on the spot if we're caught.

My friend Barb is working next to me with the same headset and virtually the same hairstyle. We started here on the same day, Barb my senior by a year. She nudges my arm, winks, points to one of the holes in the switchboard. She wants me to plug in and listen to the call she's just connected.

I look over my shoulder for Mrs Harding, or Vinegar Tits as the other women call her, our supervisor. She's at the end of the row, far from us. I plug in.

I can't hear now what I'm hearing then but can see my face and Barb's lighting up. It could be an apology call – there were lots of those and they were always entertaining. They rarely started with the actual apology, but you could tell one was imminent. Contrition has its own cadence. Typically, the caller would ask how the person on the other end was getting on. The response was almost always muted or defensive. From there, sometimes at great length, the caller would circle in nervously to their reason for calling. They were sorry – for an argument they'd had, for stealing something, for not taking the other person seriously, for the death of a loved one they should have been looking after. That last one, nobody ever said that, not on my watch. Sorry. It was a small word, a treacherous sea.

More likely this one's a dirty call, judging by the blush creeping over Barb's face and mine. There were lots of those too, including, I shouldn't say this, but who cares, between high-profile public figures, even royalty. Like the rest of us, they craved, could be depraved. I once heard a man who may or may not have been a prince refer to someone's pulchritudinous décolletage. At home, I looked both words up in the dictionary and even then it made no sense.

Sometimes callers even craved us, the operators. What knickers were we wearing? What colour were they? I never knew. Mint. Maybe sage. *Oh. Hang on. Please keep talking, anything, say something, please, your knickers. Oh. Oh my god.*

Barb and I look at each other, eyes goggling, and pull our jacks out at the same time. She laughs so loud it catches the attention of Mrs Harding, who comes over. I'm laughing too, can't help it, but Mrs Harding hasn't seen it and we both get a lid on it before she arrives. It's not easy. I laughed a lot as a young woman, was full of joy, Barb too, she loved a laugh.

'What's going on?' Mrs Harding asks.

'I'm terribly sorry,' Barb says. 'A long-distance caller just told me a funny joke about a man and a–'

'We're not here to be entertained,' Mrs Harding says. 'We're here to assist people, is that clear?'

'Of course,' Barb says. 'I'm sorry, Mrs Harding.'

Mrs Harding lingers and it's not until she leaves that we can relax and have a giggle again, mindful that she might look back at us at any second.

Chapter 2

2014

The bedtime stories Rachel tells her boys are about things that have happened, things she or they would like to happen, things – in one way or another – she is scared will happen. Like all myth, their purpose is to tie people to people, and people to place – the way the details contort over time can be logical or illogical. That doesn't matter.

They mostly star two boys, Ilya and Alyosha, and are open to requests.

'Can it have lollipops in it?' William might ask.

'And balloons,' Ewan might say.

'And poo,' William might counter. They love faecal matter, those boys, can't get enough of it.

Ilya is five like William, Alyosha three like Ewan, their ages changing in line with the boys'. The length and complexity of the stories depends on how tired Rachel is, how late it is, and how much of the story is a rehash of previous Ilya and Alyosha adventures.

Right now, she's tired, her eyes, her slumping shoulders, you can just see it. She didn't need to have kids . . . but that's not helpful. People said the same to me – I didn't need to have kids, especially two at once. As if I'd not only chosen to procreate but had expressly requested twins with a side of gestational diabetes. In Rachel's case, it was more planned – completely planned and paid for, in fact – but she still deserves sympathy.

She's the one who changes the boys' pyjamas and bedclothes in the middle of the night when they wet their beds and cry out, even though Gem, her wife, is woken too. I like Gem, love her even, but to me that's unfair. Both boys mewl sometimes because they're filled with mucus. They're edging towards the winter equinox and their house holds cold more efficiently than heat, its front door rattling as Melbourne tries to sneak its way in. Gem, I should say, is an architect and is overseeing an extension to their house, so she could probably deal with the draught if she wanted.

Even without the boys crying, Rachel often wakes with a start and sits up in the darkness, breathing rapidly, holding her jaw – she's ground her teeth for years, decades, it's a wonder there are any teeth left. Her eyes are lined like mine, dark brown like mine, they scare, stare and settle like mine. I know what she's thinking in those moments, or feel like I do. Stones, chairs, bottles – these are inanimate objects that exist as part of the world. Rabbits, fish, people – they're powered by a force they've been granted but don't own, that can be employed only until it leaves of its own volition, at which point those rabbits, fish and people no longer exist autonomously. Is that even what she's thinking? Is it close?

Or is she thinking about trees and how, in Buddhist philosophy, trees don't exist, can't exist, are actually just a confluence of air and sunlight, water and earth, a meeting point of elements, a natural and illusory knot. If they fall in a forest, nobody will hear them because forests don't exist and neither do people beyond the fiction – or friction – of the self. *And all the lives we ever lived and all the lives to be are full of trees and*

16

changing leaves. The Dalai Lama wrote that, or Virginia Woolf, I forget which.

I don't know what Rachel's thinking, can't read minds. But she does scribble notes on the pad next to her bed before falling back under. Sometimes it's a single word – anima, animus – and I wonder why she's written it.

She kneels on the carpet between the boys' beds, William's feet and Ewan's head with just an arm-span between them, tells them that once upon a time there were two boys called Ilya and Alyosha who lived in the Fantastic Forest. One day, Ilya went out to chop some wood for the fire, to keep his family warm.

Gem has her legs crossed on the floor, her head propped on one of her hands, curly, coily hair corkscrewing through her fingers. The boys look at her dreamily, at Rachel.

'Ilya stopped at a beautiful tree he'd never seen before. It was gigantic and would give them firewood for years. He spat on his hands, swung the axe behind his head, and heard–'

'No, no, no,' Ewan says, anticipating.

'Ilya turned round to see who had spoken but–'

'There was nobody there,' William says.

'That's right,' Rachel says. 'But there was a bird, a beautiful bird, who told Ilya that this tree was the Augury Tree and he shouldn't chop it down. At the top, way up through the clouds, there were amazing things, beyond Ilya's wildest dreams. He should climb up, he would see. Ilya dropped his axe, spat on his hands again, and started climbing. Holding onto one branch then another, he got faster and faster until he was climbing as quickly as he ever had.'

'That must be really fast,' Gem says. 'He's such a good climber.'

'Really fast,' Rachel says. 'And then, to go even faster,

he started farting as hard as he could, shooting up one branch for every fired-up flatus.'

'Gross, love,' Gem says, but Rachel knows her audience. Both boys are laughing, blowing raspberries. I hope this is a passing phase. 'OK, enough now,' Gem says.

'He turned and saw his house,' Rachel says. 'So small, so far below, with smoke coming from the chimney. The fire, he thought. My family. Soon, he was up above the clouds and noticed something funny on his hands.'

'A feather,' Ewan says.

Rachel winks, nods. 'And then another feather, and another. He rubbed the back of his neck because it was itchy and found more feathers, and realised–'

'He was turning into a bird, squawk, squawk,' William says, flapping his arms.

Gem laughs, Rachel and Ewan too.

'The talking bird from the forest was hovering beside him,' Rachel says. 'It told Ilya he was safe and could let go of the Augury Tree. Ilya was scared – but his hands had changed into tender claws and he couldn't hold on much longer. He let go and started falling, then he waved his arms about and . . . he was flying! Oh, he loved it! He soared this way! He soared that way! He was happy, he was free . . . flapping–'

'My tummy hurts,' Ewan says.

'Aw, does it, mate?' Rachel rubs his stomach, kisses him on the nose. Gem moves closer to William, crosses her legs again, strokes his forehead.

'One day, a long time later, Ilya was back in the forest, flying around, when he saw a boy coming towards him carrying an axe and a basket. It was his brother, Alyosha, looking older and bigger than before. Alyosha stopped in front of a tree – the Augury Tree – and swung the axe behind his back. Ilya shouted–'

'No, no, no,' William says. 'But Alyosha only heard–'

'Tweet, tweet, tweet,' Ewan says.

'Alyosha ignored the strange bird. He swung the axe as hard as he could – whack, whack, whack. When he had cut the Augury Tree to the ground, he chopped it into little pieces and carried the wood basket home. Ilya followed him to the cabin and perched outside on the windowsill looking in. His mummies were sitting by the fireside with droopy heads and looked as if they'd been upset for a very long time. Ilya tapped on the windowpane with his beak, but they didn't hear him. Alyosha threw the wood from the Augury Tree onto the fire. The flames were so bright! His mummies smiled and stroked his hair. Ilya flew up to the roof and sat on the edge of the chimney, feeling warm and sad.

'The end.'

Gem looks . . . is she relieved?

Ewan claps half-heartedly. William stares at the ceiling. Neither boy looks particularly drowsy.

'It's late,' Rachel says. 'Off to sleep now. Mummy loves you.'

'I love you, Mummy,' Ewan says.

'I hate you, Mummy,' William says.

2014

Oil-rig-bound helicopters take off and land, spreading choppy white noise. I like the sound, of course I do, but no . . . I don't like helicopters, I hate them really, I don't know why. Because they look stupid, maybe, especially the Chinooks. They're filled with men, mostly, heading off or returning from two weeks in the North Sea, where they are paid handsomely but never enough for what could happen and has happened before.

The noise they make lulls and sensitises me all the same, I can't help it. I'm sleepy, could sleep, can't sleep, have thrown up into a bowl, will need to empty it.

I'm in my car behind the main airport carpark, don't want to pay. Champ is lying with his head on his front paws on the back seat. On the radio, quiet under the hum of the helipad, a man and woman are discussing the referendum, saying it's only three months away. Independence – I like the idea, won't live to see the reality, more's the pity.

Eva knows where to find me – I waited here last time – and she'll have landed by now, must have. I try calling her but her phone rings out. I look a little annoyed, will find her eventually in the pick-up zone where I expressly told her not to wait. She'll look shivery because it's significantly colder here than in Spain, summer be damned.

I'll roll down the window. 'Hi, dearie, have you been waiting long?'

'Just half an hour or so.' She'll smile reluctantly and scan the car for Rachel, who isn't with me – she arrived a few days ago and was going to come but said she had a headache. We've all had headaches – stabby, hypnic, psychosomatic, fake. I don't need the girls to get on, necessarily, but I don't want them to not get on, have had enough of that for a lifetime.

'I was parked over there,' I'll say, but she'll be distracted by my voice and how strange it sounds.

Champ will headbutt the back window, thrash his tail, bark and I'll try to calm him while Eva gets her suitcase into the boot. Dogs smell it, the death, that's what they say. Did Champ? And, if so, was it my ending or his own he was smelling?

When Eva gets in and reaches to hug me, she'll see the bowl in my lap with liquid – some clear, some black. She'll notice – how could she not? – how much bigger my legs are now, each one nearly as wide as my emaciated top half, as if I'm a reflection in a funhouse mirror.

'How are you, Mum?' she'll ask.

'Yeah, fine,' I'll say. 'How was your flight? Can you pass me that bottle, please?'

I'll gulp down some Irn-Bru, my cheeks billowing, sagging back into their hollows.

'Do you want me to drive?' she'll ask.

'No, I'm fine.'

I'll check the side mirror, pull out, feeling suddenly conscious of my pocked hands on the steering wheel, my concentration-camp wrists, my ankles spilling across the sides of my unlaced trainers.

'God, my teeth were sticking to my lips,' I'll say, my voice back to normal. 'Now, how are you?'

'I'm OK,' she'll say. 'I'm more concerned about you.'

'I've actually been feeling pretty good. I don't know why I threw up. It's probably just a bug.'

'How's your leg?'

I told her about it before she left Spain. Champ jumped up on me playfully, punctured me accidentally, and I've been leaking oedema ever since.

'It's fine, dearie. I got a fresh— Oh, you bloody idiot.' A driver will overtake us, swerve back in front of us to avoid oncoming traffic. 'The nurse put a fresh bandage on last night.' We'll pass billboards advertising oil companies, another with Aberdeen's civic motto: *Happy to meet, sorry to part, happy to meet again.*

I was happy to see Eva and Rachel, would be sorry to part, unhappy to never see them again.

She'll gawp through the windscreen, her head swimming, no doubt, not knowing what to say. The trees, bushes and grass were nicer than Spain's – in my opinion, anyway. Those poplars

21

in Madrid, they had nothing on our elms, although many of the elms, like me, were diseased.

'Does Juan know you've arrived?' I'll ask. Juan is Eva's new boyfriend. I've seen his picture but never met him, never will.

'Not yet, no, the WiFi . . .'

'Use my phone,' I'll say, nodding at the glove tray.

We'll drive along Anderson Drive and see people in their T-shirts mowing their lawns, memories splattering the windscreen.

'He's not answering,' she'll say. 'He must be busy.'

Juan was a teacher like Eva, taught at the same international school. He was younger than her by two years – a toy boy, very handsome too. Lots of stubble, though; I wouldn't like that. Henry, when he grew a patchy beard once, or on our caravan trips when he was too lazy to shave – it caused a rash that would last days.

We'll drive past what for a time was Henry's Handyman Services, the pinnacle of Henry's career and, for a while, my workplace too, past the turn-off to the girls' childhood home.

'Does Dad know yet?' Eva will ask. 'I mean, how serious it is.'

'Yeah, the basics,' I'll say. The traffic will be light and Eva will be home again, home again, jiggety-jig, Rachel too. My girls, returning to watch me leaving. 'I wonder how he's doing, poor sod,' I'll say as we drive past the turn-off for the mental hospital.

2014

Gem waves and holds her hands up apologetically as she approaches Rachel and the boys at the Royal Children's

22

Hospital. They're sitting on teal chairs beside a red, black and orange sculpture that might be a sea creature or an ant, it's quite abstract. It will be an hour, maybe longer, before the staff can see Ewan and put a cast on his fractured wrist. Rachel has the X-rays in a big radiology envelope on her lap. They're more flexible, young bones, tend to bend under pressure, but they can break too.

'Sorry,' Gem says to Rachel. 'I couldn't get away from work.' She looks good in her fancy pants and cashmere winter coat, very professional. Rachel, in a grey beanie and pilled green scarf, less so. 'How long have you been here?'

'Too long,' William says.

'Not long at all,' Rachel says. 'It was a nightmare getting parked.'

'And how's that wrist?' Gem asks Ewan. 'Good,' he says, shrugging.

'Why don't you and William head home for a bit,' Gem says to Rachel. 'I can call you when we're done here.'

'Are you sure, love?' Rachel asks.

'Please, Mummy,' William says.

I was with them when it happened – not in a corporeal sense. They were in the hills near Lake Eildon, at the weekend house Gem's parents, Tash and Pete, bought with two other couples.

They were sitting round an outdoor fire, the adults, while William and Ewan played nearby on their bikes.

'So, yeah, that's what we're thinking, maybe moving to Spain,' Gem said.

To be closer to Eva, that must be why, although Gem didn't say that and Rachel looked content for Gem to do the talking. She wanted to be closer to her sister, for the boys to be closer to their aunt, maybe because I was dying and she was reassessing her life choices, there was nothing wrong with that. She hadn't told me, but that was OK. She would have wanted it to be a surprise.

Tash dragged a serrated knife through a salad roll, passed it to Pete. He stared at it, gave a plaintive sigh. His diet had taken a hit since his mesenteric excision, his digestive system wasn't what it used to be.

'Spain, love?' Tash replied, scooping out an avocado. 'What if the boys get sick or, you know, have an accident?'

'They have hospitals there,' Rachel said.

That's when William shouted, 'Ewan!' and everyone looked around, me included, and saw Ewan tearing down a dirt hill on his little bike with its training wheels, his legs out, laughing, and for a second – not even a second – it felt like maybe he'd be held upright and safe by something bigger than him, bigger than any of us. Rachel was already scrambling down the hill by the time the front wheel collided with a stone and he cartwheeled through the air.

His silence wasn't followed by the usual wailing – just soft sobs, measured sniffles. He was belly-down, looking at his arm. Pete laughed – what was he thinking? – as he came down behind Rachel, followed by Gem, Tash and William. I looked on, did nothing at all. But I would if I could. I'd die for you, Rachel, and those boys.

'This is bad,' Rachel said, kneeling next to Ewan. 'I know,' Gem said, holding Ewan's head.

'Why did you let him do this?' Rachel asked William. 'That was stupid, William, really stupid.'

'I'm sure he meant no harm,' Pete said. 'Ewan's a daredevil, that's all.'

Rachel shot him a look I knew well, shot the same one at William, a direct hit. She had four shots left in the barrel, enough to take out everyone there.

They would never go to Spain. The travel gods were angry with them – they had spoken.

At the house, Tash got some gauze from a first-aid kit and gave it to Gem, who set about wrapping Ewan's wrist in a tight figure-of-eight. Pete lifted him from Rachel's lap, laid him on the sofa, covered him with a blanket.

Rachel and William are in the car now and Rachel's anger is a distant memory for her, and hopefully for William too. Siblings. They had to look after each other – I'm sure that's all she meant by it. She drives back to Brunswick with him and they agree to go for a pizza. The place they choose, I recognise it, went there with them on my one visit to Australia, managed a coffee, nothing else. They make the coffee strong in Melbourne, give it funny names. They're seated quickly and she helps take off William's hat and gloves.

My darling William. It's exciting for him, the pizza, being out with Rachel, the fizzy orange drink, the whole experience. I can see that. It's exciting for me to be there too. I would ask questions if I could. How is prep going? Who are your friends? Would you like Grandma to sing you a lullaby? How about 'I See the Moon'?

After eating, they agree to walk around the block slowly, looking in the windows of closed shops, their breath coming out as steam in the cold air. They stop outside a tattoo parlour that's still doing business, watch a man on a reclining chair being inked.

'Can I get one, Mummy?' William asks. He loves his tattoos, the stick-on kind. He loves Rachel's too. She has his name, Ewan's name, some others, I think, I've never seen.

'They're forever,' Rachel says. 'Not the stick-on ones. Do you want to have one that lasts forever?'

'I do, I really do,' he says.

'You just can't,' Rachel says. 'You're too young.'

'But Mummy . . .'

'You just can't, mate.'

William relents grumpily. In a few days his mother will be in Scotland, visiting me, his grandma who he'll never see again, except on FaceTime, during which he'll get bored, put on silly voices, mope out of view, run away.

Chapter 3

I'm running along the Esplanade with damp hair, in training. I've recently turned thirty-five – my claret velour two-piece, a birthday present from Henry, still looks new. This is the first time I've seen it with my body inside, in motion, and I'm not unhappy with how they look, the tracksuit and my body. Shorts and a T-shirt wouldn't block the chill rolling off the water, even less so the bits of me swelling and crashing. The sea is grey-green, a philodendron uprooted and laid out under dull pearl skies.

I say running because jogging sounds too fancy, even now. But I'm in expensive – it's all relative, isn't it – jogging shoes and I'm moving forward much like a novice jogger might. I've already been passed by three runners, two men and a woman, each of whom said hello as if we were one of a kind, likeminded in our choice of locomotion.

'That's nearly a mile,' Henry shouts. He's in his big white Transit van, over my right shoulder, supporting me as he's done every Sunday morning since the start of the year. My face is the colour of a robin's breast, my eyes focused and tense.

The girls are at home, I assume, watching *E.T.* or *The King and I* on VHS. Or maybe they're at my parents' house, ciggie smoke cladding their lungs with hydrogen cyanide.

The traffic, what little there is, has to crawl along below the speed limit – it's not very fast, and neither am I.

'You're doing great,' Henry shouts, his hazard lights on, before turning to flick the Vs at someone in an Astra who revs aggressively and toots as he passes.

I'm loping slightly, some pain just under the ribcage, my left elbow tucking in, a bird with a sore wing. I don't want to make a big deal of it. Sam's in the van, too, I suppose, though I can't see him. The girls – I wish I could see them, would rather be with them than here – don't have a say. Hello, just popping by. You both fine? How's *E.T.*?

'How you feeling, Marg?' Henry shouts as I approach the Bouley turn-off.

'Fine,' I shout, panting, clearly lying.

I've committed to a five-mile charity run in July with our neighbour Alison, whose tickly cough will turn out to be cancer, and I don't want to let her down. I won't. We'll finish the run in a respectable time and have tea and scones to celebrate. Alison will lose her hair in September, find a wig in October, have a funeral in November, but I don't know that yet.

From memory, I'm less than pleased with Henry stalking along behind me. Sometimes I quite liked it because it kept the sexual predators away, hypothetical or otherwise, but on the whole, it wasn't very helpful.

'You're doing well,' he says again.

I don't turn round. My stitch, my breathing, needs to settle. I'm up against the pain barrier, have to push through. At least that's what my father always told me. He used to run, won the Hill Race at the Highland Games several times back in nineteen-oatcake. The pain barrier was like the sound barrier and once you broke it, everything would be quieter and easier. Like being on Concorde over the Atlantic just after the sonic boom, I imagine – yes, please, I'll have some strawberries with my champers and, by the way, what's the temperature in Manhattan today? Post-stitch, I'll be supersonic. As it is, it looks like my heart is a jellyfish stinging my chest.

'Pick up the pace,' Henry says.

'OK,' I say. What a pain in . . . my side and chest, mostly. Henry was a cox in the Navy, had a yummy swimmer's body for years, knows the motivational lingo for us sporty types. Now he's the sole trader of Henry's Handyman Services – and maybe that's why he likes coming with me. His stencilled van is a slow-moving billboard for his lifting, cutting, papering, wiring, sanding, hammering, welding, callusing, tiring nine-to-five. My stitch is easing, I can see it in the way I'm running.

Henry keeps track of my distance on the odometer. When I hit the one-and-a-half-mile mark he'll let me know, and I'll turn round and head back to the Links. Or stop before that if I just can't do it. Like now, I could stop now – why don't I? We could have a cold drink at the Inversnecky, head home early, see my parents or sit on the sofa with the girls.

'No shame in giving up,' Henry says.

'Right, thanks,' I say.

I canter slowly, inside myself, probably trying to put Henry and everything else out of my mind. My vibrating denture plate – ignore that. My ballooning knees – ignore them. The groin chafing – ignore it. The two teenagers laughing at me as I pass – ignore them, their mohawks, the acne round their mouths that makes me suspect they're glue-sniffers. I'm running, that's what I'm doing, all that matters.

Waves foam into the pier, I watch them, the whitecaps, keep going, keep going. You had to be careful around water, on it, under.

'That's it,' Henry calls. 'One point five. Let's head back to Dodge.'

Wasn't getting out of Dodge what you were supposed to do? As in, let's get the hell out of Dodge? I don't think you were meant to head back once you'd made it out.

Henry does a U-turn, quickly, expertly, his eyes on the tarmac briefly before locking back onto me. Watching him as a young man on the water, calling time to his rowing team, I'd been surprised by the love I felt, and by the coach, who cycled along the riverbank barking instructions through a megaphone. Wasn't he worried about falling off, riding one-handed like that, not even watching where he was going half the time? Was Henry hardwired to be the same? A dog, and me his bone.

Because he was the cox, he was always the first to hold the trophy when his team won. Everyone – but me especially – applauded as he raised it above his head, lowered it, took his medal. The eight men in his crew took their turns lifting the trophy and gathering their medals too, and we'd applaud each one, even though it always got boring after the first two. As the last man accepted his medal, they would grab Henry and lift him by the legs and underarms. They'd get him to the water's edge, bare feet on the bright green grass, and everyone would laugh, including me. I knew he'd be all right, probably, but what if they threw him and he hit a rock, broke his spine, spent his life having to blink once for yes, two for no?

They'd start the countdown – three – swinging him like a ragdoll – two – even higher, the momentum building – one – and then Henry was airborne, a study in angular velocity, his arms and legs waving, before crashing into the water. Cheers from everyone. For he's a jolly good fellow. And as he surfaced and swam gracefully back to the shore, I'd start cheering too.

I'm heading north, into the wind, and it's much harder, by the looks of things – my grimace could launch a thousand ships, have men jumping from the oil rigs, those poor men.

'I think you might be slowing a bit,' Henry says. His tone is friendly, but really, what a thing to say.

'Thanks,' I shout over my shoulder. 'You're not helping.'

I pick up my pace, as if the wind resistance is negligible. The girls, they'll be proud of me, or maybe they won't. But at least I'm practising what I preach: the trying, that's what counts in the end. And being there for each other. Lending a hand when a loved one is sinking, pulling them up from the depths.

'We can stop for a 99,' Henry says.

It's tempting, of course it is. I nod, and seem to be considering it, a little break, yes, a tutti-frutti or a 99 would be nice, but look at my feet, my legs, I'm moving quicker than I was before, stitch be damned; stiff northerly, eat my dust.

Henry hasn't noticed yet or if he has, he's not saying. It probably doesn't register on the Transit's speedo but it's registering with me. I'm through the pain barrier. Boom. I've smashed right through it. New York, here I come.

Henry has to brake to let a campervan negotiate a parking spot near the Bouley turn-off. He probably expects me to jog on the spot, waiting, but clearly I'm not doing that. I'm speeding up. Just knowing, just seeing, that he's had to pause puts wind in my sails.

The last half-mile back to the Links is usually a slog but, as my velour tracksuit bottoms flap around my calves and my trainers pound the pavement, I can see that, by my own standards, I'm sprinting.

I look over my shoulder quickly: Henry still hasn't caught up, and for a second, maybe more than a second, it seems he won't. This must be adrenaline. My arms slicing up and down

31

through the air, my knees coming up higher with every step, leaning into the wind, jaws gritted, pupils dilated. My heart must be going like the clappers, lactic acid flooding my muscles, lungs labouring, but I don't look uncomfortable. Au contraire – my legs are propelling me.

I have the Links entrance in sight by the time Henry draws nearly level with me – I know the sound of the engine, don't need to turn round.

'Jesus Christ, Marg, what's got into you?' he shouts, his voice whipped in the wind. 'Want to slow down a bit?'

'Not really,' I shout, powering ahead. I don't want to slow down, Henry. Not now, not ever. I look so light and happy and free.

2020

What a racket. I'm in Madrid, at night, on Eva's balcony. Juan is clinking an empty wine bottle with his keyring. Eva is applauding, as are her immediate neighbours and people on other balconies. Air horns are honking, dogs barking. It looks like Hogmanay but there are no fireworks, at least none I can see or hear. Maybe they don't do that in Spain.

'*Qué bueno*,' Juan says, clanking the empty Rioja as if his life depends on it.

'*Sí, increíble*,' Eva says. Her accent sounds good to my untrained ear. My father and Eva were blessed when it came to foreign languages. I like the Spanish words that look and sound like their English counterparts. *Increíble. Religión. Televisión*.

Do they have babies yet, Juan and Eva? I can't see any, but they could be in the apartment, sleeping – I don't know how – through the almighty stramash. Or have they given up?

Exhausted their options? Ungirded their loins? She looks younger than her forty-odd years but that's superficial. As I always said, it's what's on the inside that counts.

A man walks a dog along the street below, the lead hooked through a belt hoop on his jeans. He's clapping as he goes and wearing a surgical face mask, must be unwell.

'*Gracias a los enfermeros*,' shouts a woman from one of the balconies above Eva's.

'*Sí, gracias a todos*,' Juan shouts. He curls a hairy olive arm around Eva's waist from behind and I feel a bit voyeuristic – of course I do, they don't even know I'm here, I may as well be in their wardrobe peering through a peep hole – but it's nice to see them being affectionate and also to have a moment's respite from Juan's incessant clinking. Eva stops clapping, turns and hugs him and they kiss, oh, it's quite passionate, I can see some tongue, even though they're standing out in the open. That's maybe the Spanish way, but I think I should look elsewhere.

I don't know what I'm doing here, and by here I mean here, there and everywhere, hopping from disembodied present to living past as if I have a foot with which to hop, a spare locomotive mechanism to employ when the first leg tires. If I was of a Catholic bent, I might think of it as a staycation in my non-existent human form, a chance for some housekeeping of my venial sins – all that Dante stuff with rivers and she-wolves. But I'm culturally Episcopalian, raised on scripture, tradition and reason, the most reasonable position being that Jesus Christ is both fully human and fully God, that he lived, died, rose, died, lives, and that we're practically unsalvageable thanks to our precorrupted souls. The strongest memories from my churchgoing childhood are the polished dusty smell of the pews, picking scabs from my knees and eating them, the smooth wooden handles and plush burgundy velvet of the offering bag, that there were words but no pictures on the walls, laments but no laughter in the songs.

I borrowed Dante from the library when Eva was in Glasgow, Rachel in London, and was transported by its playful imagery – a Hell that's cone-shaped like a poke of chips, rivers that circle downwards like a helter-skelter before joining an ice rink, or iced lake, that imprisons the Devil. And threes, there were so many of those – three rivers, three beasts in the forest, a dog with three heads, all of it rendered in three-line stanzas in three main sections that each have thirty-three cantos.

The pre-Christian Pythagoreans were also three-huggers, put the number on a pedestal, or tripod, above all others, saw it as the beginning, middle and end of everything. They also believed in transmigration of the soul, that we were trapped in a continuous cycle of death and reincarnation, and that breaking wind should be avoided at all costs because it let the soul escape.

Preceding them, but not by much, Thales of Miletus made a case for water as the be-all and end-all of creation. Water made the universe, was what the world floated on, our watery selves waving to each other in a cosmos of liquid, vapour and ice. It was a radical position to take six hundred years before Jesus in that it gave no role to the Olympian – or any other – gods, whetting and wetting an appetite for science over superstition. But where would we be without a touch of superstition? Probably not with Dante, sailing from scene to scene – *The little vessel of my genius hoists sail, and leaves behind a sea so cruel.*

Dante himself is the narrator in the *Divine Comedy*, having been granted permission, it seems, to undertake a journey that's ultra-mundane – outside the known world – for the purpose of ethical and religious enlightenment. And maybe that's how it is for me too – I'm on a divine mission (I don't believe in divinities) that is ultra-mundane (it can be that sometimes, it's true) for the purpose of . . . Is there a purpose? I don't know. I really don't. Maybe I can save someone? Save myself? Send myself an SOS: ...---...

Eva and Juan have uncoupled their unctuous mouths, thank god.

Two young women amble up the street in the opposite direction to the dog walker, cheering and waving their arms. It's quite the party. They're wearing face masks too.

It might be Halloween, although who cheers and hollers on All Hallows' Eve?

2014

I'm still alive. That's probably what I'm thinking, what I often thought on mornings like this, taking Champ for his walk.

Some days I walk all the way from the house, up into the Gramps, down the other side of Kincorth Hill, back to the house, but that's unrealistic today. I've driven with Champ to the foot of the hills and parked – I look heavily pregnant, my legs bipedal blimps.

It can't be much later than five in the morning, that's my guess, but it will have been light for a couple of hours already.

Champ runs in circles, his chocolate coat shining, urges me, *Come on, come on, let's go, it smells so good, we might see a rabbit, a deer, come on, get my lead on, or don't, I don't care, but please, for the love of Anubis, let's get going.*

'You go ahead,' I say, pointing at the dirt path that leads up the hill.

He runs, stops, looks back at me, smiles, bounds past some trees and out of sight.

It'll take me a while to get up today, but there's no rush.

I enjoy the pop and scrape of dirt and boulders under my Frankenfeet, the aural dance of leaves and breeze, the tepid sun lifting dew from bracken, birch and heath. I can't breathe – no, I can, I'm fine, I just have to take it easy. Champ comes running back down the hill to make sure I'm on my way, wags his tail and tears off again, content.

People say if they knew they were dying, they'd dive headlong into their bucket list – snorkelling in the Seychelles, a genital piercing, visiting the Taj Mahal – but I don't want anything more than this, right now – the Gramps on a fine summer morning, bees in the gorse, me and Champ. If I can bend far enough to get one, I'll throw him a stone up top and he'll chase it excitedly, if not as quickly as he did when he was a pup.

I stop for a second, hold a quiet branch, catch my breath. It's not far now. I remember what day it is, I think. If I'm right, Rachel will be on her way to Tullamarine Airport already and will arrive tomorrow, Eva will be here from Madrid by the end of the week. Will they be nice to each other? I hope so.

I keep walking, stopping, walking again, find Champ at the picnic spot entrance. He runs over to me as I sit in slow motion on the bench – there are fire marks on it, hooligans. I pat his head.

The grass around the miniature headstones has been recently cut. They're not real, the headstones, nobody is buried here – they're commemorative only. I could look, have read them all before, but that's not what catches my eye, then or now.

'Not a bad view,' I say, pulling myself up heavily and waddling closer to the edge of the clearing. Champ agrees or seems to, ambles, lies down, tail wagging, his snout in the grass.

I watch a bee, let my eyes follow the River Dee past oak and Scots pine, under the old Brig o Dee. My parents' old house, our current house, the university, Marischal College, Old Aberdeen, the beach arcing northwards – you can see it all from here. Supermarkets that don't close, a city's worth of curtains not yet open, the sky streaked white with wispy summer cloud, wild cherry and greens circling granite shops, roads and houses. The Granite Hill telecom tower the girls used to think was a spaceship and always wanted to visit. It marked the edge of their known universe.

'Imagine going right to that line,' Eva said once, pointing at the horizon. 'What would we see when we got there?'

'Another line,' I said. 'And some astronauts getting ready to blast into space.'

I never told them what the spaceship really was, didn't want to thwart their expectations.

1970

Henry and I are living in Portsmouth, although something tells me he's away, in Singapore or Hong Kong, on distant waters. My hair's in curlers and I'm in my nightie and red dressing gown, looking at a picture of myself in a newspaper clipping, one of several cuttings, photos and letters I've emptied onto our double bed from a hardbacked manila envelope. I must be twenty or twenty-one in real life, eighteen in the newspaper cutting, grinning through a veil, wearing the thin gold necklace my parents gave me.

Telecoms Personality Girl Stakes Claim for Another Title

THIS YEAR'S North-east Telecoms Personality Girl, Margaret Bryce née Taylor (right), is the Evening Express Bride of the Week.

> Margaret wed an electrical mechanic (air) with RNAS Lossiemouth, Henry Bryce, at St Clement's Church, Footdee, on Saturday.
>
> Margaret receives two Premium Bonds from the Evening Express and has a chance of becoming Bride of the Month for November.

The black and white clipping will go missing but my parents' copy will survive, turning yellow with the passage of time and the fug from their B&H Filters.

I had my first cig at thirteen – a Rothmans King Size from Karen Stewart that sent me home, head spinning like the carousel at Codona's, believing I would never smoke again. I did. But it takes time for tar to discolour and my smile in the clipping is polished ivory.

I lay the cutting on the floral bedspread, pick up another printed a few months earlier: 'Two With a Title in Mind'. A photograph of me and my friend Barb, who's looking directly at the camera while I, clean and coiffed, gaze into the middle distance. We're holding rotary telephones to our ears but they're not connected to anything.

> BEAUTIFUL girls come in pairs, it seems, and these two attractive young ladies are determined to bring the title of Telecoms Personality Girl 1968 to the Granite City.
>
> Margaret Taylor, 18 (left), and Barbara Milne, 19, were chosen yesterday in the Aberdeen round of the contest and go forward to the area finals to be held later this month.
>
> Both girls are engaged, although the sound of wedding bells is still a long way off.

Barb did better than me in the area finals, and I was happy for her, I suppose. She came runner-up to a woman from Kilmarnock, and I was happy about that too. She never lorded it over me and I loved – still love – her for that and so many other qualities. She didn't see herself as a great beauty, but I always did and wish I'd told her on occasion. You can love a friend, move in together if you like. It seems so obvious these days but I'd have laughed back then.

As it transpired, wedding bells were just a few short months away for me, a year away for Barb. Like me, she'll be in the paper the day after her wedding and again nearly twenty years later when her son, Michael, becomes one of the first local men to die of AIDS, although she'll insist at his funeral it was pneumonia. Which it also was. Fluid in the lungs. It could happen to anyone. I'll back her up with this, with anything. The terror of losing a child, my brain (I have no brain) refuses to go there, barricades itself, and I saw that with Barb too. She was never the same again. It's one of my abiding memories – Barb and me hugging in her lobby.

Crying.

Me consoling her, her consoling me.

Weeping

both of us at sea.

Losing a child

I couldn't

Barb, I can't

if it was me

Her husband Des, it felled him too. He was a master baker (we used to laugh about that a lot) and had just registered a new business name and put up the signage for Des Cowie and Son Bakers, Michael, barely eighteen, throwing his lot in with the family business. In the end, they changed the name back to Cowie's Rowies, a celebration of the butteries Des was particularly famed for. According to legend, rowies were invented on behalf of Aberdeen's fishermen, the winning combination of lard, butter, salt and sugar ensuring they stayed edible for at least a fortnight on the boats. Des's – fresh from the big oven, with an extra dab of salty butter on top – were widely acknowledged as the best. Even thinking about them makes my mouth (no mouth) water. But even they tasted bitter after Michael's death.

How do you help someone after their child dies? Do you bring it up? Wait for them to bring it up? With Barb, after her initial grief, when the razor-wire fencing was still easy to traverse, her pain a wild, open plain, she ran off and buried what had happened, returning after swearing herself, it seemed, to solemn secrecy.

Chapter 4

2010

Did Henry ever want children? He said he did, I'm almost certain. I have a recollection of us waiting in The Capitol to watch *Planet of the Apes* – in what, 1968, 1969? We were newishlyweds, in any case – Henry in a pink shirt, which was unusual for men at the time, and me in a pea-green miniskirt and jacket, cerise blouse. He was on leave from the Navy, must have been. We would have come up to stay with my parents or his, always alternated. He said, 'I'm ready to try, Marg. I'd love to give it a go,' or words to that effect. He was clean-shaven, handsome – still is, although with fewer teeth, greasier hair, the same shaky hands that eventually made gutting fish hazardous for his father.

He went funny for a while when I miscarried later that year, wasn't aware of a second embryo abandoning ship the following spring. He probably didn't count on having two girls at once – who does? But you make the most of it with twins, count your blessings twice over, do your best. I always have. Henry too, I suppose. He made them laugh, worked hard to put grub on the table, rarely got cross and, when he did, could uncross himself relatively quickly. He did well in all the ways that meant something until the girls hit early puberty and his drinking took on an adolescent verve. I'm not suggesting those things are connected, merely that they happened around the same time – 1988, the summer of the Piper Alpha oil platform disaster.

A safety valve on one of two essential condensate pumps had been removed during routine maintenance and replaced with a temporary cover. When the day-shift engineers clocked off at six, they left a written report about the missing valve for their night-shift colleagues. Divers were working in the sea beneath the rig, meaning, as per protocol, an automated fire-fighting system designed to suck water in vast quantities from the sea in the event of a fire was switched to manual.

When the second of the two pumps tripped that evening and couldn't be restarted, there was a scramble to maintain production on the rig and a search for any paperwork that might indicate the first, currently inactive, pump was unsafe to operate. A docket was found saying work hadn't yet started on the pump itself, but not the one warning the valve was missing and the pump couldn't be used under any circumstances.

Within seconds of it being turned on, high-pressure gas sprayed out, causing an explosion that threw workers in the accommodation block from their chairs, shook others from their beds. Shrapnel from the blast ripped through a smaller pipe, sparking a fire that engulfed the helipad. A mayday call was issued from the heavily damaged control room in haste before it was abandoned, leaving nobody to coordinate an evacuation or reinstate the automated fire-fighting system.

Twenty-five minutes later, a high-pressure pipeline connecting the rig with another nearby platform ruptured, the explosion releasing thirty tonnes of gas a second, all of which immediately ignited, devastating much of the rig. Another pipeline ruptured half an hour later, adding a further 1,200 tonnes of gas to the conflagration, the noise of which was said to be like a thousand blow torches at full capacity. Those who could jumped the height of a twenty-storey building into the flaming sea before another major gas line connecting the Piper Alpha to a nearby rig erupted, the fourth and final explosion adding even more fuel to a blaze that could be seen for seventy miles and had already buckled the 20,000-tonne platform. Not that anyone with a heart cared about the platform. They cared about the poor workers leaping or falling from the rig into the North Sea, on fire, into fire. Some of those who survived the drop would be crushed by falling steel or drown, hypothermia slowing them to a halt. There were sixty-one survivors, but nearly 170 men perished, a few dozen of whom were never found, their families, then and forever after, lost to what psychologists call complicated grief. The not-being-there, followed by not seeing a loved one's lifeless body – it does things to the minds and bodies left behind.

I'm not suggesting the Piper Alpha drove Henry dipsomaniac either – only that it gathered, condensed and reignited whatever pain was already there that summer.

We never discussed the why of his drinking. Even if we had, I expect we'd have disagreed on the detail. False recollections move like water, their rivulets cohering and combining until they're powerful enough to carry you away. The mind is a lifeboat and if it capsizes, you're in trouble.

Henry's mind – I can see now, but not then – is already listing when we visit Eva in Madrid. If you'd told me at any point previously I'd be in the Spanish capital, I would have laughed – I was a landlubber and, without my girls, would never have crossed the sea. But Eva always knew. As a child she was determined she'd either be a teacher or would master Spanish and live in Spain. And now she does both, teaching at an international school and living independently. Her life is a dream, although she still dreams of having children.

'Even now?' I ask quietly. We're sitting at a table outside a restaurant with pigs' legs hanging from its ceiling and I've no idea who else here might speak English. 'At thirty-four, without a partner?'

'Thirty-four's hardly old, Mum. And in any case, I'm thinking IVF, like Rachel and Gem. I've been doing some research.'

They've upped sticks for Australia, Rachel, Gem, William, have been gone a few months, leaving me, leaving everything, behind. Eva hasn't met William, had her chance but didn't take it. She could have asked Rachel and Gem about their IVF journey, didn't want to.

I look at Henry, his eyes trained on the alcohol-free sangria he's lifting slowly to his mouth. It's a shame he can't have the real deal, especially now, on holiday, but the AA Big Book was clear about abstinence. It was also clear about God, that He with a capital H existed and should be thanked and consulted regularly during recovery.

Henry must like the combination of grape juice and sparkling water. The young waiter has motioned twice already to offer more, and both times Henry has nodded slowly, almost calmly, as befits his anti-anxiety meds.

Eva miscarried at twenty-seven and thirty-one – maybe other times too, for all I knew – and they were real for her, those missing children, real for anyone. They'd been living inside her, bowels growing, bones fusing, little hearts syncing with hers. She told Henry and me about her first pregnancy just after the twelve-week scan, showed us the ultrasound picture. A head, a body – boy, girl, other. Her partner, Thom, was beside himself with joy, as was Eva, as were Henry and I. By week fourteen they were beside themselves with grief.

All children die eventually – in utero, in lecto, in ICU. Ten weeks, twelve years, nine decades – we leave denial, confusion and anger in our wake, if we're lucky.

With Eva and Thom's second pregnancy, she told me much earlier, thought it would make her baby more real, and I told her not to worry – what were the chances of lightning striking twice? One hundred per cent, it transpired. But Thom would stay with her, wouldn't he? They'd keep trying? Yes, they would, but only for another eighteen months, after which their nine-year union would come to an acrimonious end. I'm not sure what happened to Thom after their split, not sure I care.

'I'll pay,' Eva says, waving at the waiter. She smiles at him, then at us. 'Should we keep walking for a bit?'

We stroll through colourful backstreets, Eva by my side, Henry up ahead looking every bit the tourist. From behind – and from the front, increasingly – he appears lost. In years to come, little William in Australia will say talking to his Grandpa in Scotland is like speaking on a phone with a bad connection.

It's late afternoon by the time we stop in yet another beautiful plaza and I look like I want to be airlifted back to Eva's apartment with its cool marble floors and tepid shower, but she wants to explain why people are parading past the plaza, chanting and playing music, a haloed statue tilting this way and that on a golden litter.

'Can we at least sit?' I ask, pointing to a bench.

'Of course,' she says.

'Henry,' I shout. 'Henry.' But he can't hear me over the drums and trumpets. He's doddering, stopping to look at makeshift stalls and busy chalk artists, won't go far.

'So, San Isidro is the patron saint of Madrid,' Eva says. 'He lived in the eleventh and twelfth centuries. He's credited

45

with loads of miracles, mostly to do with animals, farms and water. He's known commonly as the Labrador in Spanish . . .'

'Like Champ,' I say. We've paid for someone to look after him while we're away. My father offered but he's been sick and will die – we don't know this yet, him either – in eighteen months, aged eighty-two.

'Labrador just means farm worker,' Eva says. 'He's also the patron saint for them, specifically.'

Henry sees us, waves, continues looking in stalls and at the slow-moving parade.

'Anyway, today's the day everyone celebrates him. The only miracle I remember is one where his baby son falls into a really deep well, causing Isidro's wife, Mary, to panic. She apparently ran off to tell Isidro what had happened and he told her they should kneel next to the hole and pray. When they did that, the water in the well started rising and swelling until it was level with the kerb.'

'So their son drowned,' I say. 'That's awful, love.'

'No, he floated,' Eva says. 'He was sitting on the surface of the water, splashing with his hands.'

It sounds fanciful, but Eva has the same wide-eyed look stories have given her since childhood, and I don't want to rain on her or anyone else's parade. I don't feel the heat now but can remember wishing for rain of the sort that lashes Union Street on a January morning. It's only May, not even summer – Eva always told us August was the hottest month.

When I tell Henry the San Isidro story the next morning, he'll nod sullenly. We'll be sitting on Eva's balcony, two floors above the street, eating the chorizo and scrambled eggs she'll prepare before leaving for work, me reading one of Eva's books called *The Shadow of the Wind*, Henry reading one called *The Sum of All Fears* that we picked up at a second-hand stall after

46

the parade. The cover of Henry's says it's an edge-of-the-seat thriller, but Henry's rump will remain in the centre of the wicker chair and he won't look in any way thrilled.

'But you would,' I'll say. 'I mean, save your child miraculously if you could.'

'Yeah,' he'll say, consumed, or pretending to be, with his Tom Clancy.

1985

We're in our back garden wearing woolly hats and gloves. Sam's tail is wagging, bobbled snow on his belly fur and legs. I would have told the girls on the walk home from school that the icicles on the gutters were growing long again and we'd have agreed to try to get them off. It's one of their favourite winter games, mine too.

Their lace-up moonboots are identical but otherwise their clothes are different. We swap them around periodically, the jumpers I've knitted, the jeans and corduroy trousers I've darned, from Eva to Rachel and back again until the holes grow too big for fixing. We're doing OK financially, have bought the house and will sell it for a profit in a couple of years, but Henry pumps as much as he can into the mortgage and money still feels tight. Their puffer jackets – red for Rachel, green for Eva – were Christmas presents from my parents.

They fashion their snowballs with bare hands, mittens dangling from the string that connects them through the jackets. It's easier to mould and compact the snow without gloves. I do the same – one ball then another, building my arsenal before our mission begins.

It's a simple enough game – throw the snowballs at the gutter

47

to dislodge the stalactites, then watch them plummet, potentially fatally, into the garden snow. It's one point for a full fall, a half-point for making contact without dislodging.

Hitting their bedroom window or the little bathroom window is obviously against the rules. Adding stones to the snowballs to further weaponise them is also prohibited – broken glass would lead to a frozen house and rouse the opprobrium of Henry when he got home from work. In the mornings, as it is, we scrape ice from the inside of the windows, the condensation frozen to the glass.

'You throw first, Mum,' Eva says, her cheeks like Red Delicious, eyes gleaming like polished silverware. She has at least ten snowballs in her pile, has probably calculated the optimal cache number against the likely time between throws and concurrent hardening of her projectiles.

'Yeah, do it, Mum,' Rachel says, eyebrows hidden under her woolly hat. She has three or four snowballs, will be hoping to intuit her way to victory.

'If you're sure,' I say.

Sam wags his tail, enjoying the camaraderie. I close one eye to aim, throw, and miss by a mile. I always do, I'm hopeless at throwing – that's part of the fun for the girls. We laugh as we always do, unless our snowballs land in Mrs Simpson's garden or, even worse, hit her house, leaving a mound of icy evidence. Mrs Simpson, for reasons unknown, abhors children. Or my two, at least. She growls at them whenever they're in the garden or playing in the street outside her house. Once, when Eva accidentally kicked her ball into Mrs Simpson's garden, she drove her garden fork right through it, three holes on either side, before throwing it back over the fence.

Eva goes next, tongue between her teeth as always, her arm going back and forth to perfect the desired trajectory before throwing. She launches and there's contact – a direct hit: the icicle drops like a swatted fly. Sam runs over to paw the transparent cone.

'Nice work, squirt,' Rachel says, reshaping her snowball ahead of her attempt.

They're competitive in ways I wasn't fully aware of at the time. I mean, sibling rivalry, of course that was there, and for twins I can only imagine it's worse. But Rachel looks every bit as stressed as Eva is happy with her throw. She's not yet slipped on the black ice that will see her flailing for years, sliding from school, skidding through hospitals and police stations. It will be nearly fifteen years before she regains her footing and starts training as a therapist, but I can see it now, the need to one-up her sister and the even greater terror of letting her down.

Sam spins in excited circles as Rachel lines up her throw. She can do it, I know she can. Eva wants her to, I can see that. I want her to. Sam wants her to.

She launches the snowball – crack – another direct hit. 'Woo-hoo,' she cries, looking happy and relieved, high-fiving Eva. 'Your turn, Mum. Let's make it one-one-one.'

2014

I'm in the living room, lying back in my comfy hospital chair. It's too big for the space, too brown for any space, but it reclines easily. It was nice of the hospital to let me have it – a short-term loan, right enough. Others will have had it before me, others after me, poor sods. Champ is sleeping under the footrest. Rachel has her feet up in the apricot armchair – Henry's old chair, not that he uses it anymore – reading *Frankenstein*. Eva might be upstairs talking to Juan or maybe hasn't arrived from Spain yet.

I look worn out or, as the girls used to say, spaced – not quite in fairyland but approaching, watched from the woodlands by the beautiful Baobhan Sith, her hooves hidden under a long green dress, her fingers fidgeting for my jugular. The doctors and nurses give fair warning that the treatment will tire you but don't explain how the drugs will make the sore bits feel so warm and tender that you want to poke and press them, even though it makes you woozy. I can't see it because of my cable-knit jumper but I'm rubbing at the shunt in my side. That's where the draining happens – I can do that at home now too. A litre at a time – any more and the nausea is unbearable. I siphon clear fluid into a small bucket, empty it down the loo.

On the TV, the weather girl says we'll enjoy a top of fifteen tomorrow. That sounds about right for mid-summer – twenty down in Cornwall, only twelve up in Orkney.

'Orkney,' Rachel says. 'That's a coincidence hearing that.'

'They mention it every day,' I say, eyes half-opening. 'Why wouldn't they?'

'Victor's just arrived in Orkney to make a wife for the monster,' she says. 'Listen to this: *My mind was intently fixed on the consummation of my labour, and my eyes shut to the horror of my proceedings. But now I went to it in cold blood, and my heart often sickened at the work of my hands.*'

'Oh,' I say, head falling back, eyes closing, flitting. I'm maybe dreaming about limbs being sewn together and how the cold climate in Orkney would help stave off putrescence in an era before refrigeration. They'll take my body for science, I hope – I might be dreaming about that. How I want them to strip, slice and dice me. Or about the Baobhan Sith, preying by night, recruiting me.

I open my eyes quickly – 'Oh Christ' – and pull myself

50

forward on the armrests, grab the stainless-steel bowl I keep by the chair, throw up kelp and barnacles.

'Oh no, there's more . . .'

Rachel has come across, is kneeling next to me, rubbing my back. The spine – she can feel it, the vertebrae, how skeletal I've become, my spindly top half at least, doesn't mention it. 'Love you, Mum.' She waits until I fall back under, dreaming about what – monsters, fairies? – takes the laden bowl to the bathroom.

Eva – yes, that's right, she's here already – comes downstairs, must have heard the retching and Rachel's movements, sees me reclining with closed eyes, sweat beading on my forehead. 'Oh, Mum,' she says. 'That's not good.'

'I'm sorry, dearie,' I say, eyes opening and closing, wiping sick from my mouth. 'I know how squeamish you are.'

'Less than I used to be,' she says. Teaching rich kids day in day out has inured her, no doubt.

Rachel returns, mid-conversation on her mobile phone, puts a glass of water on the sideboard, looks at me, barely acknowledges Eva.

'Yeah . . . that's right,' she says to whoever she's chatting with. 'I know . . . I think she'll need a jab from her Just-In-Case bag.'

'What's your Just-In-Case bag?' Eva asks quietly, standing behind me, stroking my regrown hair.

'Just medicine,' I say, reaching for the water, sipping, placing it back on the sideboard. 'A few different things. I just feel . . .'

My eyes close and my mouth – oh, that's unfortunate – falls open under the work of Eva's hands. My hair's being tugged at gently, the follicles straining like gums against toffee-clad teeth. She could ease my chair and head back even further if she wanted, I'd not resist, tap at my jugular – tap, tap, tap.

Chapter 5

2017

It hurts where my head used to be – my heart, in the phantom sense, aches. I don't know why, only that some days, I call them days, are like that, while others I can have a laugh, so to speak. If you'd heard my chortling – once upon, I mean – you'd not have forgotten it. Some people have a gift for making others cackle but my special talent, one of them, was to give in to my guffaws, my contracting diaphragm a magic carpet onto which all and sundry were invited, the only judgement being how funny – funny haha – their foibles were.

We're all flawed, our ointments flecked with flies. When someone tells you differently, what they're really saying is they're scared to admit how vulnerable they are, a flaw we all share. How could it be otherwise? We're squished through pelvises or pulled through incisions onto a moist grain of dust that twirls like a mote within a logically impossible universe, bereft of direction until we learn the accepted rules and behaviours of a socio-religious framework we'd be literally crazy to believe in but abide by nonetheless because that's what our parents, teachers, lovers and peers do, and being ostracized during our infinitesimal glimmer of consciousness, bookended as it is by eternal darkness, is more than many, maybe any, of us can bear.

Some days people walk on me, that's how it feels. The seagulls down by the beach, thousands of webbed feet stomping on grass to mimic rain so that the worms come up and they can eat them. Some days it's like that, and I can even smell things, or so it seems – a curry someone's eaten, the fabric conditioner they've used on their corduroy jacket, but the mulchy aromas are much stronger, have their own shape, or range of shapes, depending on the season – the world turning in its earthy grave, its sweetly decaying breath and humic elbows, its isosceles knees in my back.

When I'm with my family, it's never by choice. I'd happily be with them all the time, of course – or maybe not of course, maybe not, what a thought, because I'm confounded, off course, unheeded, not needed.

Henry's sometimes in his assisted-living flat, sometimes not. When he's there, he watches TV and I sit on the chair next to him, same as always, until one of us falls asleep. I forget myself on occasion and start talking, say something during a quiz show like, 'That's going to cost her,' but he either doesn't hear me or doesn't want to turn around. He's in a dwam, forgets to take his pills, looks as lonely as me.

His flat is sparse: his TV, the two chairs. Framed photos on the windowsill – Henry and me in Madrid, me when I was young, me looking wan with William in Melbourne. The cupboards are bare, the fridge practically empty. But the view offers consolation.

His flat's on the second floor, with an unbroken vista of the harbour. There are cranes, heavy industry, boats with Norwegian names, Scottish names, Dutch. Pelagic trawlers, mostly, their crews of young and old knocked around in the water or falling overboard in some cases, dragged to the depths with laden lungs in their hunt for the mighty haddock. The sheer size of their nets takes away some of the romance, the Biblical connotations, but it's still very impressive, even though I can't help feeling sorry for those creatures, rammed eye to eye, gill to gill, with so many of their tear-shaped compatriots. Still, I do like a fish supper, can't deny it.

Henry's father worked in the fish, would scrub himself scarlet in the bath and still sweat omega-3, his pores incessantly releasing oil.

At night it's quite something, sitting at Henry's window, watching the lights streak across the water, the reds and whites of the tugs, the oranges and yellows of the big boats. Does Henry ever do that? Just sit there and watch, I mean, in those stretches when he's not in hospital. I've asked him more than once – he doesn't seem to know or have thought too much about it.

1986

We're at His Majesty's Theatre, named after Edward VII, in the stalls – me in the peach dress and cream jacket I keep for weddings and special occasions, Henry in his navy suit jacket, the girls both in cotton party dresses – Eva's green and white stripes, Rachel's lemon and black zig-zags – a touch of rouge on their cheeks, their idea, not mine. We're overdressed, everyone is. Builders in blazers, shopworkers in shoulder pads. It's hard to fathom why we make ourselves up like mannequins for the theatre and wear tracksuits to the cinema, given both involve sitting mostly in the dark.

It's the intermission – the girls are scooping the last of their icecream from cardboard cups. People stream back into the stalls, the dress and upper circles – it's a packed house, although the royal boxes are empty. We're about ten rows from the front, bang in the centre, the tickets a surprise gift from Henry for the girls' eleventh birthday.

He employs three people now – another time-served electrician, an apprentice and me, part-time, as his receptionist. I take calls from as far away as Banff and Buckie and feel at ease on the phone as always. *And what time might it suit for someone to be there tomorrow? Would between two p.m. and five p.m. suit? Oh, how lovely, I'll book that in now and we'll call again in the morning just to confirm.* I'm proud of Henry, feel sad – then and now – about his burnt and bandaged hands. That was Neil's doing, his young apprentice. Henry was under someone's floorboards in Mastrick – I'd arranged the job, an electrical fault, the elderly man a repeat customer. Neil wasn't the brightest, was known a little cruelly as Feel Neil, the Doric word for daft, so it was always worth double checking he'd understood instructions.

'You're sure?' Henry had asked. 'The power's off?' 'Aye, it's aff,' Neil had said.

'The mains? You're a hundred per cent sure? You've flicked the switch?'

'Aye, Henry, good to go, pal.'

The second Henry's hands made contact, he was thrown back through the floor hatch and into the hallway, where he came to, stood quickly and started punching Neil. Neil apologised, Henry too. 'Sorry, Neil, I shouldn't have hit you, it was just the shock.'

He claps but not too forcefully as the lights dim again, the red seats and gold leaf fading.

The Corries walk back on stage to thunderous applause, wearing brown leather waistcoats and yellow shirts. My favourite is Ronnie Browne with his devilish white hair and beard, a Scottish Kenny Rogers, but I've also got a soft spot for Roy

Williamson, the Paul Simon of the pair. He wrote 'Flower of Scotland' and will die at fifty-four, aware of the song's popularity but not that it will go from being a rugby anthem to the de facto national anthem for the de facto nation, replacing the insipid shortbread ditty 'Scotland the Brave'. They'll sing it this evening – will finish the show with it, from memory – and we'll all feel roused by the prospect of sending Proud Edward's army – Edward II not VII – back to England after the Battle of Bannockburn to think again. Most importantly, we'll sing along, as loud as we can, and The Corries will encourage that, always do, could build a nation from bonhomie.

They open the second set with 'Will Ye Go Lassie Go', its lyrics based on a poem by the Scottish weaver poet, Robert Tannahill.

Roy and Ronnie pluck their guitars and the audience of, what, a thousand people, maybe more, is rapt. Roy's voice is the only one we hear until the first chorus, when Ronnie comes in with the high harmony.

We do The Corries' harmonies at home, the girls and me, even Henry sometimes. We know all their songs inside out. 'The Skye Boat Song'. 'The Massacre of Glencoe'. 'Lowlands Away' – Eva and Rachel sang a hauntingly beautiful duet of that one:

I dreamt my love was drowned and dead
Lowlands, Lowlands away

Eva marched round the living room behind me and Rachel once, all of us singing, hitting a pan with my spurtle to mimic the big bodhrán drum Ronnie played on 'The Blue Bonnets'.

It's a really nice thing Henry's done, getting the tickets. The girls' eyes are lit up and – I don't look at the time, remember not wanting to jinx it, but can look now without fear – they're both singing, as all of us do during the chorus. It's mournful and gorgeous and the truth is I love my family, my girls, Henry and his melted mitts.

'Once more,' Ronnie calls and we sing, all of us, asking a lassie if she'll go, if we all can, to pull wild mountain thyme all around the bloomin' heather.

1978

Excuse the bellbottoms, although my figure – what a babe! – there's no need to excuse that. I'm at Nana Jean's house with the girls, who are two or thereabouts and recovering from whooping cough. There's not much to like about *Bordetella pertussis*, but they're over the worst of it, for sure. They're lying listlessly in the big, awkward pram I'm forever hauling them out of, lifting them into. I could hoist them out now, or maybe . . . no.

Nana Jean, in her early sixties, is trying to fish her brown leather purse from the pot of Scotch broth on the kitchen stove.

'Here, let me help, Nana,' I say, taking her wooden spoon and rubbing her diminutive back gently.

She's made the soup for lunch, seems to have confused it with a wishing well. 'Fit's ma purse deein' in there?' she asks, embarrassed.

'Och, I don't know, Nana. It must have fallen in.'

She pulls her cardigan round at the front, releasing a cloud of jasmine talc, shakes her head. I wonder what she wished for.

Her husband – my Grandad Duncan – leapt from a burning Lancaster bomber just outside Würzburg in Germany in 1945. He was twenty-eight, the oldest in the seven-man – or six-boy, one-man – crew. As wireless operator, his job was to transmit all messages to and from the aircraft, including their position as smoke filled the flying carcass. Würzburg would have been ablaze already as he jumped, the sixteen-year-old pilot and bomb-aimer already dead, the navigator and gunners tumbling to earth. He seemed to struggle to deploy his parachute, took longer than the others, but got it open eventually, only to land in a lake where the chute dragged him under like a purse in a pot of soup.

All green and wet with weeds so cold,
Around his form green weeds had hold
That first gulp of water
if he was conscious
the need overriding his body's defences
there's no air now
Just water, but water has oxygen, just one percent but
Swallow, breathe, drink it in

The war in Europe had been over for eighteen months by the time Jean could start adding colour and contour to the black and white sketch of Duncan's last moments. Sandy, the rear gunner, had seen it happen, was lying in a field nearby with broken legs when Duncan hit the water, drove prisoner-of-war thin from Chester to Aberdeen to tell my Nana the whole story. She's been a widow for more than half of her life already, raised my mother with the help of her mother, Janet, and great-aunt Connie.

I rinse her sodden purse, pick barley and mashed carrot from the plug hole. I dry my hands, lift the girls onto the floor, where they sit, look at each other, start mewling. We can't stay long, never can these days. It's a mile from Nana Jean's to ours – a short walk that feels much longer with the twins, especially when they're poorly.

Jean birthed my mother at sixteen, my mother had me

at seventeen, the last two in a parade of early pregnancies that ended with me at a geriatric twenty-six.

'Will the bairns hae some soup?' she asks.

'I don't think so, Nana. They're still too wee.' They're lying down now, both of them on their backs next to the washing machine, red cheeks and mottled skin.

Nana Jean pulls on her rubber gloves and takes two soup plates from the oven – always heats them in there – ladles them to spilling point with broth from the pot, places them shakily on the table and sits. Her soup is the best, my mother's second, mine third. It's the way she mashes it, the pot she uses, an excess of x-factors that can be imitated but never matched.

'Oh, that's really fine,' I say, blowing the soup on the second spoonful. 'Just delicious, Nana.'

'Braw. Glad you like it, Peg.'

Nobody else calls me Peg. In a few years I'll have to explain to the girls that it's short for Margaret, as is Daisy, because a daisy is *marguerite* in French.

I wipe sweat from my brow, lift my turtleneck jumper over my head. My arms, the tops of them, don't look too big, do they? To me, they look fine – all that pushing a heavy pram with wheels as frustrating as a wonky shopping trolley's. I can't compare my upper arms with Nana Jean's – her cardie will stay on, always does, even in her sweltering surrounds. The lump beneath her sweater, I know, is the oblong locket given to her by Grandad Duncan. It's filigreed with a Celtic eternity knot and contains his miniature, mildewed likeness.

'Ye ken, the weirdest things keep happening,' she says, before leaning closer and whispering as if the girls are old enough to understand. They're more likely to pass out, are both looking glassily at the ceiling. 'I think I hae a ghost in the hoose.' She smiles, her pale blue eyes creasing. She's being serious – that's what I thought at the time, that she actually believes her house is haunted. But now her smile seems to be acknowledging what she knows and is struggling to articulate, that the house she's referring to is her head.

Jean doesn't like hugs, or pretends not to, so I lean in to kiss her cheek as I'm leaving, tell her I love her.

'I love you too, quine,' she says. 'Always hiv.'

Within months, she'll set fire to the living-room curtains and insist it was an accident, even though her neighbour Sandra will see her striking match after match to coax flames from the fabric. Shortly afterwards, we'll start visiting her at Cornhill, the new name for the Aberdeen Royal Lunatic Asylum that was founded in 1800 through the largesse of the city's dancing master, Francis Peacock, who donated the substantial profits from his bestselling treatise *Sketches Relative to the History and Theory, but More Especially to the Practice of Dancing*. It was a short walk from Cornhill to Foresterhill Hospital, where the girls were born and I died.

The girls will come with me to Cornhill when I visit Nana Jean, my parents too sometimes, and Henry when we visit on weekends.

He'll make us laugh, Henry, with his impressions of the psychiatrically impaired. If a man with sunken cheeks and hollow eyes sits up in bed and shouts 'arse' or something similar, Henry will sit up in his chair and whisper 'arse'. The girls will find this hilarious, me too. My parents think Henry can do no wrong, and even Jean, on a good day, will laugh. You'd have to be unlucky to end up in a place like this – that's what he'll be telling us with his jokes, unaware of how hard he's pushing his luck.

Jean will die suddenly when the girls are six, not from dementia but the flu, which the doctor will call a blessing.

It won't feel that way. To me, she'd been the smallest person in our family and yet somehow, in a trick of perspective, gigantic.

Her tiny body, more angular in death, will look so brittle in the coffin, her mouth a closed question as to whether the mortician has applied too much lippy.

We'll go back to my parents' house after the funeral tea, have dinner there. When we get home, Henry will fix himself a drink – must have been gasping for one all evening – while I help the girls brush their teeth. It'll be a late night for them, ten-thirty or thereabouts, the gloaming still gnawing at their orange curtains.

'Don't be scared about anything that happened today,' I'll tell Eva as I pull her covers up to her chin.

'I'm not scared, Mummy,' she'll say.

'Me either,' Rachel will say as I'm tucking her in.

The football highlights will play on the TV downstairs while I lie in bed in my nightie, the light finally leached from the sky. A draw, they'll be hoping for a draw. Who hopes for a draw?

I'll see a flare of green through the gap in the curtains – the northern lights, the heavenly dancers, before they too fade to darkness.

And then . . . the smell of jasmine talc. Nana Jean will be there with me, in the bedroom.

'Peg, hey Peg,' she'll say.

My eyes will stay shut, tighter than before, but I'll feel her standing, not sitting, at the foot of the bed.

'It's me, quine, Nana Jean.'

I'll pull the blanket further over my head, hands on the inside, all of me covered, none of me exposed.

'Margaret, it's me.'

I'll remember how she taught me Scottish country dancing when I was a girl, how we made treacle together, its cloying, purple sugariness, her hugging me, the only time she did so from memory, when I fell and skinned my elbows badly on the path leading up to her house. Stewing rhubarb together. The charred curtains and her purse in the pot of broth.

'Peggy, love.'

I'll take quick shallow breaths and play dead – my only thought: don't sit on the bed. But I'll feel her, her shape, the displaced night air. Don't sit on the bed.

'Wid ye like me to go, pet?'

Please don't touch my legs.

'Are ye sleeping, Peg?'

Don't sit on the bed. Go away, go away, Nana Jean, go away.

Chapter 6

2014

I attach my seatbelt, try not to look at my legs – they're dropsical, swollen popsicles, what a laugh – adjust the rear-view mirror. Rachel's on the passenger side, her eyes puffy from too much or too little sleep. Or lingering jet lag – that's maybe it. She'll be missing the boys and Gem, stewing over the prospect of missing me. I reverse out of the driveway, into the glare. It's unforgiving, the morning light – it's not Rachel's fault, how time dates the dermis, its cutaneous callousness. The skin of the earth too, its natural oils liposucked for profit, its surface patchy-dry and inflamed.

Champ pants happily on the back seat, curled into the corner, watching me, good boy. He's unaware his days are numbered – a couple of dozen at most.

Eva has the rest of the back to herself but still looks cramped – she's not overweight, is average on the BMI and outstanding in other ways. She too is showing her age – her flavescent fangs, the little lines round her mouth. But in other ways she's ageless. The soul – I don't believe in souls – dances endlessly, never opening its eyes.

I didn't think of my car as small when it was just Champ and me, even us and one of the girls. I thought of it as adequate, and it is, I suppose, even today. I look focused, happy – it's not cold, the solstice is coming.

My father always had big cars, swapped them every eighteen months or so for the latest model. He knocked a cyclist from her bike the last time he drove, didn't see the problem – what was she doing, the bloody idiot, riding along a road like that? – didn't see himself very clearly at all. The rider was concussed, my father's licence, after a compulsory eye exam, revoked.

I open the window slightly, am enjoying the air, can almost – but not quite – smell it now. Use your nose (I have no nose) and breathe deep (no lungs). Roses line the verges, plump with red and yellow life.

The druids will be amassing at Stonehenge, are maybe there already, revering nature, but I'm with my daughters, my standing stones. I'm glad they're getting along, suspect they've both decided to be nice for me, or maybe that's my sassy self-regard. So much time has passed, magical time, just like that – *poof* – no rabbit and, look, no hat.

I pull into the Shell, need to inflate the tyres – they'd felt soft for weeks, even more so now with extra sardines in the tin. 'Where's the air pump?' I ask myself out loud. 'Oh, there it is.' I draw up to it, sling a sandbag foot onto the brakes.

'Back soon,' Eva says, reaching for the door handle.

'I'll get it,' Rachel says, turning to me. 'You stay there.'

I can get behind this type of sibling rivalry, fully endorse it. A fight to the near-death is fine when I'm the beneficiary. There's blood on my trousers – dammit – just a spot, a nick from catching myself on the door getting in.

'Stay there, mate,' Rachel says to Champ, gently closing her door.

I squirt some water from my plastic bottle onto my trousers then, with some difficulty, into Champ's bowl on the floor in front of him. He laps at it noisily as I rub at the little red flower on my leg. We sit there, Eva and me, the windows steaming. I lower mine further, wave to Rachel in the side mirror.

'Pretty lucky with the weather,' Eva says.

'I'm thrilled,' I say. 'Just being out of the house.'

'I feel I could come back here to live on days like this.'

'I'd love that, dearie. I mean, if I was going to be here.'

Rachel pushes a foot against the front tyre, gives me the thumbs-up.

Inflated, elated, I drive us west along the South Deeside Road, prefer it to North Deeside Road. When a Scottish person dies in a foreign land, their spirit journeys home by the low road, that's how the story goes. It's more efficient than the high road too, according to the song 'Loch Lomond' and Google Maps. We pass dry stone walls, furrowed fields, and before long are surrounded by vibrant greens, a chlorophyll cacophony of branches arching over us like arms at a ceilidh. I miss those. Loved them, Henry too. Barb and Des sometimes came with us, sometimes didn't. Strip the Willow, the Virginia Reel. Eight sets of partners facing off in two parallel lines, taking three steps towards each other, nodding, three steps back. Meeting in the centre and spinning each other by the right elbow, the left. A two-handed clockwise turn followed by a do-si-do – I enjoyed a do-si-do, they were joyous and daft. The head couple joining hands and gliding to the bottom of the set, back to the top, the other pairs clapping and laughing and shouting yee-ooch. The head couple spinning each other with right elbows before crossing to the person opposite – boy to girl and girl to boy traditionally – spinning with their left elbows, back to the centre, turning each other again, and so on, moving along the set like laces in a bodice, joining hands at the bottom and gliding back to the top before peeling off, the two lines following them in single file to what was previously the bottom of the set. Raising their arms to form an arch under which the other pairs, now reunited, will pass and repeat the process. It was jolly, everyone got a turn, our hearts (I have none) beating hard.

We're self-consciously creating a memory, Eva, Rachel and me, doing something fun together for the first time in what feels like forever. We'll watch the salmon leaping at the Bridge of Feugh, applaud those that make it up the waterfall, dodging heron, surviving the side-splitting sharpness of rocks, their gills red and raw, swimming wounded to calmer waters, where they'll lay their eggs and die of injury and exhaustion. A good day out for all.

Remnants of rain are preserved in puddles that barely ripple. 'Feughside,' I say, to myself more than anyone.

'You know that Scottish *ch* sound helps with Spanish,' Eva says.

Feuch, loch, *yee-ooch* – as if you have a herring bone caught in your throat and need to clear it.

'*Trabajo, broch* . . . they both employ the voiceless velar fricative.'

'That's fascinating,' I say.

'Of course, in Spanish, a lot of sounds, including that one, are transplanted from Arabic.'

'Is that right?'

I listen to Eva talking while Rachel leans against her window, cheekbone propped on her hand. I'm keeping her from her family at the other end of the world.

Ewan asked her once if he was a real boy – she told me about it on the phone. It wasn't about his in-vitro fertilisation, although that was her first thought and she was about to offer him their pre-approved positioning statement, just as they had with William, a flan case suitable for a three-year-old, to be filled with choice ingredients at a later date. But they'd been reading *The Adventures of Pinocchio* and he wanted to know if he was made of wood. That's what she'll be thinking about, looking out at the trees – I'm wildly speculating, she might not be thinking about that at all. Eva slides seamlessly from linguistics to the Moors to books, always books, her own, mine, Rachel's.

'Lots of things in *Frankenstein* are *a priori* implausible,' she says. 'We're invited to believe, at least not disbelieve, that Victor has gone out at two in the morning on a little skiff in the Orkneys, the day after his monster storms off in a boat bound for Ireland. He lies down and falls asleep, waking in a panic from a reverie that sees him "swallowed up by the immeasurable waters" now roaring all around him. He makes a sail from his clothes, as you do, struggles to keep hold of his rudder in the heavy swell. All of this only to land in a small Irish harbour town 500 miles away – which would take days – where he's thrown in jail on suspicion of murder. And the murder victim? Well, that just so happens to be his estranged bestie who has washed up in that very same town, of all places, having written to Victor a few days earlier from landlocked Perth. I think she asks a lot of our credulity.'

I catch her eyes in the mirror, nod and smile. At the time, I don't think about it, but now I do. She's always wanted to impress me, I know that, and she always has, with her imagination and outlook, if not her big words. I could live without those – the way she unfurls them like a bullfighter's cape, hoping people will throw roses at her and shout *¡Olé!* Those poor beasts, meanwhile, their horns shorn to expose the nerves. I refused to go when we were in Madrid. 'But Hemingway,' Eva had said. 'Hemingway nothing,' I'd said.

They cut the horses' larynxes so their screeching won't upset the baying crowd when they're upended and eviscerated by the bulls. But it's not just me Eva wants to dazzle – that's what I'm finally realising. She wants to impress Rachel – it's so obvious, and that's why she's worked so hard for so long to hide it. It's to her that Eva's fluttering cape is directed, causing genuine hurt when Rachel sees red or, even worse, refuses to engage.

'Percy Shelley, Mary's husband, was a sailor, of course, and famously couldn't swim,' she says. 'A curious anomaly that came back to haunt him at twenty-nine when his boat overturned during a storm in the Gulf of La Spezia, sending him to his watery grave. He could definitely have helped Mary with some of the realities and specifics of sailing.'

An oncoming car flashes its lights – the police must be up ahead but it's fine, I'm safely under the limit.

'So we have Victor's father, brother, fiancée, housekeeper and best friend all murdered without witnesses, and Victor, who just happens to be in the vicinity when each of the killings occur.'

'Oh?' I say. I don't care, if I'm honest, but you can't really tell your children that, especially when they've taken to the skies to say goodbye. I nod again, try to look impressed, wait for a break in the traffic before turning left onto the A93.

'We're in the realm of *Jekyll and Hyde*,' she says. '*The Private Memoirs and Confessions of a Justified Sinner. Fight Club.*'

'I've only read *Jekyll and Hyde*,' I say. 'What's your view, Rachel?'

'Hm?' She sits up, wipes her mouth. 'I think I was drifting off. My teeth feel a bit loose.' She holds her top incisors, winces.

Eva sits back, looks spent, while I look like the portrait of Dorian Gray, every last sin scarred into my marred and withering face. I should be hidden away, put to rest, soon will be.

I draw the car to a halt in the disabled bay in the Bridge of Feugh carpark. Rachel gets out first, stretches, opens the back door, takes Champ by his lead round to my side, opens mine. 'Give me your arm, Mum.'

'Actually, I might just stay here, love,' I say. It makes no sense, I know. It might be my face, how it looks, my giddiness from the drain the night before.

Rachel looks flummoxed.

'I feel embarrassed walking,' I say, leaning over to pat Champ, his tail wagging at the open door. 'You both go. I'm quite content just sitting here.'

Rachel makes a big deal of looking around – there are no other vehicles in the carpark, we're out of season, the salmon leap mainly in spring and autumn.

'You're not getting out, Mum?' Eva asks from the back seat. 'I might just stay here as well, then.'

Rachel bites her bottom lip, shakes her head. They both want to be with me, and I want to be with both, but the maths doesn't always work out.

'You just go,' I say. 'Wait . . .' I lean over as she turns to leave, rummage in the glove compartment for a bag. 'Take this in case Champ does a poo.'

'Catch a salmon for our tea,' Eva calls as Rachel walks away, but she doesn't hear or care enough to turn around.

We say nothing for a while, me breathing as if I've climbed the stairs too quickly, Eva looking out the side window, drumming her legs. I itch through my top where the shunt is, try to make it look casual.

'You're feeling rough,' Eva says.

'I'm fine,' I say, laughing. 'I'm just getting lazy in my old age.'

The minutes empty, start filling with guilt.

'I might just head over,' I say. 'Will you come too, love?'

'Let's go,' she says.

It takes a while to get out of the car, even with Eva's help. We start walking, shuffling really, our arms interlinked – she the loving daughter, me the doting mother, wishing I wasn't as weak as balsa, as woozy as wood glue. I drained too much the night before, wanted to lessen my load.

It's not far to the bridge, a couple of hundred metres through the trees. It could take some time. Eva pats my hand and I pat hers. We'll get there, together.

'The Feugh sounds strong,' she says.

'It does,' I say. 'Not a good day for swimming.'

Our long-gone summers in Aviemore, both girls bobbing with goosebumps in the River Spey, it was always so green there.

'Remember *The Water-Babies*?' she asks.

'How could I forget?'

For a time, it was her favourite story, may even have been one of the reasons she carried on swimming in high school while Rachel dropped out. Tom the little chimney-sweep hurries from the window of an upper-class girl's bedroom, having been caught admiring her alabaster skin by the stout old maid. He climbs down a magnolia tree, its flowers almost as big as his head, and runs barefoot from a growing band of pursuers, into the woods, across hill and dale, for what feels like an eternity. Eventually, desperate to be clean for once and slake his aching thirst, he tumbles into a fairy-infested stream and succumbs to the best sleep of his life, dreaming of green meadows and elm trees.

'*Clear and cool, clear and cool,*' Eva says. '*By laughing shallow, and dreaming pool.*'

There was a moral to the story, something about the dangers of child labour or something about Darwin – I forget. There was a moral to Rachel and Eva's divergence in the water too, Eva's shelves increasingly lined with swimming trophies and rosettes, Rachel's with record sleeves and badly hidden cigarettes.

My breathing, it's . . .

'It's OK, Mum,' Eva says. 'You're OK.'

Rachel's up ahead with her arms on the bridge railing, watching the waterfall. Champ's off his lead, his tail wagging. He could have been looked after by Henry if Henry could look after himself. Or by Barb if Des didn't have severe cat and dog allergies. Champ was an old dog – ten – but not that old, poor thing.

'Oh, you made it,' Rachel says.

'Didn't want to miss all the fun,' I say.

'Well, so far we've seen, what, three fish, Champ? I remember there used to be thousands. It feels great to be here, though.'

'Childhood memories are often exaggerated and false,' Eva says. 'I thought you'd know that as a psychotherapist.'

Rachel is impassive, feels the hook, refuses the bait.

'It's just not spawning season,' I say, pocked hands on the railing, trying to catch my breath. The grating is rife with padlocks, hundreds of them, with love hearts and initials. Whatever happened to carving your initials onto a tree?

'Let's at least get a selfie,' Rachel says, her phone already in hand. 'I'm just . . . I feel a bit emotional, Mum, like it's finally starting to hit me.' She rubs the undersides of her eyes, sighs. 'It's probably best if we turn this way.'

We stand, the three of us, huddled, the frame showing the beech trees, the river, and just a hint of the fall. I look lamentable but the girls look good, as does the scenery.

'OK, cheese,' Eva says.

'Cheese,' I say.

'Cheese,' Rachel says.

We turn and watch the waterfall. Another salmon. A leap . . . she's unsuccessful, will try again.

'I'm in denial,' Rachel says. 'I know that – I've been that way for so long.'

'Me too,' I say. 'It's a lot, isn't it, love? A lot and also so little, as if it's not even real.'

'I've been seeing one of the therapists I know in Melbourne. She's good, she really helps. She reckons I'm blaming myself.'

'Well, that makes no sense,' Eva says, laughing derisively. The chill wafting from the water has nothing on the one rolling from Rachel.

'I'm sorry,' Eva says. 'I shouldn't have said that. It's all valid, all of it. I wish I could have been here more. I feel guilty about that too.'

It works well like this, all of us watching the water, not each other, like when we used to speak in Henry's Transit van – all eyes to the front, no risk of bruising from heavy eye contact.

A salmon – maybe the same one – leaps half-heartedly, gets spun back into the spume.

'I don't suppose you're hungry,' Rachel says. 'I'm feeling a little peckish.'

It takes an age to get back to the car, longer than I'd like for me to get back into it and catch my breath.

'You sure you're OK driving?' Rachel asks. 'I'm more than happy to.'

'Yes, I'm fine, dearie. I just need to get this stupid seatbelt in.' Champ panting on the back seat, good boy.

I drive us towards Banchory, need to find a restaurant or bakery with parking directly outside, such as . . . yes . . . I swing us into the big supermarket carpark, stop in front of the adjoining café.

We leave Champ in the car and shuffle towards it.

Eva takes a free, slightly blackened banana from beside the till, looks sullen. Rachel orders a bowl of pasta and pesto. Me, a prawn cocktail sandwich.

I sit opposite the girls at the window, catch my reflection, recoil.

'Back in a sec,' Rachel says, standing and hurrying towards the bathroom.

'Actually, me too,' Eva says, getting up, banana peel in hand. 'I'll go get us something for dinner. How does roast chicken sound?'

'Like a live chicken,' I say. 'But quieter.'

Rachel's pasta and pesto is on the table when she returns – it's pre-cooked, reheated. She forks it into her face. 'My period's come,' she says. 'I need to get some tampons real quick. Do you need anything?'

I wipe my mouth, am struggling with the bread and tiny prawns. 'I'm fine, love.'

I'm glad she's bleeding. As a teen she had amenorrhoea – not that we knew it by name at first – and would go months without menstruating. Doctor Gordon said it could be stress-related. It wasn't particularly unusual in teens, and perfectly understandable in Rachel's case.

I'm sitting at the table with my head in my hands when Eva returns.

She sits opposite, reaches across to stroke my hand.

'I hate feeling like this,' I say. 'Will you walk me to the car?'

'Yep, come on.'

We take itsy-bitsy steps, the girl at the till looking away out of respect or unease, Eva's arm hooked through mine.

She takes the keys, opens the car door, sits me on the passenger side, my legs outside, and, oh yes, I remember this bit – a burp and then vomit in my throat, my mouth, trying to swallow it. Eva opening the back door, grabbing Champ's plastic bowl, emptying it on the ground, telling him to stay put. I try to spew in silence but can't. Eva turns to look at the hills, give me privacy with my nemesis, emesis. I'm expelling but thankfully, now at least, unable to smell it.

Eva turns back, has been crying, trying not to. She shouldn't have come over from Spain. Rachel shouldn't have come over from Australia. I don't like them seeing me like this, should have shuffled into the Gramps to die alone, my meat a treat for fox and fungi. Wolves did it, all the canines – left the pack, to pass in peace.

'Let me empty that,' Eva says, nodding at Champ's bowl.

It's frothy, scummed like lentil soup, home to chewed crustaceans. Eva walks it gingerly towards the café, will presumably empty it down a toilet.

Rachel emerges from the supermarket, an open box of tampons in her hand.

'What's going on?' she asks on approach. 'I was looking for you inside.'

'Are you still OK to drive?' I ask. 'I probably shouldn't have had that sandwich.'

Chapter 7

1983

The girls. I'm not sure how old they are – seven, let's say – but we're at the beach, on the sand, in knitted scarves, hats and gloves, negotiating the north-easterly. It comes from Siberia – I've been told that before. When it's like this, so burly, we sometimes unzip our coats and hold out the flaps, pulling them as taut as we can, to form a webbing. You can lean right into it like that, forty, forty-five degrees, won't fall over, might even fly away, a pterodactyl exploring new territories. But for now, our heads are down, the girls with a woolly hand in each of mine, grimacing and grinning through it.

There are imprints of Henry's Chelsea boots in the sand, the right heel gouging slightly deeper than the left, little paw prints patting alongside. He's up ahead with Sam, in a bad mood, I think, but I can't remember why. Because we've bought our council house and have just seen the new interest rates? Because his toast wasn't hard enough at breakfast time? That's the way with moods, isn't it, they're all-consuming and forgettable. He's not powering away from us, that would be an exaggeration, but with the Baltic wind, the girls' little legs and the fact we've come to the beach for some fresh air (mission accomplished) and not to audition for the Olympic walking team, he's put some distance between himself and us.

'Henry,' I shout. 'Wait for us.'

'He can't hear you,' Rachel shouts, pushing her hat back from her brow. 'It's too noisy.'

'The tide's coming,' Eva shouts, pointing.

'We'll be fine,' I shout. 'It takes a while.'

The water groans, white spittle sloshing around its convulsing mass, the clouds, or cloud, a grey blanket pulled tightly over our heads. Reach up and you'd poke right into it, a world sapped of colour and hard edges. The oil rigs on the horizon look like black scratches against their charcoal surrounds.

We stop to pick up shells, keep moving. Henry usually parks about half a mile up the Esplanade and we're heading that way now. To check erosion, the beach is divided by groynes, long wooden barriers with barnacled posts slinking into the sea. They're about waist-high for an adult, and easy enough to clamber over, but can be slippery from seaweed and slime.

'Woah,' Eva shouts, slammed by a stray gust within the overall press of the gale.

'What's Daddy doing?' Rachel asks, pointing.

Henry's up on a groyne with Sam, and, rather than climb across, he's walking tentatively towards the sea. Water crashes into the posts, swallowing the structure maybe ten feet ahead of them.

'Henry,' I shout. 'Henry.'

'He can't hear you,' Eva shouts.

But he does, or just assumes we'll be watching, because he looks in our direction and waves, his hair whipping. He keeps walking slowly, carefully, Sam just ahead of him.

'Is he being a silly billy?' Eva asks.

78

'I think he might be,' I say. 'Come on, let's run up to see what he's doing.'

We forge ahead in gasping, slow-motion movements but before we get there Sam has slipped, back paws first, and is now in the water, his neck craning. Henry kneels and straddles, his groin on the groyne, tries to drag Sam to the surface by his lead, which is mercifully still attached. But the water, the weight of it, he could lose him any second.

'Bloody bampot,' I shout.

'Mum!' Eva cries, shocked.

'Pot of bams,' Rachel shouts.

'Enough,' I shout. 'Come on.'

For a moment, Sam disappears and it's hard to know from our vantage point whether he's been dragged back under or the swell is blocking our view, but it's precarious, we can see that. One wave, that's all it will take, a pusher, to knock Henry in too, *boof, glug,* under he'll go, his head into the corner of a wooden post, his temple punctured like a shaken beer can with a needle hole, an intake of breath, sharp, salty, take it in, breathe deep, swallow the brine, let the brine swallow you. But he gets Sam, somehow, back onto the groyne, his front legs at least, lifts him up, Sam's mouth open and seemingly yelping, a frantic blur of frantic fur. Henry holds him to his drenched chest.

The girls cheer. Their dad, once again, is a hero – it doesn't matter that he's also the villain.

Henry leaps to the sand, puts Sam down and approaches, shivering, his skin blotched purple, hair blowing wildly. He'd benefit from a good shake, like Sam, who is trailing beside him in a state of what appears to be shame. They both look so much smaller than before. Sam, most obviously – he's soaked, his fur flattened. But Henry too – not so much in the moment, at least, not in ways I could fully understand back then, but revisiting it all now.

1986

The girls are ten. It's the first of three summer holidays to Aviemore, two with me, one without, and Henry is stoked – to borrow one of Rachel's Australianisms – with our caravan.

We could have waited until morning to travel to the campsite, it's only a couple of hours' drive, but he insisted we go as soon as possible after work, to maximise our time there, time in which we'll swim in the river, eat food from cans, and get eaten by midges.

It must be coming on for nine in the evening and the Transit's shades are down for Henry and me, Sam sleeping at my feet – we're heading west down the barrel of the A96 straight into the eye of the sun.

'You sleeping yet?' I ask the girls. We've set them up with sleeping bags and pillows in the back of the van – they're lying on the floor, feet facing the back door.

'As if,' Rachel says.

I know they're not, of course I do – they're too excited. I look behind me, through the plastic grating, and see Rachel hugging her Cabbage Patch doll. From the beeps and music, I already know Eva is playing her Pac-Man, and so it is – the music has quickened, meaning she's chasing the ghosts and not vice versa.

'A bit blustery,' Henry says.

'Sure is,' I say.

The van is one thing, the caravan we're towing quite another – both are being walloped by the wind, forcing Henry to grip the steering wheel. I like watching his forearms like this, the muscles, their strength. He's our protector, spends his days hammering, sanding, wiring and sawing so that we can be here, out of danger, with him.

'I still can't get over the deal,' he says. 'What a bargain.'

'Such a bargain,' I say. 'You did really well, love.'

It's come to us, the caravan, in fits and starts. Henry had spotted it a couple of months earlier, propped up on bricks outside a farm he was driving past on the way to a job. On finishing, he'd driven up the gravel driveway to the farmhouse, found some chickens but no humans, and stuck a note to the front door asking if the caravan was for sale and leaving our phone number. A man phoned a fortnight later, introduced himself as Bill, said that aye, maybe, aye, the caravan might be for sale – his mother had lived in it for a few years but she was dead now, she'd died at the hospital, not in the caravan – so yes, maybe, how much were we thinking of paying? Henry said he didn't know, that he was just looking for a caravan to go on holiday with his wife and daughters. Bill invited him to come out any night of the week to have a look and make sure he wanted it, and then they could talk turkey. But when he drove out there, he couldn't find Bill, just the chickens again. The same happened the following evening, and again the following Saturday, and for days to come. Long story short, it took weeks to sort out, but here we are, heading west with our blue and white, slightly rusted caravan in tow, thanks to Henry's chutzpah and perseverance.

'I feel like singing,' he says.

'Sing then,' I say. 'What's stopping you?'

At that, he breaks into 'Summer Holiday' by Cliff Richard and, try as I might – I don't even try – I can't stop myself from joining in. The girls, too young to feel mortified yet, chime in above the beeps of Pac-Man, the thumps of the wind, and before long the four of us are belting out lyrics about blue skies and the wonderful times ahead.

'You're the best dad ever,' Rachel says, when we finish.

'I maybe agree,' Eva says.

Henry looks at me, sees me smiling, looks ahead, grins, drums the steering wheel.

2014

Rachel parks my car, sighs and gets out, Eva too. She feeds the parking meter, returns with a ticket, sticks it to the inside of the windshield, lifts a couple of polo shirts out on hangers, locks the doors. For a second, it looks like they'll cross the road and get on with the task at hand. Instead, they pause, saying nothing to each other but clearly of a similar mind. They stand at the passenger side, their behinds against the car, squinting through the afternoon sunlight into the park. Children slip down slides, soar on swings.

I stand next to them (have no legs), admiring the sycamores, shrubs and rhododendrons, and the grass, even the grass, just look at it, so luscious, its silky roots snaking into earth and practically begging to be pulled like hair.

We came to this park often when they were little, after visiting Nana Jean, played I Spy and ate sandwiches at the . . . *What starts with an 'f', girls? Fountain!* Eva once got chased by an Alsatian, and Rachel fell another time and scraped her knee, but other than that, it was a safe haven for us, just as it seems to be for them now. They've still not turned to look at the tired granite walls of the lunatic asylum, the border between childhood permanence and their first glimpse of minds on the fritz.

It's getting cold – I don't feel it, but Rachel does, she has goosebumps. They cross at the lights and head into the hospital grounds. They zig-zag in search of the right door – I told them exactly which ward he was in, how to get there, but never mind – pick the wrong one, read a sign with directions, walk down a corridor hung with hospital art.

'Uhhhhhh.' A young man groans, his face pressed against the wall, marching on the spot as if he's reached the edge of a computer game and wants to keep moving. 'Uhhhhhh.'

'Excuse me, can I help you?' Eva asks. She reaches out, tries to be gentle, but the man turns to look at her and starts screaming, terrified.

'It's OK,' a staff member says, appearing from a doorway and running towards him. 'It's OK, Mark, it's OK.'

The girls nod and forge ahead, the polo shirts swinging from their hangers in Rachel's hands. They're for Henry's birthday and have cost next to nothing, but it's the style of shirt he's worn for years: collared, three buttons, bland. When we became a couple, in those early years, he would cut the labels off his clothing, telling me he wasn't interested in advertising on behalf of companies and that branding was for cows. Now, he just doesn't care – it doesn't matter anymore and, though I respected his stance at the time, it maybe never did. They've bought the shirts in medium, on my advice, rather than large or even extra-large as they would in the past. They were sceptical that he'd fit into a medium – even more so when I warned them it would still be too big.

Another young man passes, talking gibberish, flanked by what I assume are his parents. They look distressed, the mother particularly. She's holding his arm.

'Farts,' the young man says. 'Leave me, haha, what, hello everyone, grind them, that's right, yeah, farts.'

For the briefest second, it looks as if Rachel will start laughing but she controls herself.

They ring the bell on the security door, wait.

A woman opens it and shouts 'Henry' before returning her gaze to the girls. 'There's no mistaking the family resemblance,' she says, smiling. 'Henry,' she calls again. 'Henry.'

Henry clearly hasn't heard. The girls are taken by another woman to a ward with six beds.

Like me, the girls don't see him at first – but, oh yes, look, he's sitting in the corner, willowy and hunched, spindly and sad. His eyes twitch towards the girls but he appears to be looking right through them.

Eva pushes her hair behind her ear, coughs quietly, looks crestfallen. It's the first time either girl has seen him for nearly a year. Sometimes he's here, sometimes in his flat, sometimes here again.

'I'll leave you to it,' the woman says, smiling at the girls and waving at Henry before departing.

'Hey, Dad,' Rachel says, crouching down in front of him before thinking better of it and standing upright again. 'It's good to see you.'

Henry grips the armrests on his chair, pulls and pushes himself onto his feet in awkward increments. He smiles, embarrassed, revealing gaps where teeth should be. They've been falling out, he's told me that on the phone, it's a shame. 'Hiya,' he says eventually, his voice a whisper.

'Shut your fucking pie hole,' shouts another man from behind a nylon curtain.

The girls look round quickly, startled, turn back to Henry.

'Happy birthday,' Rachel says, brandishing the shirts.

He reaches towards them slowly, as if they're suspended in gloop just behind a forcefield. Rachel meets him halfway, hooks the hangers over his fingers. He looks at the girls, at me – at least, that's how it feels – at the shirts, before doing an eight-point turn to look at his locker. His arm still extended, clothes shaking on their hangers, he stops and turns back again in stages to face the girls. 'They'll get stolen,' he says. 'Things go missing in here all the time.'

They were made by small children in the Far East, I want to say. You have already contributed to their economic enslavement and unenviable life expectancy just by accepting such gifts. We've stolen from them, Henry – it's only fitting that their wares should be stolen from us. The girls spent more on the parking ticket coming to see you here than they did on your stupid supermarket shirts. Nobody cares, Henry. I'm dead, you'll be dead soon, live your bloody life and stop worrying about trivial nonsense.

'I don't know what to do,' he croaks. 'I could lock the door, I suppose.'

When eventually the shirts are stowed safely, the girls walk him inchmeal, one at either side, to the communal area. Places have been set at a long wooden table but there's no sign of forthcoming victuals. A TV blares behind a thick brick pillar – there's a suggestion of the bodies watching, a tapping foot, an elbow, someone's hand.

The girls sit at the table, opposite Henry, cast their eyes towards an exercise bike with missing pedals, an acoustic guitar with missing strings, some puzzle boxes with – almost certainly – missing pieces.

'Fancy a tea, folks?' asks a bearded man in casual clothes who is either a staff member or a patient who enjoys playing host.

The girls smile, shake their heads. Henry looks at them, at the man, back at the girls, searching desperately for the right answer. What is it? What could it be? Does he, or does he not, want to commit to a warm beverage served with too much milk in a cup whose lip has been smoothed by a succession of sick people's mouths?

'No,' he whispers. 'No, thank you.'

The man leaves. Henry purses his lips, looks lost. The girls have already asked him how he is – 'Crap just about sums it up' – and now . . . now what? Maybe, I don't know – how were their flights, Henry? How are your grandchildren? Do you know Ewan has broken his wrist? How is Rachel's life going in Australia otherwise? How is Eva's life in Spain? Is she enjoying teaching? Is she happy?

He lowers his elbows onto the table, drops his face slowly into his palms. 'I'm sorry,' he says, looking up. 'This is terrible. Your mum, how is she?'

'Oh, you know . . . dying,' Rachel says.

Henry's face descends slowly back into his hands.

'She's off the medication,' Eva says. 'So, barring a miracle, it's–'

'I wish I could make things right,' Henry says, cutting her off, maybe not even hearing. 'I wish, oh god, I just wish that . . .'

'You could help her?' Eva prompts.

'. . . that I could sleep,' he says.

'What tablets are you on?' Rachel asks.

'Diazepam,' he says uncertainly. 'Laxatives.'

'Laxatives?'

'I haven't been to the toilet since I came in here. It was the same last time. They're so dirty, the walls are crawling . . .'

With the TV's volume holding steady and Henry's diminishing, it's getting harder to hear him. Like the girls, I lean towards him, getting closer to what he is, what he's become. I don't want them to experience this. I'd prefer it if they got up and left. So long, Dad, thanks for all the fish. There are too many pauses, caesuras, non-sequiturs. He looks pathetic and that makes me feel pathetic. He can't help it, he really can't, but I don't care. He's a stupid, stupid man who has let us down and I want the girls to leave. He doesn't deserve them. I do. I should live. Not him.

He looks up briefly, plants his face in his hands again.

'Do you want to go outside, Henry?' asks the man who offered the tea. He's standing next to us, smiling in a patronising way.

Henry stares at him, draws his mouth into a silent whistle, the muscles in his forearms spasming. 'Not really,' he says. 'I don't have any shoes.'

The girls and I instinctively look under the table, all of us no doubt expecting to see him in socks, but he's wearing the white trainers I bought him only months ago.

'You need shoes?' Rachel asks.

'For the service,' Henry says.

'You're going to church?' Eva asks.

'For the funeral,' he says, correcting himself, his face clenching.

'We can buy you some shoes,' Rachel says. 'Just some black ones, yeah? I can bring them to you here, if you like. Or I can take them to your flat.'

'You've been there?'

'This morning, yeah, just checking for mail. Nice view, isn't it? Better than staring out at a brick wall.'

The orderly, if that's what he is, walks away again, content. Henry looks at the girls, eyes twitching. 'How long has it been since Australia?'

'Couple of years,' Rachel says.

Chapter 8

It might sound strange to say I'm short of breath, but that's how it feels. I'm struggling to keep up with my childhood self as I run along the streets that lead to the prefabs, my leather satchel bouncing on my back. My shoes – I remember those – are unyielding, nip my toes, but I'm speeding, skirt flapping. School's out for the day and I want to get home to play on the back green. But wait . . .

I stop suddenly at Alan Bisset's shop – Mr Bisset, as I know him at the time. He must be forty, decrepit to me then, a baby to me now. There's a brown terrier on a big table at the window, a curled-up ginger kitten in a cardboard box, two blue budgies in a hanging cage, but they're not what catches my eye. Up close to the glass, in another box, are three snowy mice, beautiful little things, their tails, oh, I want one, the smallest, it looks sleepy, resting its head against the price tag as if it's a pillow.

I take off again – holy heck – sprint all the way back to our prefab.

My father's already at home, in the kitchen, must have finished work early. His chiselled jaw, his kind eyes. Dad, oh Dad. He's snipping thin strips of apple into bite-sized soupçons for the sparrows. Once that's done, he'll mix in some seed and furnish the feeder at the window. He's equanimous in his actions, a Zen master by way of Aberdeenshire, and there I am, sweating and panting, struggling to contain myself.

'What's the hurry, love?' His smile melts my heart, then and now.

'I've . . .' I try to catch my breath. 'I've seen this mouse, Dad, a pretty wee mouse. Do you think I could get it? It's at Mr Bisset's and it's got these little pink feet, with teeny toes. And its tail, Dad, you should see its tail. It's got this funny wee twitchy nose.' I twitch my nose, a decent impersonation. 'Dad, he's gorgeous.'

'You seem quite taken wi' it,' he says, laughing. 'I'm nae sure your mother would appreciate a mouse, though. She set Elsie's tabby from doon the road on the last one that was here.'

'But this would be different, Dad. I'd look after it. I'd love it. I really want it, Dad. Please, Dad.'

'Well, I dee hae some coins here for the coupons,' he says. 'How much is it, love?'

'They're thruppence each, Dad. Mr Bisset must want rid of them.'

He takes a sixpenny bit from the bundle, gives it to me. 'See if ye can get a boxie for it to live in too.'

'Dad, thank you,' I say, kissing his head, hugging him.

'Mind those roads,' he shouts as I race out the door.

I'm going as fast as I can – in case the shop shuts early today, in case, no, please no, the mouse gets sold to somebody else. That would be the worst. What would I do? Take another? I didn't like the others, not as much.

The traffic's light by modern standards but I still need to stop before haring across a couple of the roads. In those moments,

I bend over, hold my bare knees, breathe deeply. I'll be fine, still have plenty of pep. I dart through a gap between buses, reach the opposite pavement and bound ahead.

I virtually skid to a halt outside Mr Bisset's – he's still open, that's good. The mouse . . . Where is it? It's there, where it was before, still dozy.

I push open the door – the bell trills – see Mr Bisset standing behind the counter. He's reading a newspaper and barely looks up – I'm the only other person in his shop but there are lots of animals looking content and bored.

I have the tanner in my hand, damp with sweat.

'Hello, Mr Bisset,' I say. 'I wonder if you could help me. I'm quite taken with one of the mice in your window display. Do you think I'd be able to have a look at it, please?'

'Ye're wanting a moosie?' he asks, peering down at me over horn-rimmed glasses. It's murky in the shop and, from memory, smells – I don't know how he can read in here.

'Yes, please, Mr Bisset.'

'I think 'at can be arranged,' he says.

He limps towards the window – a war wound from North Africa, according to my father – moves the box with the ginger kitten, reaches over the table to the mice.

He's picked up the wrong one, I just know he has.

'It's the dreamy one,' I say. 'Closest to the price tag.'

'They're a' the same, dear. Same mither.' He lumbers towards me, opens his hands. A mouse, dazed but unthreatened.

'I'm sorry,' I say. 'It's just . . . It's the other one I want. Can I show you, please?'

He tuts, mutters something I can't make out then or now, collects himself. 'As ye wish, quine.' He gestures for me to get the mouse myself, shuffles closely behind me. I stand on tiptoes at the table's edge, crane my neck, make sure I'm happy with my choice – yes, I'm happy, it's a perfect little thing, but I can't reach it, my arms aren't long enough.

'Can I kneel on this, please?' I ask, pointing at the table.

'As ye wish, dear,' he says.

I test the weight of one knee on the table, hitch up my skirt, climb on with my second. I can't see it at the time, but Mr Bisset is reaching out behind me, about to make contact, when – No! – the budgies start flapping and chirping, several dogs start barking, baring their teeth, the kitten in the box starts hissing.

'What in the name . . .?' Mr Bisset says.

'I'm sorry,' I say, backing slowly, carefully off the table. 'Is that me? Did I make that happen?'

I carry the mouse to the counter in my cupped hands, put my nose to its nose, feel its toes on my fingers. Mr Bisset wipes his forehead with a dark handkerchief, looks relieved that the animals have settled down.

'You'll be needing a box,' he says, pressing the keys on the till.

'If you have one, yes, please,' I say. I open my hands a little to look at my furry friend, its red eyes, so sweet. Mousey. Is it a boy or a girl? A girl, I'll later discover, but either way I'll call it Mousey.

'So, 'at's a shilling for the moosie and thruppence for the box,' he says.

'A shilling?' I say. 'I'm sorry, Mr Bisset. Isn't it thruppence for the mouse?'

'Nuh, a shilling,' he says. 'They're actually quite rare, white mice.'

'But it says on the box . . .'

'The box?' he repeats. 'Oh no, dear, 'at's just an old box I had lying aroon.'

92

Is he angry with me? Have I upset him?

'I only have sixpence,' I say.

'Right,' he says. 'Well, I do need to shut up shop for the day.'

'I only have a tanner,' I say.

'That's right,' he says. 'Ye telt me just a moment ago. If you could pop the moosie back in the box afore leaving.'

I start walking towards the window with Mousey, stop, turn. 'Can I please just take it home, Mr Bisset? I'll come back with the rest of the money another day, cross my heart. I'm scared someone else will take it or something bad will happen to it.'

'I'm afraid I canna bend the rules,' Mr Bisset says. 'The ither bairns would start takkin advantage.'

'Oh,' I say, looking into my cupped hands at Mousey. 'The thing is, Mr Bisset, I'd not tell anyone. I'm very good at keeping secrets, Brownie Promise.'

I'm not in the Brownies but my friend Anne is, and I know the Brownie Promise is sacred.

Mr Bisset drags the back of his hand across his lips, looks unsure. 'I'll tell ye what,' he says, 'I hae some nice boxies through the back, up high on a shelf and it's a pain to reach them wi' this blasted leg. If ye help me get them doon, ye can hae one for free, and I'll gie ye the moosie for half-price as payment. How does that sound?'

'I'd be happy to help,' I say.

Mr Bisset takes Mousey from me and returns him to the box at the window, leads me, limping, towards the cramped back room. 'The ladder's just there,' he says. 'If ye ging up it, I'll stand at the bottom here holding, to make sure ye're safe.'

A couple of the dogs are getting jittery, low-level grumbles, their jowls tightening. I'm on the second rung, four more to go, when the door trills.

'Hello.'

I know that voice.

'Hello.'

It's my father, he's here, my father.

'Oh, there you are,' he says as I emerge from the back room, cheeks flushed. 'I remembered I had this.' He holds up a box – for shoes but converted with care for a pigeon he nursed back to health.

'Terrific,' Mr Bisset says. 'That's just what we were looking for. Let me get the moosie for ye . . .' He limps past the till to the window, reaches over the table.

My father, tall and proud, stands next to me, rubs my head.

'Now, is this the right een?' Mr Bisset asks.

I look into his cupped hands and yes, it's Mousey, my Mousey.

My father opens the box – there's shredded paper, some cut-up apple and carrot – and Mr Bisset places Mousey gently inside.

'There you go, love,' my father says, passing me the box, smiling.

'Let's call it thruppence,' Mr Bisset says, pressing the keys on his till.

1997

I'm in our hallway – the *Evening Express* is on the phone table with the headline 'Horror Smash' and a photo of a contorted car. I can hear Rachel clearly at the time, and also now, looking on.

'People are losing their minds,' she says. 'The funeral's going to be nuts. They reckon they were doing more than a hundred miles an hour through that tunnel.'

She's calling from Brixton, where she lives in a squat with

her friend – that's what she called her back then – Gloria. The two of them ran off to London like Dick Whittington and his cat the day after Rachel and Eva turned seventeen, and have been living there together, and sometimes apart, ever since. I haven't met Gloria, never will, even though she grew up in Aberdeen. She's a tattoo artist, painter, sometime protester, will go on to work as a town planner for local government. I haven't visited their squat either but can picture its low ceilings and dumpy walls – it's just the name, isn't it . . . squat.

Is Rachel on smack? Cocaine? I don't ask, now that she's an adult. You learn to back off. All that time you've invested, all that care, the tending, deadheading, watering. You can retreat now. Bugger off. Let them be. Stop worrying. What do I care if she's shooting up, gets HIV, dies of an overdose, has to sell herself in Soho to fund her habit? I don't. I care. I care. I really do. She doesn't sound angry, though, and that's always a relief. She's working in a bar, apparently, pulling pints – no shame in that, I did it for years, had a laugh.

I imagine – now, and maybe back then – that the phone box she's calling from reeks of ammonia and nitrogen, the handset of burnt plastic and sweaty palms. London has been on the news for days, since Princess Diana was crumpled in a car with Dodi Fayed, triggering mass psychosis. That's not the horror smash I want to talk to Rachel about but, still, it's been everywhere. Tens of thousands of people congregating at Buckingham and Kensington Palace: grown men displaying serious psychogenic symptoms, gnashing their teeth and bawling publicly; distraught families, their faces scrunched as if one of their own, maybe a child of theirs, had died, holding up banners with *Queen of Hearts* and *We Love You* and *True Inspiration*, the infectious hysteria just a few steps short of the dancing plagues that swept Europe in the Middle Ages, crowds of people unable to stop dancing until they collapsed, even died, from exhaustion and injury, the musicians who joined them and tried to settle them with calming tunes only making matters worse.

Teddies – who were all the teddies for? Diana's boys were twelve and fifteen – mounting in gigantic fluffy body piles. Photos and printouts of Diana everywhere you looked – the golden hairspray years, the edgy mousse era, the yellow blouse, the white two-piece, meeting Mother Teresa, who will die the day before Diana is laid to rest. More than 60 million blooms will be laid across the city, a health and traffic hazard that will get in the way of the funeral car, its windscreen wipers struggling to bat away orchids and peace lilies. Boy and Girl Scouts spending weeks in that saccharine scent, wading through indole and putrescine, taking fallen but still presentable flora to nursing homes, toys to children's wards, the dead and dying bouquets to Kensington Palace where they'll be used as fertiliser. A city in the grips of clammy decay.

I could bring Rachel up to speed with Eva – she's graduated from Glasgow with a First and is heading to Spain for a gap year before hopefully returning to do a postgrad teaching course in Edinburgh. But first I have bad tidings to share, as per the *Evening Express* I'm lifting from the table.

'Remember your friend Barry?' I ask.

'Barry Winter?'

'Yes, Winter. He's been in an accident, dearie. It's on the front page of the paper.'

I read the story into the phone with impeccable 'hello girl' diction. Barry is in a full body cast, spiral fractures in both femurs, broken arms, cracked ribs, ruptured vertebrae, whip-lash, bruising. 'He's lucky to be alive,' I say. 'I mean, when you think of Diana . . . They reckon it'll be months before he can even start physio.'

Car horns honk in the background. Someone with a cockney accent shouts obscenities. 'Poor Barry,' Rachel says eventually. A series of beeps as she feeds more coins into the phone. It's a lot to take in, the news but also the timing, a nationwide dirge for Diana, people painting their pain en plein air, and now this, the sorrow of young Winter, more consequential than Diana's demise for those to whom he's connected but somehow still subsumed into the broader mourning sickness.

'I feel for his parents,' I say. 'What were they called again?'

'Joyce and Ian,' Rachel says.

'That's right,' I say. 'Joyce and Ian. A lovely couple.'

'I saw him just before leaving Aberdeen,' she says. 'Complete coincidence. He gave me a lift home from the beach and told me he had a secret for getting from A to B quicker than anyone else. It was pretty simple. He just drove at the speed limit, never above or below it, even at roundabouts and junctions.'

'That sounds dangerous,' I say.

'Evidently,' she says.

'I can send some flowers and a card,' I say.

'That'd be nice,' she says. More coins going in. 'Do you remember that thing with his Smurfs?'

Another secret of Barry's that Rachel had told me years ago in confidence. I'd forgotten but remember it immediately then and now.

He had all the Smurf figurines, knew all their names. Joyce and Ian had even built him a replica Smurf Village with chipboard and AstroTurf from B&Q. By day, they were just rubberised figurines, Smurfette and whatever the others were called. But by night, when the curtains were drawn, Barry would sing 'Kumbaya' to them like some god of the Smurfs, at which point they'd start milling around the village, chatting with each other, telling jokes, feeling blue.

'He wasn't joking,' Rachel says. 'He really believed it.'

'Did you?' I ask.

'I don't know,' she says, laughing. 'We were kids. He was pretty convincing.'

'Did your sister believe it too?'

'I'm not sure she knew.'

'She was up here last week,' I say. 'She says hi.'

Silence. 'That's . . . good, I guess. Look, Mum, I have to go, I'm out of coins.'

'Listen, love, do you need any money? Are you eating OK?'

'I'm fine, Mum, love you, got to go.'

1987

I know exactly where and when we are by the sky, the way it looks. A poet might call it splenetic, but I doubt the sky feels emotions. It can certainly inspire them, though. It's the second – my last – year at Aviemore and Henry, me and the girls – they must be eleven – are in the caravan, kneeling on the miniature sofa, looking out the side window. Sam is lying on the rug, waiting for something, anything, to happen. From our spot, we can just about see the river through the pine. The trees, grass and other caravans are illuminated by the brightest sunlight I've ever seen, the clouds as ominous as an ogre's mouth.

A thunderclap shakes the caravan. Rachel screams and we all start laughing, jolt and laugh again as fork lightning stabs the air. A moment's repose. Another crack, the sky, the air, is taking damage. It's as if God herself is stamping on and hitting us with 300 million volts. The heavens open, rain falling not as individual drops, it seems, but solid sheets. The sun cowers behind a cloud that snuffs out its light, watches as water bounces waist-high from the concrete path. Another crack, another electrostatic discharge. Nervous laughter from the caravan next to ours, loud enough to pierce even the racket of rain crashing onto our cold tin roof.

'It's the end of the world,' Rachel cries.

'We're doomed,' Eva shouts, feigning a swoon.

Henry and I laugh along with them, pretend we're praying for mercy – 'Please save us!' – or maybe we're not pretending, it's hard to tell. If pressed, we'd probably express a high degree of confidence that the rain will pass, as all things must. We'd laugh incredulously at the notion that, just this once, it might not, and indeed could fall far heavier than it is now, a deluge washing bodies and buildings along rivers old and new into rapidly conjoining seas, the lightning reanimating or annihilating corpses.

'I'll pop the kettle on,' I shout between thunderbolts.

'That'd be nice, love,' Henry shouts. 'Girls, shall we play Connect Four – you both versus me?'

I mooch to the kitchenette, a picture of late-thirties puppy fat, followed by Sam, his legs already failing, switch on the kettle. Eva ducks into the bathroom with something in her hand, pulls the door shut quickly. Rachel starts setting up the Connect Four. I snap a water cracker in two, feed both halves to Sam. His tail wags, he wants another, and he can have it, yes he can, good boy. The kettle clicks, nickel leaching into the water. The cups, I get those, the teabags.

There's an extra thud within the reckoning of rain – someone has left the caravan.

'Marg, quick, come look,' Henry shouts.

'My god, Mum, check it out,' Rachel shouts.

I hurry back over, kneel next to them on the sofa, watch Eva waving to us from outside, in her swimsuit and cap. She must

99

be cold, the rain ricochets off her, but if she is, she doesn't show it. She tiptoes to the inundated path, puts her hands on her hips, and starts strutting, her legs crossing in front of each other dramatically as she moves forward, her bare feet all but submerged. She stops, throws her head back, turns a full circle and, as the thunder claps, keeps walking, a model in the making, nature be damned. Rachel wipes the window with her sleeve, is beside herself laughing, Henry and me too.

'She's definitely your daughter,' I say, nudging him. 'She's yours too,' he says.

We're not the only ones enjoying it. Happy faces appear through holes rubbed in condensation – kids, adults, elderly. She's putting on a real show, defying the water gods, and we all think it's bloody hilarious.

Chapter 9

2005

I've long admired Edinburgh Castle. Not its interior – I've never seen that – but how it looks from outside, perched on that big rock, the sheer drop down one side where Mary, Queen of Scots secretly lowered her newborn son, James, who would grow up in exile before returning – a Protestant, no longer Catholic – to become the first monarch of Britain, all but guaranteeing Scotland's cultural oblivion and slide into centuries-long servitude. A traitor, then? No. Well, who knows? Apparently, it didn't happen, the whole lowering-down-the-cliff bit, or the exile – that was just a tale my mother used to tell me, part of a suite that included the Glencoe Massacre (Clan MacDonald's women, men and children betrayed by the Campbells and slaughtered in their sleep) and Robert the Bruce hiding in a cave and taking solace from the perseverance of a spider. That's how it goes with stories: if at first you don't succeed, lie, lie again.

I read once that King James wore baggy clothes because he feared being stabbed and thought generous tailoring might confound his assailants. I read too that his mother Mary's beheading at Fotheringhay Castle was a particularly gruesome affair, her head hanging on for grisly life thanks to a blunt blade, her mouth still moving a quarter of an hour after the hacking began. What was she saying? *In my end is my beginning*, or some such. But you just don't know.

What I do know, and can reconfirm as I watch myself and Eva move along the stands in search of our seats high above the castle esplanade, is that my marriage is over. Maybe not divorce – we never will, it transpires – but in the sense of it having a happy, or potentially happy, trajectory, our union is dead in the water. That's why Henry's not with me, even though we'd planned the trip together and bought tickets for the Tattoo. You can't drive down there alone, he'd said. Oh yeah, just watch me, I'd said before slamming the door. It's also why – I'm guessing, but it's a safe bet in this era – he's getting torn into the drinks cabinet back home in Aberdeen. It comes in waves, his hankering for stupefaction and his inability to resist, a tidal swell that corrodes his sandstone defences. It's been sixteen years, give or take. The Big Book talks about the Four Horsemen – Terror, Bewilderment, Frustration and Despair. And to me, looking at Henry, that's fairly accurate. There's no mention of the horses, just the riders, and I imagine all four huddled on the back of the same beast, elbowing each other and jockeying for position. If you loved me, you would stop, Henry – how many times have I said that? I do love you, Marg. That's why I got you, Champ. I love you. Then stop drinking, Henry. I will, Marg, I will.

We've been retired, or as good as, for a couple of years. He sold his business at its high-water mark – twelve employees, eight vehicles, a storage and office space for spare parts and me, a large and loyal customer base. The name lives on, even though three of his handymen were handywomen, but Henry's Handyperson Services didn't sound right. He was fifty-six at the time, not young, not old, and that could have been an end to it – down tools, down fewer cask ales. It behooved him to stop, but those hooves – Henry's Horsepeople of the Alcoholalypse.

Eva and I lay empty shopping bags on our folding plastic seats. It's not raining now, but it was. The castle is lit up, its brickwork caramel, the sky purple. It's the most besieged place in the UK, Edinburgh Castle – a couple of dozen times in armed conflict, countless more by the tourist hordes since. There must be, I don't know, five thousand people in the stands, maybe more.

'Lots of Americans,' Eva whispers.

'So many,' I whisper back. Those accents, there's no mistaking them. Sometimes they call the city Edinbro, and the people Scotch as if we're a broth.

Eva's new shoulder-length hairstyle suits her – a lob, she called it. Mine is perilously short – what was I thinking? From memory, I wanted a pixie cut like Keira Knightley . . . more like Margaret Unsightly.

I open the chocolate eclairs, nearly drop the bag and glossy Tattoo programme when fireworks fizz from the ramparts. We applaud as the massed pipes and drums of the Scottish infantry regiments march through the gatehouse, under the portcullis, over the drawbridge. The sound is overwhelming, an almighty stramash of snares, bass drums and bagpipes being thumped, rattled and blown by the Royal Highland Fusiliers, the Royal Scots, the Scots Guards, the King's Own Scottish Borderers, the Black Watch, the Highlanders, the Argyll and Sutherland Highlanders . . . Oh, and going by the programme, an Australian outfit too, the Rats of Tobruk Memorial Pipes and Drums. They fan out, following their respective pipe majors and playing 'Cullen Bay'.

It's the sixtieth anniversary of VJ Day, six decades since the end of the Second World War. They play a tribute in slow time to the heroes – that's what the programme calls them – of the Battle of Kohima.

Eva leans into me, mumbles something about tomorrows, todays.

'What's that, love?'

'John Maxwell Edmonds. It's an epitaph for the fallen.'

'Oh right.'

I like when they're referred to as the fallen, would be delighted if those young men ripped from their communities to gun each other down in places they'd never heard of had merely fallen, if wars were won or lost on the ability to push people over, trip them up, after which they're out, game over – I'm sorry but you have to go home now, we're heading to Kohima to make them fall over too.

I recognise this one. They're playing 'When You and I Were Young, Maggie'.

The green grove is gone from the hill, Maggie,
Where first the daisies sprung . . .

How old am I? Fifty-five? Fifty-six? I have more fingers than years left to live.

No sooner have the infantry bands marched back through the gatehouse than a troupe of small children roar into the esplanade on motorbikes – the Imps Motorcycle Display Team, the brochure says. Seven- and eight-year-olds on Yamahas. They do cross-overs and other stunts to riotous laughter and applause – because they're kids, just as they were in my Grandad Duncan's Lancaster bomber over Würzburg, in the hundreds of other planes bombing Germany that night, in thousands of tanks, shivering in trenches, caught up in barbed wire, in firing lines, behind machine guns, trampled on, decomposing.

'It's so good to have you here, Mum,' Eva says, squeezing my arm.

'Wouldn't have missed it,' I say, angling the eclairs in her direction. 'I mean, the show, it's great, but I wouldn't have missed seeing you, Eva. I'm just sorry your dad couldn't come.'

'I hope he's OK,' she says.

'I think he's struggling,' I say, eyes on the mini bikers. 'I don't know what to do.'

To be young, or younger – that would help, although you don't know how tight the escape tunnels are going to get until the walls start closing in, don't even think they're going to narrow, you're just enjoying or destroying what you have. Eva's content with Thom and, as far as I know, he's content with her. They had a miscarriage, of course, but that was some time ago and it's a year or two until the next one. They rent a lovely flat in the Grassmarket, at the foot of Castle Rock. It's not cheap but it's a nice part of the city, the one-time setting for public executions, not least the Covenanters during the seventeenth-century Killing Time. Eva loved all those stories, the lore, took me to the White Hart Inn, just a short stroll from her flat, told me it was not only the oldest pub in Edinburgh but its most haunted. She was greeted heartily by the staff and patrons as soon as we entered, an admired and accepted Aberdonian abroad.

From the Grassmarket, we had to walk up so many steps – one hundred and eighty-seven, I counted – to get to the castle but, still, my legs, just using them, my hot lungs – I'd settle for that now. How many women were marched up those same steps to be burnt at the stake on the esplanade for witchcraft? A few hundred, thanks to the satanic panic of King James, a steady stream of witches – and sometimes warlocks – who in truth were herbalists, mentally ill, or had just annoyed someone.

Only the guilty were set ablaze, though – they condemned themselves by surviving being dunked in a loch while the wrongfully accused spared everyone the bother and drowned.

Thom revelled in those tales, was a story nut like Eva. He's in Cambridge with his family – the schools are shut for summer so they're having a break from work and each other.

The Trinidad and Tobago Defence Force Steel Orchestra and Drums play 'Jamaica Farewell' as they leave the esplanade and most of us are clapping along. The moon, nearly full, is yellow, the sky a chimney-sweep's broom.

'And what about you, Mum? How are you doing?'

'In what sense, dearie?'

'Well, in any sense. I don't know . . . with Dad. Are you happy?'

Eyes front. Some buglers come through the gatehouse, replacing the steel drums, and it's not the most pleasant sound, is it, the bugle, but apparently it carries well on the battlefield, providing top end to the cannons and machine guns. The players are hopping from foot to foot in double time, the witchy flames heating the soles of their feet.

'That's a hard question to answer,' I say, and I'm blinking more frequently than usual – Eva can't see it, but I am. Of course I'm happy. How could I not be? Rachel finally – *finally* – seems to be sorting herself out, has just finished her Gestalt therapy training in London, where she lives with Gem. It took a full five years to gain her qualification, with a gap in between . . . that doesn't matter. She's managed to turn everything around before thirty, to atone. And I'm with Eva – how could that not make me happy? My gorgeous daughter who lives in a beautiful city and teaches at a prestigious school. I'm happy with my loyal husband who at that very second is probably knee-deep in Tia Maria or – are things that bad yet? – doing shots with my Fiori di Capri perfume.

'I'm happy about your sister,' I say.

'Me too,' she says. 'That's really good news.'

'You haven't spoken to her?'

'No. I want to. It's just difficult with us.'

'Why?' I ask. 'In the past, I get it, but why's it still hard now?'

'Oh, you know,' she says.

Oh, Eva, just . . . I get it. She swam away from us – you lost a sister, a twin. But from where I am, it's so clear that bygones should be bygones, that it's water under the bridge, that any number of old sayings and idioms are nudging us towards the same fundamental imperative: don't lose touch with blood relatives – they can be replaced to a certain extent but it's never the same.

'You'd have plenty of advice for her,' I say, offering the bag of eclairs blindly. 'About life after graduating, I mean.'

'I suppose,' she says.

We watch the next few acts in silence and, if I'm honest, it becomes much of a muchness. My biggest takeaway is that the industrial killing machine of the modern military exists alongside all sorts of performance training – how to play drums while riding a bicycle, how to backflip while playing the trumpet, skills that may or may not prove useful in a battle scenario. But as the lights cut out completely, I sit up attentively and reach for Eva's hand.

A single spotlight, trained on the castle ramparts, illuminates a lone kilted soldier in red, with bagpipes. He starts playing a mournful rendition of 'The Skye Boat Song', one of my favourites, and walks slowly along the battlements. *Carry the lad that's born to be king, over the sea to Skye.*

It's hard not to think of Bonnie Prince Charlie, Mary Stuart's great-great-grandson, dressed as an Irish maid while his supporters smuggle him over the water, passing himself off as Betty

Burke for days while the blood of his Jacobite followers seeps into Culloden's fields, the last pitched battle on British soil. His calico gown and quilted petticoat, his large hood, stockings and garters, his pointy shoes and fancy head-dress.

'Look, Mum,' Eva whispers in my ear.

She points into the sky, and I see it: the silhouette of a passenger plane against the nearly full moon, the strains of the lone piper, the fact I'm here, right now, with my daughter – I know I'll never forget this moment.

'I love you,' I whisper, squeezing her hand.

'Love you too.'

2014

'I've never noticed that your toes are the same as mine,' Rachel says. 'How weird's that?'

She's massaging my feet, my legs up on the footrest of my big brown hospital chair, Champ sleeping underneath. I'm holding my side where the shunt is, trying to make it look as if my hand is resting there casually. I nod, don't open my eyes.

'They curl up and to the side a bit,' she says. 'Your big toes especially. Mine do that too.'

'That feels so good,' I say. My legs are hideous – don't look, Margaret. It's the first time I've had a massage from either of the girls, apart from when they were children and they gave me pale imitations of an adult massage, or what I imagined an adult massage might feel like. Henry never gave them, wasn't big on other people's pain – either because he didn't believe in it or didn't want it to exist. And because of that, anything even vaguely corrective, including neck or back rubs which, let's be honest, are as much about giving and receiving pleasure as removing pain, were out of the question. I'm enjoying this one, though, even if I've left it a little late. The toes Rachel is rubbing, the feet, ankles, sinew and bone, they'll be ash soon enough.

'They're like fingerprints,' Eva says from the couch. 'Every toe is unique. Criminals have even been prosecuted because of their toeprints.'

'Lovely,' I say, eyes still closed. Going by the plate on the sideboard, we had enchiladas for dinner – or the girls did, at least, I've barely touched mine.

'You know the film *Frankenstein*?' Rachel asks.

'Not really, love,' I say. 'Maybe. I don't know if I've ever seen it. Oh, maybe a bit softer there, please.' She weakens her grip on the ball of my foot, keeps massaging.

'The black and white one,' Rachel says. 'With Herman Munster.'

'That's Boris Karloff,' Eva says. 'James Whale, the director, used him again in *Bride of Frankenstein* a few years later. They're both classics of the pre-Code genre.'

'I don't know that I've ever seen it,' I say again.

'Well, me either,' Rachel says. 'But I watched some of it last night on YouTube. Just the bit where the monster comes to life. I wanted to compare something from the book.'

'Films and books present different exigencies,' Eva says in a tone that, thankfully, Rachel lets slide.

'There's a lightning storm outside, and the flashes illuminate the other people in the laboratory – a romantic couple, I don't know who they are, and another, older man. Victor's assistant seems to be invisible to him. "Quite a good scene, isn't it?" Victor says. "One man, crazy – three very sane spectators."'

Oh, my feet, the relaxation in my face – keep going, Rachel, don't stop. The endorphins – I miss those.

'Victor cranks the monster up to the open roof on a trestle, so he can be struck by the lightning.'

'Three hundred million volts,' Eva says. 'That's going to sting.'

'When he cranks it back down, he sees its fingers are moving and runs around like a fruitcake shouting, "It's alive, it's alive." But in the book there's nothing about lightning. Just yellow skin that *scarcely covered the work of muscles and arteries underneath*, a spark of being.'

'It's implied,' Eva says. 'Shelley was inspired by galvanism, the idea that scientists could use electricity to stimulate or restart life. It was a well-known theory at the time.'

'That's strange,' I say. I don't know if it's strange or not. Is it strange? I do know that this is nice, the three of us being together, Rachel's knuckles pressing into the sole of my foot.

2021

Here's something I've seen twice recently: Rachel and Gem putting on masks before leaving their house – not Halloween masks, although I did see them do that once (they weren't very scary). These are more like the ones the doctors were wearing when they nixed my necrotic gallbladder, or the ones those people were wearing outside Eva and Juan's apartment in Madrid. Blue on one side, white on the other, with elasticated straps for the ears. It's not just them, either. Their neighbours – *G'day, mates!* – have them too. Even some of the kids. William – he's so tall now, such a handsome lad – is the first to put his on at their front door. Ewan doesn't, and I've noticed the same with the smaller kids who live nearby. Ewan must be ten now, or thereabouts, which would make William twelve or so.

Puberty, if it hasn't arrived yet, is on its way. I can't speak for mothers with boys, but if it's anything like it was for me with the girls, I feel sorry for Rachel and Gem. And for William, of course. Puberty's a riptide at the best of times, its hormonal undercurrents dragging kids under, their bodies thrashing, lashing out and repurposing before bobbing back to the surface, transformed.

Eva somehow managed to keep a foothold in the best bits of who she'd been before, came up for air easily enough, but Rachel, the Rachel I'd known and loved, took so long to re-emerge.

Ewan has a couple of years before his change, I think. They stroll past gum trees and other masked people, into a small park: two mothers, two sons, one grandmother walking (I have no legs) by their side. Like Ewan, I'm wearing no mask, have nothing to hide.

'Shall we go over and look at the veggie patch?' Gem asks.
'Do we have to?' William asks, shoulders slumping.

'It's important to get some exercise,' Rachel says.

'You said we'd be out for five minutes,' Ewan says. 'It's already been more than that.'

Both mums continue walking to the veggie patch and the boys reluctantly follow.

'Do you remember what this one is?' Gem asks, pointing at . . . I don't know what it is, maybe a potato plant.

'A hamburger tree,' William says, adjusting his mask, shoulders slumping again.

'Lettuce?' Ewan asks hopefully.

'Actually, I don't know either,' Rachel says. 'What is it?'

'A potato plant,' Gem says. 'And that one there's silver beet.'

'What's that one there?' William asks.

'That's a weed,' Gem says.

'Why's someone growing weeds?' Ewan asks.

'They're not,' Rachel says. 'They just grow.'

Chapter 10

2012

I'm at Tullamarine Airport in Melbourne, waiting for Henry and me to appear through the sliding doors like sequinned dancers from a cake, and it's boring, not just standing here with no legs – my days are not even days and I'm over it all.

Our plane has landed – I saw it on the board, Rachel too. She's standing behind the Arrivals barrier looking tired but excited and somehow healthier than she ever does in Aberdeen. William – he's about to turn three – is standing between us, holding a cardboard sign, with some felt-tip squiggles, that says *Grandma and Grandpa*.

Henry and I have flown 10,000 miles to see their new life in Australia, to mark William's birthday and to meet Ewan for the first time in the flesh. I do miss it, the flesh – take issue with my lack of soft tissue. The girls, my flesh and blood, I miss them even though I see them all the time.

'Just keep the sign up, mate,' Rachel tells William. 'They'll be here soon, I promise.'

After a long pause, the Arrival doors swoosh open again and a young woman with dreadlocks and dirty-looking clothes emerges and gazes around, sees her family, laughs.

Nearly everyone around us is smiling or laughing – that must be the Australian way.

'I'm tired, Mummy,' William says.

'Won't be long,' Rachel says, smiling down at him, looking up and grimacing at the doors.

Grandma loves you, I say.

He turns and looks up at me briefly, where I am, I mean, turns away.

The doors open again and . . . it's us, hallelujah. I'm pushing a trolley piled with cases and have looked better. My make-up, applied at 30,000 feet, is struggling at sea level. The grief from my father's death – what, four months earlier? – smeared like white face paint through the rouge.

Henry teeters next to me as if he's slipped on the stairs, come down hard on his coccyx, a man of eighty trying to operate a sixty-four-year-old's body. He hasn't seen us yet but I have – the *Grandma and Grandpa* sign first, then William, then Rachel. I steer the trolley towards them, leave it against the railing, open my arms the way I've seen people do in films.

'Hello, dearie,' I say, hugging Rachel.

'Hey, Mum. Hey, Dad.'

Henry totters in for a noncommittal backslap and I bend as far as I can to hug William. 'Did you make this sign for Grandma and Grandpa? Oh, you're so clever, sweetheart.'

'I see you before,' he says.

'That's right,' I say. 'On the computer, and in London when I came to visit. Remember the red bus? And the big clock? I've missed you so, so, so much.'

I miss things, am missing something and have a feeling it's something big . . . What have I missed?

Rachel drives us down the freeway – that's what she calls it, the freeway, as if we're in a cop show. These days, she says kilometres instead of miles, eggplants instead of aubergines, zucchinis instead of courgettes. I watch William in the visor mirror, pull funny faces.

'It's been swollen for a couple of days,' I say, turning to Rachel, holding my ant-like abdomen. 'None of the clothes I've packed are going to fit. What a bloody state.'

'Well, we've got loads planned,' she says. 'Walks. Restaurants. Trips to the Dandenongs.'

She's spoken often of the Dandenongs and I've told her often I'd like to see them. The eucalypts are evergreens but the introduced species will be turning by now because it's the beginning of March, our late winter, their early autumn. I want to see those colours, smell the aromas. And Hanging Rock – I want to go there too. Henry took me to see *Picnic at Hanging Rock* at the cinema a week or so after the girls turned one. I remember it more for the break it gave me (my parents took the girls for the afternoon) than the film itself. White dresses and boater hats – I recall those. Girls being seduced and swallowed up by nature – is that even what happened?

I rub my stomach, read some billboards along the side of the motorway. 'I think it might be because of my gallbladder.'

They'd found necrosis while they were removing it six months earlier, said they had a good poke around while they were in me but found nothing untoward. The swelling – could it be a by-product of that? Short answer: no. But Living Margaret doesn't know that yet, doesn't even suspect.

'You can just rest,' Rachel says. 'We have five weeks ahead of us.'

'Maybe longer,' I say. 'I'll give you a laugh, dearie. We were at the–'

She's not listening – maybe she's focusing on the freeway – but I had my Tarot cards read in Aberdeen before leaving and was told I'd be going on a journey that would see me staying away from home for longer than I'd anticipated.

'Oh?' Rachel says, then, 'Oh shit.' I grab the overhead handle and yelp as she swerves across two lanes to make the exit, three generations of our bloodline in her hands.

William – I look in the visor mirror, he's fine, hasn't even noticed. Henry has the reflexes of a sloth.

We drive in near silence along a concrete slipway, through traffic lights, past shops, parks and houses. It takes a while for Rachel's breathing to settle.

'So, this is Brunswick,' she says, nodding at the windscreen. 'Oh, lovely,' I say, letting objects and elements pin their tails to me. Lemon trees. Wedding dresses. Street art. Tram lines. A whippet. 'What's that there?' I ask, pointing.

'The tree? That's a bottlebrush, I think.'

'What about that one?'

'A river red gum. Actually, no, it might not be. I've got a book at home – we should look at it together. I'm trying to get better at identifying them.'

She drives us down a quiet street, draws the car to a halt. I get out and unbuckle William from his seat, stand with him on the pavement while Henry and Rachel retrieve our cases from the boot. It's a much bigger car than mine.

'Thanks for coming to get us,' I say to William.

'That's OK,' he says, smiling, little darling.

Rachel rolls one of our cases towards me, gestures towards a white and green wooden house. 'Oh, look, there they are.'

Gem appears barefoot in the doorway with Ewan, little Ewan, on her hip, his cherub head, chubby body. The house, the garden – they've done well for themselves. The neighbours' houses too, it looks like a nice area.

'How you going, Margaret?' Gem asks, slinking out through the wrought iron gate, onto the street.

'Hello, sweetheart.' I hug her and Ewan together, try to prise Ewan gently from her.

'Oh my god, he's just gorgeous,' I say, tickling his chin. 'Nice to meet you, Ewan. I'm that funny lady from the computer.' I try and fail again to coax him clear.

'Are your hands still shaky?' Rachel asks Henry.

'Yeah,' he says, holding up his fluttery fingers.

'Look how bloated I am,' I say to Gem, laughing.

'Oh no, Marg,' she says. 'That looks uncomfortable. What time's it? Let me take you round to our doctor to see if she can give you anything. We should hurry, they'll be closing soon.'

'Oh no, what a hassle, no.'

'It's not a problem,' she says.

She's a decent person, Gem. I'm glad for her and Rachel, and feel embarrassed that I haven't always valued her enough. It's not that she rescued Rachel – that sounds too dramatic – but she steadied her, or provided the right conditions for Rachel to steady herself. She helped Rachel financially through her degree, continued working late into her pregnancy with William and right through Rachel's with Ewan.

I had nightmares during both gestations in which the boys looked like they'd been made in labs, their bionic bodies obviously manufactured, wires and circuit boards crackling, but you'd never know. The doctors and donors helped, but it was Gem and Rachel who turned the tadpoles into frogs and then princes.

I'm struggling

Dead Margaret feels heavy all of a sudden waterlogged

I don't know why

Gem sits with me at the doctor's, translating as if I don't

speak the language – and maybe I don't. Medicare, bulk-billing
. . . I look confused as the doctor scribbles something on her
pad, can barely hear her now and

feel confused

all out of puff as if

I

have slipped from the lily pad of my own despair into
something sloppy and brackish.

Rachel has hung lots of party decorations by the time we
return. Henry's sitting with his arms crossed on the sofa bed
Gem and Rachel have set up for us, has probably helped by not
hindering. Ewan bobs in his bouncer next to William, who's
sitting on the carpet sucking a wedge of orange, watching a
cartoon.

I make the hush sign to Henry, sneak up behind them,
bend over, holding my stomach, kiss Ewan on the head, lean
over, kiss William. They're unsurprised, less impressed than
I would like.

Gem's bringing Rachel up to speed in the kitchen, I can
hear her. 'She says we should go down to the Royal, to
Emergency, just to be sure.'

'Emergency?' Rachel says.

'I'm not going,' I say, strolling breezily into the room,
laughing and not holding my stomach, seeing their kitchen in
its entirety for the first time. It's rustic, very Gem – she's drawn
up initial plans for an extension, new rooms for the boys, a
second lounge, has explained it all on FaceTime.

Above the polished hearth, on what would have been a
working chimney, are framed photos of Gem's parents, Tash
and Pete, several of the boys, but also one of Henry and me
when we visited them in London and another of Henry, me,
Rachel and Eva in Aviemore. It looks so old, the colours

corrupting, too much ochre and red, a green blotch across one of Eva's arms. Has Rachel hung those for our sake, or are they always there?

'Come on,' Rachel says. 'I'll drive you and Dad down there now. It's twenty minutes away, tops. Dinner's made – we can eat when we get back.'

'Seriously, love, I'm fine.'

And I was. I am. Fine. In Aberdeen, depending on the intonation, fine means OK, average, amazing, moderately attractive, drop-dead gorgeous, barely edible, delicious. So . . .

So nothing . . .

We're waiting in Emergency as if waiting and emergencies are compatible. The man sitting next to Henry has sliced a hacksaw blade through the webbing between his thumb and index finger, its rusty teeth lodged in the trapezoid bone and cartilage. The woman a couple of chairs up from me, in her nightie, has dropped something heavy on her foot, going by the blood on the tea towel wrapping it, her toes poking out like strips of beetroot from a burrito. Others have burns, bruises – I try not to look. Rachel is focusing on the floor.

'Help me out, would ya,' the sawman says to nobody and everybody.

Rachel likes hospitals even less than I do. She wanted to give birth to Ewan at home but couldn't in the end. She declined a water birth at the hospital because she worried about him drowning. But they don't – newborns are amphibious, their journey one of aqua to ashes, fluid to fertiliser.

'You must be hungry,' I say to Henry.

'Not really,' he says, barely turning round because it's all so inconvenient, isn't it Henry, having to be in the right place at the right time when a so-called loved one needs your support and assistance.

I'm angry with him.

Not then – or maybe then too.

But definitely now. Why am I here and not in the lunatic asylum watching Henry drawing rivers and trees on the wall with his doo-doo, scrawling *I'm to blame, I'm to blame, I'm to blame*? Why don't I see that? Why don't I ever see that?

'Let me go get you something,' Rachel says. 'I saw a vending machine as we were coming in. Maybe a drink too?'

'I'm fine,' I say. 'I just wish they'd hurry up. For you, I mean. What a waste of your time.'

At five past eight a woman in scrubs calls my name and leads us down a corridor, motions for us to go into a booth.

'Now, Margaret, if you could just sit on the bed here. And you can both sit there.' She points to the chairs, smiles at Henry and Rachel.

'Yes, it bloody hurts,' a woman says in the next booth.

'Redback,' the nurse whispers to me, winking.

'It's a spider,' Rachel says, clarifying.

'I'll be back in a little while,' the nurse says. 'Can I get you some water or anything?'

'I'm fine,' I say.

'Me too,' Rachel says. Henry says nothing.

I try not to yawn but haven't slept in more than thirty hours, and since dying haven't slept at all. I'd like to, really would: could someone just pop the light off now, please, thank you.

According to the GPS on the in-flight TV, Henry snored from Singapore to Alice Springs.

There's someone new in the booth next to ours, another woman but less of a cry-baby. I lean back against the pillows, watch Rachel texting (Gem, I suppose) and reading on her phone. Henry would be gazing at the roof if his eyes were open. He occasionally gurgles, snaps his head forward, falls back under. I look at my phone – it still has battery – put it back in my handbag. Clipboard-carrying nurses pass the booth but don't stop.

'Dearie, you go,' I say to Rachel at ten-thirty. 'Go on – you have people coming in the morning.'

'No way,' she says. 'I'm not leaving you.'

'What's the routine for getting a taxi round here?' Henry asks, eyes like puff pastry and ketchup.

'I'll wait with you,' Rachel says.

She's doing the honourable thing, doesn't want to leave a family member in need, but I feel bad about it, so she should go. My guilt gets higher billing than hers, that's how it works.

We could catch up, there's so much to discuss, but it's better to sit there – or recline there, for me – watching the minute-hand judder on the wall clock. Champ, he's with a dog-sitter. Eva, a green blotch across one of her arms, ochre and red tones making all of us look sickly, otherworldly.

Ten, twenty, thirty, forty minutes. 'Dearie, please, go home. Take your dad, I'll be fine here.'

'What?' Henry says, eyes opening.

Another ten. 'Rachel, please,' I say. 'Henry, you too, love. Go get some rest.'

They look at each other sheepishly, baa.

Ten more minutes.

'Will you call me when you're done?' Rachel asks, standing. 'I'll come back and get you.'

Henry tries, fails, pushes himself up from the chair.

'Don't worry about me,' I say. 'I'll get a taxi. I'll ask the nurses to call one for me.'

Rachel leans over and gives me a hug, a nice one, full flesh. Henry mouths, 'Are you sure?' and looks guilty – as he should – before leaning and patting my hand. They turn to leave,

Henry shuffling, head down. Rachel glances back from the booth entrance and waves, then walks off as if she can't quite believe they're abandoning me in hospital within hours of me arriving in Australia. Me either. You should have been there, Rachel. You too, Henry. It's your fault, both of you, all of it. I'm joking.

I'm not joking

I'm tired

should get some sleep

I sit up, plump the pillow, get my phone to text Eva. It'll be lunchtime in Spain, maybe later. But she said to text when we arrived, and she'll worry if I don't. I write: *Here safe and sound X*, then delete it. Then: *Can't believe how warm Australia is! Here safe and sound! X* – I delete that too. Then: *All good, love. In hospital now, but don't worry! Xxx.* I scrub that one even quicker than the others.

Poor Eva.

A green blotch on her arm, trapped in a photograph in Aviemore.

It'll have to wait.

I'm pleased to see myself falling asleep on the bed, even though at the time I thought I was awake. I'm less pleased to see myself awake with a consultant at two in the morning, even though at the time it felt like a bad dream. The night passes with dozing, waking, dozing, another nurse, the same consultant.

I keep vigil over myself because it's imperative that I'm here in both living and dead form, a spare part for a vehicle that's already been written off and scrapped.

I text Rachel at seven in the morning: *Still nothing. Have seen one doctor, waiting for another. What a pain* ☺ *X*

The smiley face is easier to pull off in a text message than when I appear at Rachel and Gem's just after eleven in the morning. William's party is in full swing. He and his pals are in the back garden playing musical chairs. Parents, friends and people I assume are Gem's extended family stand around watching, laughing, munching party snacks. Gem has Ewan on her hip. Rachel is on music duty – the kids are running around. Between pausing and restarting a pop song, she grabs two of the disqualified chairs for Henry and me to sit on: she looks worried, hugs me tightly, but I reboot my smiley face and wave her back to the game.

I don't want to sit. Ideally, Henry would pick up the social slack but he's useless, a useless man, his two years of (almost) flawless sobriety intersecting with a daily cocktail of anxiety and depression meds, further muddying water that had been clear for only . . . I don't even know, not very long, maybe never.

He follows me over to Tash and Pete, who I've only ever spoken to online. They looked nice then, even nicer now in the flesh. Pete looks a little too thin but is kind and warm. Gem has Tash's eyes, her winning laugh.

'You've had a rough time of it,' Tash says. 'You poor, poor thing.'

'It's nothing,' I say, laughing. 'I'm just glad to get back in time for the party.'

There are cheers as the music stops and another chair is pulled away. A girl with pigtails mopes off towards a sprawling aloe vera plant.

'Can you believe the little fella's three?' Pete says.

'He's such a gorgeous wee boy,' I say.

'And meeting Ewan for the first time,' Tash says. 'My god, you must be thrilled. He's such a character.'

'I've hardly had a chance yet,' I say, glancing over at him on Gem's hip. 'I can't wait for a cuddle.'

They don't ask what happened at the hospital, must know

we haven't told the girls yet, don't want to jump their turn. Henry knows. I phoned him as soon as I was told, swore him to secrecy.

'And how are you going, Henry?' Tash asks.

'Very well indeed,' Henry says.

I've heard this response from Henry so many times that on most occasions it no longer registers, but today . . . I blame Henry for everything, or not everything, just the bad things. Drag the worst moment of my life into a quiet room and squeeze it – undoubtedly the sound it will make is: *Henry*.

Gem approaches and places Ewan in my arms. And, oh – I can almost feel it, the warmth of his little body, the softness of his skin, the breeze from his eyelashes, his beating heart. He starts crying almost immediately, but that's OK, I've settled bairns before, two at once, like a ping-pong player with two bats, never missing, never clipping the net. I bounce him in my arms, sweat beading on my ashen forehead. It's fine. *I suppose a cry does us all good at times – clears the air as other rain does.*

Rachel appears at the patio doors shading the candles on a sponge cake and we all sing 'Happy Birthday'. William looks self-conscious but blows out the candles and we all cheer.

'Mum, Dad,' Rachel calls.

I give Ewan back to Gem and go over to sit next to William and his cake, posing as best as we can for a photo together. It's a proper camera, too, a fancy one. William smiles as if we've had a chance to connect during this horror show of a holiday. Henry gets up, shuffles away, and I'm about to join him, just need to find the strength to stand, when Rachel tells me to wait.

'William, that's it, just go back a bit to Grandma,' she says. I look less than impressed – watching myself now, I mean. I'm doing my best in the moment to hide it because nearly everyone at the party is watching us and waiting for a slice of cake. My eyes are trying to scupper my sense that this is going to be yet another disappointment of a photo but William says 'Grandma' and I bend closer, at which point he cranes his head up to kiss me and I move forward to kiss him.

'Oh, that's lovely,' Rachel says, looking at the back of her camera. 'You're going to love this one, Mum.'

I do, as it happens, will have it framed on the sideboard next to my big brown hospital chair. Henry will print a copy too. My eyes are closed, hiding the heinousness of what I've been told, and my lips are connecting with William's. He looks so innocent, so full of life, I love you, William.

Tash and Pete are the last to leave the party.

'So, Lake Eildon?' Pete calls from the driveway.

'That sounds lovely,' I say. 'Can't wait.'

We won't go there, won't see their holiday home, even though I'd have liked to. It's hard to reconcile a vision – my previous vision – of life as an ever-extending line of stepping stones with the sudden realisation you've reached the final one and those that were behind you are gone.

Henry unpacks his suitcase while I take slobbery blocks of Duplo from Ewan's mouth, play with him on the carpet. He's building a tower, and now another, and now another.

Rachel and Gem tidy their house and bring us snacks, tell us to take it easy. When the boys go down for the night, we'll talk, that's what we've agreed.

William is happy to play with ghosts, as are Henry and I. He lines up his fleet of Matchbox cars and tells us we can take our pick as long as Henry has the white police car and I have the emerald safari truck. He pushes his one, a yellow Ford with a twisted front axle, along the carpet, makes it skid, looks transfixed. Henry puts as much oomph into chasing with his police car as he does into anything – the Ford's getaway is all but guaranteed.

'Grandma, this way,' William says.

'OK,' I say, laughing, not feeling like it, but Jesus Christ, you have to laugh, let kids feel there are things to laugh about, unless you're a despicable child-hating monster, or Henry. I run my safari truck along the carpet behind William's car.

'Tell the driver to skid,' he says.

'The driver?'

'Yeah.'

'OK, driver, skid,' I say, drifting the car along the edge of the sofa.

'You too, Grandpa,' he says.

'What?' The driver of Henry's chase vehicle is as doddery as him.

'Tell the driver to fly,' William says.

'OK, fly, driver,' I say, whooshing my truck into the air behind William's, up past the window frame and back towards earth quickly, the g-force pooling blood in my driver's head, her face swelling, her lower eyelids forced over her eyes, losing spatial awareness, temporal awareness, blacking out until . . .

Click – the living-room door shuts. The boys are in bed. Rachel and Gem have brought us cups of tea.

Henry sits next to me on the sofa bed. They sit opposite us on the armchairs, trying not to look tense, and I tell them, not graciously or with any of the preamble I'd rehearsed in my head, but like a dropped lasagne: my initial diagnosis, that it's still unconfirmed but highly likely.

'Oh fuck,' Rachel says.

'Oh, Margaret, no,' Gem says.

'They think it's in my ovaries,' I say. There are tears in my eyes, my lips keep pursing, but this is the worst of it – now, right now. It'll all get better after this. 'And here was me worrying about Pete,' I say.

We'd all been worrying about Pete and his forthcoming prostate operation.

'Anyway, I need to go back to the hospital tomorrow, if you wouldn't mind driving me again, dearie.'

'Mum, of course,' Rachel says, approaching and kneeling in front of me, hugging, crying.

Gem's in tears too. Henry (I wasn't watching him at the time) looks blank – not uncaring but wiped clean like a blackboard.

Gem comes closer, kneels next to Rachel on the carpet, and the three of us hug – it feels good, I remember that hug. I reach out my left arm for Henry. He leans in, stiff but softening, starts crying too.

And then he's snoring again, has been doing so for hours – I don't even know what time it is. He's worn out, we all are. I get up from the sofa bed, tiptoe past Rachel and Gem's room, past the boys' room and into the bathroom, close the door. I have Eva's number up on my phone already but still have to work out the code for calling Spain from Australia. Maybe it's the same as it is from Scotland? I could try, just try. I press the call button, sit on the edge of the bath. Gem's shampoos line the shelf, or Rachel's, they probably share. It's ringing – she'll pick up if she sees it's me. Still ringing. This is the worst of it – now, right now. It'll get better after this.

Chapter 11

2010

Eva's working today. Henry and I woke at five and tiptoed from her apartment so as not to disturb her, have come to Ávila by coach. We've already marvelled – I did, Henry not so much – at the town's medieval walls and turrets, the sierra stripped of snow. It must be eight-thirty in the morning or thereabouts.

I'm glad Henry likes (liked) walking as much as I do (did) – I don't know if we'd have survived for as long as we did (have) without our shared love of ambulation.

His gait is pretty good, relatively speaking, his lower limbs lithe beneath aquamarine shorts, camera strapped over his clavicle, hands clasped behind his pelvis and bowels. I know what happens today and could do without seeing it again, but anyway . . . My legs are sixty and, let's be honest, sexy – a treat of well-turned ankles and chewable calves. We pooh-pooh our palatability when we're alive lest we eat ourselves – slap a little ketchup on those bony but delectable hands, those flavorous forearms.

I shove my linen scarf into the laden daypack, squirt on some sunscreen, offer the bottle to Henry – no thanks.

He's of a milieu that deemed it unmanly and therefore unnecessary to shield its skin from a 15-million-degree plasma ball, nonplussed that his pastel pigmentation has evolved to better absorb UV radiation in settings – Aberdeen – where it was lacking, not on the skillet of the Iberian Peninsula.

I burn easily and tend to overheat – at my cremation, I went from eighteen degrees to nine hundred faster than you could say factor fifty.

We amble through ancient streets, past sandy buildings. It's thirsty work. From memory, the paella we had with Eva for dinner sloshed with salty seafood, so that will be partly why. We're heading towards the Cathedral of the Saviour, a twelfth-century wonder described in Eva's guidebook as *majestic and powerful*.

'Hey, Marg, can we stop for a bit?' Henry asks.

'Really?' I say, pausing, waiting for him to catch up. 'That's not like you.' It's actually very much like him since he started his medication. He'll go downhill unrapidly over the next few months, from a stride to slow steps to a shuffle.

'I just need to catch my breath,' he says.

We stand and breathe. He still looks handsome at sixty-two, nearly seven years into retirement, one into sobriety, six months into the benzodiazepine. If I didn't know about the unforgivable and immemorable mistakes he's made, I'd assume the weathering on his face was from bog-standard buffeting, not irremediable remorse.

That's mean, Marg, stop it.

I went with him to the doctor – of course – as if I was his mother. Did Henry know what was causing him to worry so much? No, not really. Had he always been anxious? No, not really. Was he sleeping? No, not really. Well, let's try you on this dosage first and up it if (when) we need to.

'Isn't this place incredible?' I say, offering him my water bottle.

'Yeah,' he says, sipping. He still has his hair, barely any greys. I dyed long before I died.

We sit on stairs dating from who knows when – their stone rendered reflective by feet long since gone. The street is narrow, golden, the high walls channelling the breeze and blocking the sun.

A man with a cart stops in front of us, says: '*Naranjas.*'

'*No hablo español,*' I say – a contradiction in terms.

'Orange,' he says, pointing. 'Orange.' In retrospect, the pile of fruit in the cart is a giveaway.

'*No, gracias,*' I say.

He smiles, waves, trundles off.

The street is slowly filling. There are more noises from inside houses: radios, TVs.

'It says the cathedral was intended as a fortress,' I say to Henry, tilting the book to show him a picture. 'It's surrounded by the Palace of the Infant King, the Palace of the Evening, the Palace of Valderrábanos. Its apse is one of the turrets of the city walls.'

'Yeah,' he says. 'Do you think they have a toilet there?'

'In the apse?'

'Just anywhere.'

'I would think so. Do you need to go?'

'Not immediately,' he says. 'But soon.'

'Shall we keep walking then?' I stand, zip up the daypack.

Eva took us to two cathedrals on our first day, another on our second. If they were anything like the church of my childhood in Aberdeen, that would have been plenty, but I find them alluring. The paintings. All those bones of the holy. The wooden confessionals. What a great idea, to sit in a narrow box in a small municipality, telling someone you can't see – but who knows you and your family – about things you shouldn't have done so they can assign you some performative penance. I sat in one of the empty booths in Madrid, drew the curtain, could hear Eva's and Henry's footsteps outside, almost wished a shadowy figure would slide back the lattice to hear my sins.

A well-dressed middle-aged man, smooth and attractive, turns a corner, nearly bumps into me. He smiles and doffs his hat, says, '*Señora*.'

We walk on in silence. 'Hey, Marg,' Henry says from behind me a minute or two later, 'I love you.'

'I love you too,' I say over my shoulder. 'Always have, Henry, always will.' Is that true? Am I mollycoddling him?

The street turns unexpectedly onto a plaza and − wow − there it is, the cathedral, part castle, part celebration of Gothic and Roman architecture, its three pairs of lancet windows like the sad eyes of God, her son and the holy spirit.

Two clumps of puffy-eyed tourists are eating breakfast a short distance away at outdoor tables under white canvas umbrellas; two men in military uniforms stand outside a beflagged building that must be the Palace of Valderrábanos.

Henry turns the corner, stops. 'Christ.'

'Isn't it awe-inspiring?' I say.

'Yeah,' he says.

There's a car in front of the palace, an unseen speaker playing Radiohead − one of Rachel's favourites − but I can see my eyes squinting as they try to conjure donkeys and smock-wearing peasants, a girl dragging a goat on a rope, a bow-legged boy rolling a hoop along with a stick. 'Can you imagine the effect this would've had on people in the twelfth century?'

'Yeah,' Henry says.

The cathedral looks open already, even though Eva's guide-book says it won't be. A local-looking woman walks past us, has probably grown immune to the cathedral's charms, but not me – I might convert. I'm joking.

'Let's go,' I say, stepping forward.

'Hey, Marg,' Henry says from behind. 'I need a shit, it's coming out.'

I spin round. 'What?'

He's holding his belly, grimacing, his bared knees bent, nearly touching. 'I need to go, Marg.'

'Let's get you to the cathedral,' I say. 'Hurry up.' I march ahead, hoping for a miracle from the patron saint of bowels, look over my shoulder.

'Go ahead,' Henry calls, pointing at the cathedral. He waddles wide-eyed towards the restaurant, dances quickly round the smiling, confused waiter. 'I'll come find you. Go.'

I stand with one hand on my mouth, the other on my hip, watching the restaurant, then walk across the plaza and pass through a door within a door at the cathedral, under the stony eyes of statues.

I pay a bearded woman, take my ticket. Maybe I should wait for Henry at the entrance, or go back to make sure he hasn't soiled himself, but he'll find me. On the entry table there's a thurible – is that what they're called? – for swinging incense around. The information sheet I've been given is in Spanish and German but that's OK – the building was designed to impress the illiterate and render them speechless.

I'm above all of that, of course, or so I think until I enter the cathedral proper and nearly fall to my knees. I hold the back of a pew and sit, feeling naïve in the nave, the daypack on my lap weighted with my *Shadow of the Wind*, Henry's *Sum of All Fears*, Eva's guidebook.

The photos didn't do it justice – the columns, arches, vaulted ceilings, stained glass windows, white stone, speckled red and grey masonry . . . The temperature, I recall, is neither hot nor cold, the overall ambience neither light nor dark – it's an isthmus between the marshes of life and death, life *in* death, death in life. Eva. If she was here, we could hold hands, weep together. Or Henry even – he'd do.

The highest painting on the gargantuan altarpiece shows Jesus on the cross, flanked by thieves, Mary Magdalene hugging the base of the wooden beam. It's something of a family album: there he is, as a baby on Mary's lap, in a red gown having an epiphany, in a white robe with light bursting from his halo and body, his disciples torn between prayer and raucous applause. The frames meld within a master structure of gold that looks soft enough to roll between your palms and rub all over your body, after which you too would emanate light.

I feel for my locket, run my finger around its filigreed Celtic knot. Its gold is unyielding, but so what, it means the world to me. The necklace was an eighteenth birthday present from my parents – the locket from Nana Jean, via my mother, some forty years later. It has a photo of the girls as babies, the only one I could find that fitted.

I stand, can do that now, feel able, saunter with the guidebook in hand, stop at oil paintings of people with arrows through them, ancient crypts, alabaster statues – here a patron saint, there another bloodied Messiah, here the interior gardens, there the choir stalls, here the . . . I stop in front of what looks like a tiered wedding cake made of silver, taller and wider than me – a monstrosity that, according to Eva's guidebook, is a monstrance paying homage to the time God asked Abraham to slit his son Isaac's throat.

Herod's massacre of the innocents, Hosea's threat to slay the fruit of Ephraim's womb – the Bible brims with infanticide by dads and father figures, unlike fairy tales, where mums and their type kill the tots, teens and tykes.

I follow myself back through the vast interior, in and out of rooms, past the same bucket-hat-wearing tourists, knowing already – now, not then – that my search is futile. Henry's still at the restaurant, hasn't left.

'*Una mesa, señora?*' asks the waiter as I arrive.

'*No, gracias,*' I say. 'I'm with *el hombre*.' I point at Henry, his cheekbone propped on the heel of his hand at an inside table, eyes closed. They open, shocked and unfocused, at the sharp scrape of my chair.

I sit opposite him, say nothing, everything.

'Sorry,' he says. 'I've got the runs. I knew you'd come back, so I thought it was better to wait . . .'

'I've been gone for nearly two hours,' I say.

'I've been watching the entrance,' he says. 'I must have dozed off.'

'I'm not going back in now,' I say. 'You've had your chance.'

'That's fine,' he says. He scribbles in the air to the waiter, takes the bill quickly off the plate when it arrives, stands and goes to the till.

Spoiler alert – he's fallen off the wagon, as will start to become obvious that evening when he keels over in Eva's tepid shower, bringing the shampoo rack down, knocking the glass shower door from its hinges and onto the tiled floor where it will break into several pieces.

Both of us will hurry in, Eva shielding her eyes, to find him, gills flapping, on the floor, a fish freed from its tank, water everywhere.

I can see the bill – now, not then. Five vodkas – hardly a Spanish speciality but the least aromatic of the holy spirits, the tight-lipped tippler's go-to. When mixed with his medication, who knows, maybe it felt great, I never asked.

We walk back slowly towards the bus station, him talking of paella and food poisoning, me nodding and not really listening.

1990

'I dinna care,' Rachel says.

'Rachel,' I snap louder than I would have wanted. She's fourteen – I remember this clearly – so I must be forty, Henry forty-two.

She's wearing a T-shirt that says *James*, and may be high or drunk or both – her pupils are dilated, which, not then but a couple of months later, I'll learn is a tell-tale sign, her blissed-out neurotransmitters triggering an adrenal fight-or-flight response, even though she looks incapable of either.

She got home just before the police arrived, was on her way upstairs when the doorbell rang.

The shorter of the two officials sits forward on our sofa. His shoes are cleaner than those of his stubbly colleague, who has trailed his dirty Doc Martens across our green carpet. Usually, it's shoes off at the front door and our visitors are always fine with that, but you can't really ask officers of the law to do the same.

Or maybe you can – the house is my jurisdiction, secured by us at great expense – but at the time I was timid. It was the same, even worse, when I was a girl. If a policeman, minister, scout leader or teacher told you to do something, you just did it, no questions, and no telling tales afterwards unless you wanted even bigger trouble.

Neither has touched his tea, although the shorter one has eaten a couple of ginger nuts, dropping crumbs on the sofa.

'You don't have to give a statement,' he says to Rachel.

'And I do need to let you know that anything you say might be used in court.'

A play park has been decimated – his word, not mine. I'm not sure how you would decimate a park without specialist maths and engineering know-how. A wooden fortress has been set alight, a couple of the swing seats melted, graffiti, including Rachel's initials, sprayed on the grass. Who graffities grass? Her so-called friends, I know that now, sensed it then, but she was there at the park with them, and that was bad enough. Fly with the crows, get shot with the crows. Kerry Black – who at fifteen has already spent time in juvenile detention and at twenty-two will die of a heroin overdose while her daughter, Zoe, cries the house down – was picked up at the scene but the others got away. She must have told the police Rachel was there too.

'So, I'll just say nithin then,' Rachel says, leaning into the Doric. 'Nithin. Nithin. Oh aye, and . . . nithin.'

Henry's knuckles are white, his legs crossed in a way that could cause thrombosis – not that you think about that at forty-two. Varicose veins either. Strokes. 'Rachel, enough,' he says. 'Stop being an idiot.'

'Oh, a'm the idiot? Says the man fa canna even keep his daughters safe.'

At this Henry stands quickly from his chair, huffs, sits again.

'We can just drive you down to the station,' the stubbly policeman says. 'You can come too, of course,' he says to me and Henry before turning back to Rachel. 'We're not charging you with anything. It's important you know that. We'd just like you to tell us where you were this evening and what you were doing with . . .' He looks at his pad. 'Kerry Black.'

'What d'ye mean, doing with her?' Rachel asks. 'Are you one o' those pervy cops? Is 'at it? Ye're a paedo, aye?'

'Rachel, please.' My eyes are glistening, I can barely look

137

at her. She never speaks like this, never, not in front of us at least. I don't have a problem with the Doric necessarily, just what she's using it for. Her friends aren't here but she's dancing for them all the same.

The stubbly policeman shakes his head, turns to Henry, who looks like a blown-up paper bag someone's about to clap between their hands. The smaller, shinier faced one lifts his tea from the table, notices the dirt on the carpet, glances at his shoes in case it was him, looks relieved it wasn't, sips.

'Look, I wisnae there,' Rachel says. 'Wi' Blacksy. I hivnae seen her for a lang time, so I dinna ken far ye're gettin yer intelligence fae, if ye even hae ony.'

'Rachel, enough,' Henry shouts.

The sound of footsteps coming down the stairs. I get up and hurry from the room, pull the door closed behind me, intercept Eva in the landing. She's in her nightie, still has her mouthguard in, was probably dreaming about going roller-skating with Tom Hanks – and now this.

'What's going on, Mum?'

'It's your sister,' I say. 'She's OK, just go upstairs.'

'There's a police car outside.'

'I know. We're just sorting something out.'

'She's in trouble again.'

'She'll be fine, dearie, just go back to bed.'

She removes her mouthguard, licks her top teeth, glares at the living-room door. 'I hate that she's like this.'

'Pigs!' Rachel shouts, loud enough for us, maybe even the neighbours, to hear.

'Rachel,' Henry yells.

'OK, off to bed, love,' I say, kissing Eva's forehead, pulling her close. 'I'll see you in the morning.'

I'm having trouble combing the nits of what's imagined from the head of what's real – assuming anything's real and I'm not an ectoparasite with no wings and weak legs using my claws to move from hair to hair. That itch on your scalp, at the crown, behind your ears, that could be me and my colonising kind, mating and moulting, laying our eggs, eating your skin and feeding on your blood.

It's the early eighties, I know that much. Assuming any of this is accurate or has a meaning . . . What's the meaning, Margaret? Can you pin down a pattern? Is there a reason for all these re-runs? I'd like to laugh about it – if you'd heard my chortling, once upon, I mean

you'd not

have

forgotten that

I'm still working at the telephone exchange but also, on Tuesday, Friday and Saturday evenings, at a big granite nightclub near the train station called Fusion, a building that's been reimagined many times already and will be refurbished many times more.

Henry's working at least forty hours a week, usually more, because we want to buy our council house, or go on holiday at some point. Maybe even abroad. Imagine that. Rachel wants to go to France – she doesn't know why, although she tasted some Camembert once at her friend Barry's house and loved it. Eva has wanted to go to Spain ever since my father raved about it. He went once with my mother, to Alicante, in the early seventies, and fell in love with it. He taught himself Spanish from library books and tapes in the hope – unfulfilled – of one day returning.

Sometimes Henry and I meet as he's running towards the house and I'm running for his van, our exchange of keys and information worthy of a professional relay team. Your dinner's in the oven, the girls have eaten, love you, love you too. I get into his van and raise the seat, shorten the reach to the steering wheel, drive off to do my shifts.

I don't usually work weekend mornings – today's an exception. I'm in jeans and a purple polo neck, my hair tied back, fake lashes still on from the previous evening. Henry's working today too, I assume, because the girls are with me. It's their first time in Fusion and they both look wide-eyed. They have clean faces and unflattering – my fault – haircuts but are otherwise hale and hearty.

'What's that smell?' Eva asks.

'Your feet,' Rachel replies.

'Beer and smoke and perfume from last night,' I say. 'Why don't you both sit over there.'

They saunter to the booth closest to me.

I need to clean the bar, the bathrooms, restock the fridges.

My colleague Jane is mopping the floor, the only other person there. 'All right, Margie?' she shouts. 'Fancy some tunes?'

'Hi, Jane,' I say. 'Yes, that would be great.'

She comes over to the bar, switches on the radio – a DJ and guest chatting and then 'Body Talk' by Imagination.

'Bonnie quines, Margie,' she says, nodding at Eva and Rachel.

'Oh, thank you,' I say.

Rachel has taken Operation from her bag and is setting it up on the table. They play for money – fake money. The aim is to use tweezers to remove Cavity Sam's funny bone, Adam's apple, wrenched ankle and writer's cramp without touching the electrified edges of the holes in his body – if they do, he'll buzz and his nose will glow Rudolph red.

'What time's the pictures, Mummy?' Rachel asks.

'Just when I'm done here,' I say. I've told them we can go see a film if they're good. Get some icecream too.

Most of the original features have been stripped from Fusion. It was formerly the People's Palace, a music hall that burnt down in 1896 when scenery caught fire during a stage show. The audience and performers fought each other to escape the blaze, many suffering serious burns and seven dying on the premises. Was it haunted? Some people thought so but I never saw or sensed anything. It became the Palace Theatre in 1898, a cinema in 1931, the city's biggest dance hall in 1959, a night-club the year after the girls were born.

It was always crowded, which meant little could be seen during a shift apart from tipsy faces and the upper halves of bodies, hands with cash, the optics and pumps, the till, the other bar staff, and Keith the obsessively handwashing manager with his soapy, gropey hands.

It's only during the day, like now, with next to nobody there, that the building's shape and dimensions become apparent. It's changed since the days when people would sit there watching Charlie Chaplin, laughing, laughing, many gone now, dead.

I slosh the spill trays into the sink.

Jane mops, sings along to Diana Ross. The girls are giggling, setting each other off. *Bzzzz* – there goes Cavity Sam's bread basket. *Bzzzz* – the butterflies in his stomach. They're getting on well, usually did at that age . . .

I watch myself loading the dishwasher, can't help admiring my shape, recoil – 'shit' – as I cut my finger on a sliver of broken glass.

'You OK, Mummy?' Eva asks, getting up and coming over to the bar.

'Yeah, sorry,' I say. 'Mummy shouldn't say bad words. It just gave me a shock.'

'Is it bleeding?'

'Just a little,' I say. 'It's fine, dearie.'

'Let me suck your blood,' Rachel says, coming over, her arms out like a vampire, and they start laughing again.

'I'll give you pineapple mixer instead,' I say, sucking my crimson finger while my other hand grabs a couple of clean glasses.

They carry their drinks back to the table like waist-high women, continue where they left off with Operation.

'Best of five?' Eva says.

'Best of eight,' Rachel says. 'No, nine.'

I've applied a Band-Aid and am crouching to sweep under the bar when Jane appears. 'Shall we split the lavvies?' she says, reaching into her pocket.

'Sounds good,' I say. 'Heads or tails?'

'Which is which?'

'Heads loons, tails quines.'

'OK, tails then.'

She tosses the coin, slaps it onto the back of her hand. Such little hands. 'Oh-oh, heads,' she says, smiling. 'Sorry, Margie. You get the loons.'

The men's toilets are a state, always are – the women's too, to be fair. The urinal trough is full of

I can smell

can I smell

browning liquid that, thankfully, hasn't spilled over. Not that the floor could be described as dry or clean, although I've read that wee doesn't contain bacteria if the kidneys have done their job. I use the head of the mop to drag clumps of toilet roll and deodorising blocks from the plughole and the liquid starts sluicing away, scoop up the detritus and throw it in the bin, pick bits from between the fingers of my rubber gloves before washing them.

The girls are still in the booth when I come out. I know from memory what happens next, or what Rachel will claim happens next. It will leave a lasting impression on me when she tells me because she's never – at this age anyway, what is she, seven? – been one to invent things. Eva was the fantasist. At four, she caused a ferocious fuss in E&M's department store when she thought her imaginary friend Tommy had stayed in the lift after we got out on the first floor. I thought it would pass, her concern, it usually did, but she started screaming and Rachel, alarmed, started crying. One of the employees ran over to assist and I told her that, look, it was embarrassing, but my daughter's imaginary friend was still in the lift. 'Not a problem,' she said. 'I think we can sort that out.'

We waited for the lift to return and took it – me, the girls and the woman – to the third floor, where Eva was happily reunited with Tommy.

Rachel wasn't like that. But the day after I take them to Fusion, at breakfast, she'll tell me she was playing upstairs, crawling about on her knees in the murk, when something terrifying – my word, but that's the sense she gave – happened. She'd spun round to see something or someone there with her. She'll not remember what it was, just the feeling, the sensation which, as she's telling me about it, will bring her arms out in goosebumps.

For now, she's scratching at her backside, itching for adventure. 'Can I go play upstairs?' she asks.

'As long as you take your sister with you. I just need to vacuum down here, then we can go.'

'Do I have to?' Eva asks. 'I want to read my book.' She's brought *George's Marvellous Medicine*, a firm favourite.

'Fine then,' I say to Rachel. 'Hold the banister, please, and watch out for broken glass.'

She skips away and disappears from my sight – back then, I mean, not now. I'm already upstairs by the time she arrives. She leans over the balcony and waves at Living Margaret down below, watches her start up the vacuum cleaner before turning away and looking around in the gloom. There's not much to see – some tables and bar stools, carpet that would petrify a petri dish.

She gets down on her knees, hums along with the vacuum cleaner, and I'd like to tell her to get up because she'll get filthy but I don't because I'm dead and dirt's supposed to be good for the microbiome. I keep my eyes (have none) peeled for anything or anyone untoward, remember how convinced Rachel will be that something malevolent lurks in or lurches from the shadows.

I turn quickly, as does she, at a sudden noise, but it's just Jane laughing down below, her cackle cutting through the drone of the hoover. I scan the surrounds as Rachel sits on the floor, leans her back against a table leg, and closes her eyes. She starts stroking her arms, tickling them, really – it's very gentle, the way she does it, each arm caressing the other simultaneously.

All is fine until, suddenly, she's off her backside and onto her knees, staring right through me, towards the back wall, not a hint of horror in her eyes. I look around, try to catch whoever or whatever it is in the act – the Ghost of Burnt Bodies Past? – but there's nothing there. I look back at Rachel, who isn't scared in the slightest but smiling broadly in my direction.

Chapter 12

I wouldn't call myself languid, but only because it sounds too romantic, as if my quill has broken and my body (none) grows weak with consumption.

The day is gone, and all its sweets are gone . . .

Who wrote that? Someone with a sweet tooth, clearly. I have no teeth. No soft hand. No softer breast. Some days (my days are gone) I can barely keep my eyes (no eyes) open. I said many times in life that I couldn't be in two places at once, and yet that's exactly what's expected of me now – or maybe more accurately, that I can be in two Margarets at once. Who expects that of me? Nobody. Not even me – it just happens.

A similar fate befell Mary of Ágreda, a nun I read about in Eva's guidebook. She was seen in the American colonies more than five hundred times in the seventeenth century despite never leaving her Spanish monastery – cloistered, the world still her oyster. She wore a blue cape like Batman and told indigenous people in modern-day New Mexico that her god was God and any others were as true to the real thing as dress-up Santas in shopping malls. It didn't matter that her audience spoke Navajo, Zuni, Picuris and Keres – Mary had angel interpreters and could make herself understood from 5,000 miles away in Castile and León.

And for that she was merely venerated, not even a saint. Would languid be the right word for Mary? Or was she as drained as I am now as I . . . what am I even doing? Was Mary annoyed? Because I am. Annoyed, imploding, awash with foreboding.

I'm standing over the girls in our draughty, dreary living room. They're lying on their backs, in nappies and dirty bodysuits, on the mat in front of the electric fire. They're old enough to walk but their limbs barely move, even as their spines arch in hideous concert, throwing off the blanket I keep laying over them. I can't stand hearing them cough like this, then or now, their wheezing in between, the enervated panic in their eyes, their lifeboat lungs inverting in a sea of bacteria. *I'm drowning, Mum. Mum, please.* I can't. I just can't. I'm useless when it comes down to it.

None of us has slept, that much is obvious. But where is Henry? Out working, I suppose, making the money to power the lava-red bars of the fire. You could cook steak on its metal grills, provided you had the means to buy steak, which, in this era, we probably don't. It has a blast radius of four feet at most, heats the room eventually, provided nobody opens the door. Apart from the windowpane and walls, it's the only thing between us and the hoar frost hanging feathery beards from hedgerows and lampposts.

Eva coughs so hard it flips her onto her side. She pitches onto her back again, wheezes. The contagion needs to run its course and, going by the dusting cloth and can of Mr Sheen in my chilblained hand, I need to run around the house, tidying.

I get to my knees, breath coming out as steam, wipe mucus and drool from their mouths and cheeks with my shivering cardigan sleeve, lay the blanket back over their infected bodies.

'I need to hoover,' I say, rubbing my arms. 'The doctor will be here any minute.'

They need to stay warm – we all do. A pipe froze once in the loft and when it burst it destroyed our bedroom ceiling, the lingering souvenir of which was an unpainted square of plasterboard from a botched council repair. I loathed the council, not always, but then, I loathed everyone who worked for it, who built its poorly insulated houses, and everyone who had no option but to live in them, especially me.

Eva coughs, spittle sizzling on the fire's bars, settles. I pull the living-room door closed behind me, grab the vacuum cleaner from the airing cupboard, unwind the cord, plug it in near the front door. Coughing, wheezing. I poke my head back inside, watch the girls convulse, Eva's eyes nearly shutting, opening suddenly, close the door, start the cleaner – *hmmm* – let it idle for a second while I stick my head back in for another look. It must be ten degrees warmer in the living room than in the lobby and, even then, the frost breathes heavily, tries to reach inside. I vacuum the lobby quickly, lift the cleaner onto the first stair, the second. *Hmmm.* Lift. *Hmmm.* Lift. *Hmmm.* Lift.

Dr Coulson, I remember him. He wouldn't say anything as crude as, 'Your house is looking a bit mucky – have you thought about, I don't know, cleaning it up, you clatty cow?' But he communicated those sentiments in the way certain things hooked his eyes and yanked them away from what he was saying for . . . a split second, that was all, you might not even notice it.

The fourth step. *Hmmm.* Fifth. Is that someone crying? I switch off the cleaner, nearly twist my ankle jumping down the stairs.

They're fine. Rachel's admiring the bars, so bright and pretty – she's on her back, out of harm's way. Eva too, a whoop, but normal, or normal for now. They're fine.

I close the door again, climb the stairs, switch on the cleaner – what's that? – switch it off, listen, just coughing, turn it on again, ignore the red itchy-looking patches on my skin. What does Dr Coulson expect, and more importantly, why do I care? The girls should be my priority, not him. Who cares if there's dust and dead skin on the carpet?

I switch off the hoover on the sixth step, hurry back down, legs stiff with the cold, nearly trip on the cable.

They're fine. They're OK. I pick Rachel up, hug her, feel her lungs vibrating – good girl – lay her down, lift Eva, do the same. I can't leave them, but I should also get the vacuuming done. It's obviously – inexplicably now – important to me. I lift and fold the teddy-bear blanket into a sling, knot it tightly, hang it diagonally over my chest, get another blanket from the airing cupboard, fashion a second sling.

I hoist Eva into the one on my left hip, shaking, breath steaming. She sinks into it, chubby legs hanging out either side, her mottled face in my boob, but it holds. She looks confused but not upset, not yet cold. 'Come on, Rachel.' I get down on one knee slowly, then the other, lift and lower Rachel – it's not easy – into the sling on my right hip. My neck's already red, the cotton scoring into it. I spread my knees to balance the load, plant one foot, then the other, and yes – it looks a little precarious, but I'm standing. Coughs crammed with *Bordetella pertussis* spray the sides of my face in celebration. It's silly what I'm doing, but it's also warm and safe relative to the other options because my body will be thirty-seven degrees, give or take – maybe a bit closer to thirty-five, the ground hatch to hypothermia. I'm carrying my girls, just as I did from blastocyst to birth, and as long as they're with me, as long as I don't back off or leave them where and when I shouldn't, they'll be fine, they'll both be fine.

I side-step to the lobby like Cerberus, pull myself up the stairs by the banister. If I tumble backwards, we're in trouble, but we won't.

I restart the vacuum on the sixth step, shift Eva on my hip, kiss Rachel's furrowed forehead.

2013

More languor, *warm breath, light whisper, tender semi-tone.*

I'm in a room that, at first glance, doesn't look like it's in a hospital, although the wall art is a giveaway: abnormally colourful flowers, vases, fruit and vistas. No sand timers or scythes, no softening apples or trypophobia-triggering holes in strawberries and crackly leaves – a wide berth given to memento mori for an audience that needs no reminding. But is that the right choice artistically? When Burns wrote that his love was like a red, red rose, it didn't feel like a plastic one in a cheap restaurant or the prints on hospital walls – he'll love his rose until *a' the seas gang dry, my dear, And the rocks melt wi' the sun* . . . even though the rose, like all roses, will die, its aliveness – newly sprung in June – spotlit against a gloomy backdrop of deep time and inexorable decline, glowing all the brighter for it.

Eva and I went to Greyfriars Kirkyard in Edinburgh when I visited for the Tattoo, saw where the Covenanters were imprisoned and the supposedly cursed mausoleum of their tormentor Sir George 'Bloody' Mackenzie. A few years prior to our visit, a homeless man had taken shelter in the tomb and fallen through the putrescent wooden floor into cobwebbed remains, his shrieks supposedly summoning the Mackenzie poltergeist. Not long after that, a couple of teenage boys were charged with violation of sepulchre, an ancient graverobbing law, for taking a skull from Mackenzie's lair and using it as a hand puppet before playing football with it on the cemetery grass. The graves there were the opposite of hospital art: Calvinistic skulls and crossbones, moss-covered skeletons and statues shouting reminders that you – yes, you! – will be mulch soon enough.

There are seven chairs in the treatment room, all plush, with vinyl covers that must make it easier to clean up vomit, blood, urine and superbugs. One chair is empty today due to a scheduling issue or rigor mortis, blowflies laying eggs that hatch and creep into wounds and body openings – mouth, nose, anus, genitals – within . . . Jesus, Margaret, lighten up . . .

I look tired – no surprises there – but also relaxed, the combined effect, I think, of the chair, the sunlight and the fact I'm grazing on a magazine. The pile on the table offers choice if not variety. The covers of the so-called women's mags look nearly identical, as do the covers of the male-oriented car mags. For children and the childlike, there's the CBBC magazine, the *Beano*, the *Dandy*. They also have some word search and crossword books that have largely been completed or sabotaged already.

The sun has found my entire body through the big sash window – a good omen. I'll be here for hours yet, always am, dunking stale biscuits into cups of tepid tea. The cannula in my arm doesn't seem to bother me – I'm a pliable pin cushion these days, connected by a tube to a drip bag with what looks like cranberry concentrate.

The article I'm reading is about knitting pattern abbreviations, most of which are self-explanatory. *Beg* means begin, *alt* means to work on alternate rows and stitches. It's hardly Emily Brontë but I don't care – the experience of reading, if not the substance, is enjoyable.

'Dinna suppose onybody brought playing cards?' somebody asks.

I laugh, as do the others – it's polite to laugh even when the joke, like this one, isn't funny – it's part of the camaraderie. The comedian's name is Bill and, like me, he's been booked for a limited run. A tube splits in two just before reaching his nostrils, delivering oxygen, I suppose. Bill is eightyish and I can tell he's working class because . . . well, you just know, don't you. I am too, but I always dress for the occasion and could be mistaken for middle class quite easily.

'I could definitely go a round of bingo,' says a woman whose name I don't know. We all laugh again. She's new, and in her twenties, for sure. Her clothes look expensive – high heels, gold lamé leggings and a Versace hoodie. She has – I might once have said – more money than sense, but what does it mean to have sense? And what difference does it make here, right now, in this room? I smile politely at everyone, making eye contact with the woman and Bill before returning to my magazine. If someone told a really good joke, we'd be in danger of pulling our catheters out, bursting our stitches.

Inc: Increasing. You have to work twice, or more than twice, into the same stitch. P: purl.

None of this is news to me. I bought wool by the barnful from British Home Stores in successive January sales, different colours for the girls, Henry and me. When the girls got older and started school, I mixed and matched – sometimes knitting, sometimes ordering from the catalogue and making monthly payments. It was good in the water, wool, would be good in the sea, a lake, a swimming pool, if the girls ever fell in.

I fall asleep, wake, don't seem to care that I'm slumped in my chair, my shoulders at my ears. The sun's moved on, or the earth has – the sun will remain unmoved even as the children choke, the seas run dry, the rocks melt. It will light the coda of our kind, as impassive to our passing as it is to its own.

My fug – or is it fugue? – doesn't bode well. The days following treatment are routinely the worst, the fatigue like nothing else. Dog-tired, I used to say. Not as tired as Sam was and Champ soon will be with needles in their legs, their hearts shutting down almost immediately, and not as tired as I've been since dying, but not far off it. If I apologise for whatever I'm meant to have done, learn a valuable life/death lesson, can I please just cark it for real?

Bill and a woman of roughly my age are talking about Kintore, the town near Inverurie they both hail from. There's a market there, they both . . . I don't . . . I can't . . . A cranberry river flows into the estuary of my arm. And the . . . I'm asleep again.

'Cup of tea, Margaret?'

'Huh?'

'Oh, good, you're still with us.'

A young woman with a nose piercing is bending over me. Bridie, I think her name is, yes, I remember her.

'You've just got . . .' She pretends to wipe her mouth, so that I wipe mine, which I do. There's saliva on my chin.

'Oh god,' I say. 'I'm a bit tired.'

'If ye just want to sit up, ye can hae yer tea then snooze again.' She looks at the drip bag, as do I – it's nearly empty. 'Just another twenty minutes or so and you'll be good to go.'

'How long have I been sleeping?'

'Maybe an hour?' she replies. 'I've actually just started my shift.'

'Mair like three,' Bill says.

It's true – it was one p.m., now it's after four.

It feels like I spent half my life, and now death, watching TV and films. But I'm always happy to see this one again. It's February, I think, and Baltic outside, going by the number of layers we've discarded. The girls and I are at the ABC cinema watching *Dirty Dancing*. It's my third time, their first. I saw it with Barb a couple of weeks after it came out. She was a changed woman back then, still is now – diminished by the death of her son Michael, in denial and barely disguised despair. Can you blame her? I'd not be able to handle the loss of a child, would burrow like a miner bee into the mud of my mind and not come out again till the earth around me crumbled. *If a clod be washed away by the sea, Europe is the less* . . . What's that from again?

But Barb really enjoyed *Dirty Dancing* too. The second time, I went on my own, a Thursday evening. How sad is that? Not at all – I loved it. I'd invited Henry but he'd dithered and I didn't want to wait. When it comes out on video, I'll buy it, and when that first tape wears out, I'll buy it again.

The girls are wearing lipstick – my idea this time because they're only twelve and the film is PG-13. But in fairness, it's a feminist masterpiece dealing with heavy but important topics such as class, ethnicity, consent and abortion, so it was imperative for me that they be educated . . . What am I talking about? I read all that later in an interview with the writer and co-producer Eleanor Bergstein. At the time, and right now, I'm thinking only of Patrick Swayze, those piston-valve pins under tight black pants, his inky vest scarcely covering the work of muscles and arteries underneath.

The girls are rapt, their emergent oestrogen eked up to the max. We all have popcorn on our laps. Johnny is barefoot on a log above a river, telling Baby not to look down.

They're dancing, of course, and they might fall in. Baby laughs, and I do too because I wish I was her, as do Eva and Rachel and the entire audience.

They're in a meadow now, practising the lift they'll need to do at the Sheldrake Hotel to cover for Johnny's regular dance partner Penny, who needs to have an abortion, but, oops, they've fallen over and Baby's straddling Johnny in that long sedge grass with those beautiful trees in the background. She's laughing again – me too, in between eating. I can't get the popcorn into my mouth quickly enough. *You know, the best place to practise lifts is in the water . . .*

Yes, I agree wholeheartedly, Johnny – you don't want to risk a herniated disc when you could whip off that vest – you're not going to need it in the water, are you?

It cuts to Mountain Lake in Virginia, even though they're supposed to be in the Catskills, 500 miles away in New York state. Maybe they're in both places at once – it's possible, there's precedent.

'Go,' Johnny says, hoisting Baby above his head with Adonic arms and impeccable pecs. She maintains decent form but his is better, in my opinion – his cranked core and exquisitely exposed chest. 'Good, now hold that position,' he says, but she can't. She plunges headlong into the water, taking him under with her. They resurface and start laughing again and finally – finally – it looks like he's going to kiss me, I mean Baby, I mean Rachel, that's what she's thinking, her and Eva both, I can see it on their faces.

The three of us will dance through frozen streets on the way to the bus stop and it will become our favourite film, the one we turn to when we're happy, when we're sad, that reminds us of the day we went to see it and all the times we've watched it since.

Chapter 13

2013

The boys have always loved my teeth trick, and now, with the wig, it's even better. Most of my teeth are mine, unlike my mother's – she had them all pulled out as soon as she could on the NHS, spent more of her life with falsers than without, kept them in a cup of bleach beside her bed. My father kept his canines, incisors and molars in his mouth until the end, was found lying on his kitchen floor with a rictus grin by his brother, John. It's hard to believe sometimes – funerals help, seeing the body even more so, but little prepares you for the avarice of the cadaverous, the way they prompt you to keep pondering them, how stressful they can be to silence. Give them a chance and they'll bid good-morrow from the garden, the oven, the bath.

I have three dentures on a plastic plate that sits snugly against the roof of my mouth, held in place with wires. The dentist did a good job – when it's in, it looks like I have no gaps. When it's out – 'Oh, look at Grandma' – it still amazes the boys.

'Again,' William cries. At four, he still thinks his teddies are alive and accepts magic without suspicion. He's getting taller every day – that's how it looks through the computer. 'Again, Grandma, again.'

'OK, shut your eyes,' I say.

He shuts them, and Rachel covers Ewan's with her hand. I pull out the plate – 'OK, open your eyes' – grin gummily into the camera.

William laughs. Ewan giggles and touches his head, says 'hair'.

'Yeah, hair,' William says. 'Hair.'

'OK, close your eyes,' I say.

William closes, Rachel covers Ewan's eyes again. I slot the plate quickly back into my mouth, pull off my brown bob. 'OK, open your eyes.'

Both boys laugh.

2014

Gem and the boys are in Australia – Rachel, Eva and I are speaking to them from Aberdeen. I'm on my big brown hospital chair in the living room because where else would I be? It's my turtle shell, a dermal bone protecting my vital but increasingly lethargic organs. The girls are kneeling on the carpet at either side of me.

'It's lovely to see you,' Gem says.

'You too,' I say. She won't press me on how I'm feeling – I suppose she doesn't want to in front of the boys. They know I'm sick, or I assume they do. If not, they'll know soon enough. It's morning here, evening there, their winter solstice just come or gone, our summer solstice just gone or coming, the earth's axis tilting back in their favour.

The boys are snuggling into Gem against their living-room radiator. I could ask about the extension – it's half-done, I believe, and going well.

'It's just thirteen degrees here,' Gem says. 'Bloody freezing.'

'Just fifteen here today,' I say.

'You'd have loved it yesterday,' Rachel says. 'Fourteen degrees and people were having barbecues in shorts and T-shirts.'

Eva smiles and nods. She looks engaged but is quieter than usual – I don't know how her relationship is with Gem but imagine, having only heard Rachel's side, that Gem puts the brunt of the blame for the girls' estrangement on Eva. Unfairly, of course, but who cares about fair in relationships? Or rather, who *believes* in it? Children, that's who. I rarely hear the boys complaining, but when I do, it's usually William whining that something or other's not fair. Poor little thing – he has lots to learn.

'They were actually hoping you'd tell them a bedtime story,' Gem says to Rachel. 'I've done it the last couple of nights but mine are terrible.'

'They're OK, Mummy,' William says.

'Ilya and Alyosha,' Ewan says.

'Oh, ow, I've got pins and needles,' Rachel says. She gets up, shakes out her legs. It's still the forenoon in Aberdeen, a strange time for the bedtime routine.

'Take the computer over there,' I say, handing her my laptop. 'I can listen from here. Grandma loves you, boys.'

'Love you, Grandma,' they say in unison.

Rachel lies back on the sofa, lays the laptop on her stomach.

'Fancy a rub?' Eva asks.

My nod and smile say it all. I'm getting used to this but will never tire of it, should have become terminally ill decades ago. She gets up and stands behind me, lays her hands on my shoulders and starts kneading my neck, the trapezius, my head falling back and coming forward again. She gets a knuckle into the nuchal ligament, the elasticated strap joining my skull to my spine. They only formed when we came down from the

157

trees and started chasing our dinner, and only exist in animals that run long distances – in giraffes they're gigantic, in horses they're huge. Canines have a thin strip of bacon like ours, connecting their chest vertebrae and neckbone. Pigs don't have them and are rubbish at running, their heads flopping everywhere. Cats don't have them, can lick their backsides and sprint but tire quickly. None of the other great apes have them. If I could have my time again there would be more nuchal ligament love and hands-on caring, more of this: my girls giving me massages, me giving them massages, even Henry, my parents, my friends, all of us. Why not? When you have hands, it's all within your grasp.

'OK, right,' Rachel says on the sofa. 'Once upon a time . . .'

I want to listen, I can see that's what I want, but my eyes are closed and it looks like I'm drifting into a prehensile paradise of fingers and opposable thumbs, a bird in Eva's hand.

'So, there was a race in the forest,' Rachel says. 'Ilya and Alyosha weren't the only siblings there. At the start line, they saw Grushenka and Pavel.'

'Who are they?' William asks.

'A brother and sister who live in the forest too,' Rachel says.

'How far away?'

'About thirty kilometres.'

'How far's that?'

'Pretty far,' she says. 'But the forest stretches for hundreds of kilometres in every direction.'

Eva's mouth moves closer to my ear. 'Does that feel OK, Mum?'

'Amazing,' I say. My eyes are still closed and that's fine, close them while you have them.

'Sounds very Enid Blyton,' she whispers before straightening her spine again.

'They had to cross the finish line first with three special green flowers,' Rachel says. 'The flowers were big and heavy, almost like people. But the most important thing was to look after each other.'

'Like me and William,' Ewan says.

'Like you and William,' Rachel says.

'That's exactly right, mate,' Gem says.

Eva manipulates my musculature, goes to town on my knotted neck. She was cooking with garlic at breakfast time, I can smell it but won't complain – she's lending a hand, coming in handy. There's a reason hands are the most symbolised part of the body. Spiritually, they represent grace and divine presence; in the physical realm, mastery, work and cooperation; on my shoulders, an oxcart of oxytocin.

'Ilya and Alyosha ran as fast as they could, jumping over logs and ferns. They were going so quickly, but so were Grushenka and Pavel and all the other kids.'

'What are the other kids' names?' William asks.

'Nobody knows,' Rachel says. 'They're just kids from the forest. I mean, there's Alexei the anvil-maker's boy, everybody knows him. And Lizaveta the lumberjack's daughter. But not the rest. Some are big, some small. Some are in turbo-charged wheelchairs, some are blind but super speedy.'

My head is lolling. It looks like Eva could twist and yank it right off if she wanted, and in many ways she might as well. The drugs were fine at the end, made everything feel pretty good, all things considered, but this would have been a novel way to go. One, two, three, *schlop* – the skull coming clean off the cervical vertebra, the nuchal ligament either trailing with it or staying behind like the banger in a Christmas cracker, a happy head in need of a plate. I'd have resisted, though, at the time. We hold on to life even when we know the game's up, can't help it, would pummel other people to a pulp if it was a choice between them and us. Henry and I watched a nightmarish documentary once, with accounts of parents stealing bread from their own children in order to survive a bit longer so they could be worked or gassed to death. I threw up watching it, had to leave the cinema.

'*Over here*, Pavel shouted to Grushenka. They'd found a green flower, their first, but hey, look, so had Alyosha. *Over here*, he shouted to Ilya. Ilya ran over and helped him pick the flower. And then they found another nearby.'

'How many flowers do Pavel and Grushenka have?' William asks.

'They also had two now,' Rachel says. 'It was very close. *You're nearly there*, said the race announcer through a speaker on the tree. *Keep going, children. Remember, the winner gets all the chocolate they can eat and fifty dollars in unmarked bills.*

'Alyosha pulled the third and final green flower on his own – such a strong boy – and started running to catch up with Ilya. Grushenka and Pavel had their three already and were approaching the finish line. *Run*, Ilya shouted. *Come on, Alyosha, run.* Alyosha ran at top speed to catch up with Ilya. They could still cross the line together if he hurried. *Run*, Ilya shouted. *Run*.'

'Run,' William shouts from Australia. 'Run,' Ewan shouts.

'About a hundred metres from the line, just as they were back together again, Alyosha tripped on a root and tumbled headlong into a massive puddle.'

'Idiot,' William says.

'Hey, watch it, mate,' Gem says.

'It was so deep that he couldn't touch the bottom but he was able to tread water and stay safe, just like you boys do in your lessons. *Take the flower*, he said to Ilya, throwing the last of the big green flowers in Ilya's direction. *Are you sure?* Ilya asked. *Yes,* Alyosha replied. *Don't worry. Go now, Ilya, run, quickly.'*

'Run,' William says. 'Come on, Ilya.'

'Go, Ilya,' Ewan says.

'Grushenka and Pavel were only about five metres from the finish line and were going to win. But Ilya remembered he was wearing his pressure pants and pressed a button that made him go twice as fast as normal. He was really just a blur now, streaking through the forest . . .'

'Come on,' William says.

'Grushenka and Pavel were less than an inch from the finish line and already high-fiving each other when – *zoom* – Ilya rushed past and pipped them.'

William cheers, Ewan copies, cheers too.

'But the race organiser wasn't happy.'

'Chocolate,' William says.

'Yummy,' Ewan says.

'She said, *Yes, you crossed the line first but your brother Alyosha is still over there in a big soggy puddle – I can see him from here. So I'm afraid we're going to give the chocolate and fifty dollars to Grushenka and Pavel. Hard cheese.'*

'Cheese,' Ewan says.

'That's not fair,' William says. He sounds indignant.

'Anyway . . .' Rachel says.

'That's not the ending, is it, love?' Gem asks.

Eva, still rubbing, leans in close to my ear again, whispers, 'Very cheery.'

'Maybe we can finish it tomorrow,' Rachel says. 'Why don't you tell me what you've all been up to today?'

Henry's having one of his episodes. No, that's not right – it's a single continuous episode that bulges and bursts like a badly stuffed sausage casing. I'm joining us, as the Aussies might say, mid-snag, which is exactly where he finds himself of late: no beginning or end, a story snagged in medias res.

We've been back from Australia for five or six months, some of which I spent in hospital, but have slept in separate rooms for years. His snoring and sleep apnoea provided enough creeping barrage cover for me to commando crawl to where I needed to be – under my own covers resting in peace, with Henry gone but not forgotten under his. But we're still sharing a house – our mortgage has been paid off for nearly a decade and the bills are minimal.

I was grateful for Henry's company on the flight back from Australia. He helped very little in practical terms, but that's probably because he couldn't. Whenever I winced and held my abdomen, he'd say, 'Is it hurting?' and I'd nod with my eyes closed. His hand on mine, the warmth of it, that reassurance – that didn't happen, but in a way, in Henry's way, it did.

I'd cried at the airport, as had Rachel, our five-week holiday was coming to a close after seven awful days. Would we ever see each other again? I don't know, dearie. But I've always loved you, even in those extremely challenging years when you turned my hair grey, worried me thin and broke my heart several times over. I'm proud of you, Rachel. I really am. The boys. Gem. I'm proud of you all.

Henry spent those last precious moments staring at the window display in an airport shop and saying nothing. But just being there beside me, listless or lumbering like Frankenstein's monster – that was something. If our plane had gone down in the Arabian Sea, I'd have sunk quickly, as would he, his watery yellow eyes following me through the murk.

He came to visit me in hospital, asked none of the questions I'd have liked him to, but again he was there, and that was something. One of the doctors seemed to imply later that they'd kept me on nil by mouth for days after an ambulance rushed me there from the airport as an act of compassion. He spoke around it rather than to it, but my understanding was that they thought I was going to die soon and that giving me any kind of sustenance – even the school dinner slop from the hospital kitchen – would only prolong the pain. I didn't feel nearly as bad as they were suggesting, which the nurse said was probably thanks to the morphine. It's warm stuff, morphine, a fitting tribute to the god of dreams it's named after and exactly the kind of sensation you'd expect from drinking magical poppy milk. I've read that it feels similar to a snipped prefrontal cortex, the brain a red, red rose stripped of thorns, but I'm not sure how anyone would know. A person with a leucotomy would surely experience morphine differently given lobotomies dull the emotions.

It brought more depth and texture to mine, at least while I was communing with the son of Somnus, swimming slowly in a soporiferous pool while my tiling cracked and splintered. I'd not make it, would slip under the surface, a shadowy shape at the deep end of the pool, but I got out, had a shower, dried myself off.

And look at me now. I'd be a hard sell for the cover of *Women's Health* but I'm at home in my own bed and feeling, from memory, far better than I did. I'm going to survive. That's what's on my mind, if not in this moment then regularly at other times. I'm going to survive.

It's easy to know what's on Henry's mind because he's switched on the light and winged ants are swarming from his brain.

163

His state would be shocking, and *was* shocking – it really was, at first – but he's been worsening gradually for weeks and I've grown used to it, bit by bit.

'I just think we need to. We need to. Clean. We need to. The walls. You saying you can't see it? Nah, you're not, hey. I don't know. The walls.'

'It's three in the morning,' I say. I don't know how long he's been standing there. 'Go back to bed, Henry. I need to sleep.' My head ploughs into the pillow. Champ, in his fluffy bed on the floor beside me, huffs and settles. After Mary Stuart's head was chopped off, her Skye terrier was found under her skirt, covered in blood. It refused to leave her, had to be dragged away, and died of heartache shortly afterwards.

'The walls,' Henry says. 'I don't know. What is it? I don't know. The fridge. Down there. Last night. The water and stuff. Earlier, I mean. This morning. It's dangerous. Not sure it's safe. Is it? Is it, though? Is it safe? What do you think? Is it safe, Marg? Are you sleeping? I'm awake, fully awake. Is it safe, though? Are we safe?'

'We'll probably keep body and soul together until the morning,' I say. 'Can you turn the light off on your way out, please. Goodnight.'

'The fridge,' he says, not listening. 'The walls. The stuff on them. Crawling, so much, creepy crawlies, wriggling and stuff. Like, yuk. Inside the freezer. Did you switch it off? The stuff. Hey. Hi. You sleeping, Marg, yeah?'

I'm not – how could I? – but I'm doing my best impression, one that, in a game of charades, would have everyone quickly shouting *sleep!*

Engaging with psychosis doesn't work – I've tried. Yes, I can see it too, Henry. You're right, the walls are moving and those trees are definitely coming for us. His doctor said to think of his

164

behaviour as an injury, a bit like a broken arm. I wish they'd wrap a compression bandage around his mouth. I feel empathy, I think I do, but I also want him to shut up and leave me alone, if not permanently then for the next three or four hours.

'Walls. Water marks on the walls. Silt, is it? Emptied the fridge. Bins. The bins. They come tomorrow, yeah? Not the bins – they don't come, but bin folk do. Scrubbing the walls with soap and a cloot, do you remember my mum's clootie dumplings – they were fine, really fine. Will that soap stain the walls? Maybe from the shops. I've cleared the fridge and freezer bit. The bins. Is the tip open tomorrow?'

'You better not have emptied that fridge,' I say, eyes opening.

'I'm like, why's it full of water? Defrosted mince or something, hey, gadz. I don't know. Heaving wi' germs and stuff.'

'There was no mince or water, Henry. Tell me you haven't thrown out my protein shakes and medication again. If you have . . .'

'The fridge,' he says. 'The walls.'

He doesn't know it yet, and neither do I, and I'm not sure either of us would believe it, but this will be the last night we spend in the same house, an end to being constantly stuck in the middle of things, if not for Henry, then for me. Our age of cohabitation is drawing to a close, more than four decades of love, laughter, tears and whatever this is now.

'The water,' he says. 'Right up the walls.'

1975

Both girls are jaundiced and weigh less than they should. They have tape on their cheeks, tubes in their noses, cannulas in their hands, but they're toasty and safe. I like the purring noise it makes, the incubator, which otherwise reminds me of a hamster box – a perspex one, better than my box for Mousey. She got stuck behind a pipe a month after I got her, Mousey, died from the heat – I cried for days.

I thought the girls would get an incubator each but was told it's better this way because sharing a home was all they'd ever known. I hadn't thought of my womb as a home until then, would see my hysterectomy at sixty-two as a gutting of the girls' first abode.

I can see the padding around the sutures on my abdomen under my nightdress. My hair looks like I've had rollers in, but surely not. I look young (of course – I'm twenty-six) but also washed out. I've lost blood, and have gestational diabetes, but more than that, I've just been sitting in a ward doing word searches and visiting the neonatal every day in my dressing gown and slippers. They'd have been called weaklings in times gone by, the girls, and would have shrivelled like mouldy figs, but the incubator is a kiln for kith and kin – the girls are fighters now, that's what the nurses call them.

We've bonded – I know that I love them. They have tiny plastic bands on their wrists, one that says *Rachel*, one *Eva*. We named them after Henry's sister, Eva, who died in childhood, and my paternal grandmother, Rachel, who I'd met, apparently, but who died before I was five.

Because she was plucked from me first, or so they told me afterwards, I think of Eva then and now as my oldest child. Only by a minute or so, but still.

It's impolite to spy on the other imps in incubators, but of course you do, especially when their parents aren't there. Some spiderlings will make it, some won't. I don't remember thinking my two wouldn't, just that it would be nice to lick them like a lioness and carry them by the scruff of their necks to our lair.

The best I can do for now is reach through the little portholes in the side of the incubator and touch them, but only for a minute because there's a risk of infection. Henry's smile was the broadest I've ever seen it when one of them – I think it was Eva – gripped onto his finger, an involuntary nerve reflex that starts in utero but emotional for him all the same. He visits twice a day, that's all fathers and familiars are allowed – it's barbaric when you think about it.

I roll back my dressing gown sleeve, slide my hand through one of the portholes. 'Hello, my love,' I say to Rachel. 'Hello, little love,' to Eva.

I tickle Eva's palm, it's so little, and it happens, the grasp. She holds on, tight enough to take her body weight, and I sit there, being held, in love.

Watching Living Margaret is fine but it's hard not to wonder if . . . I stand (have no legs) at the other side of the incubator and reach my hand (no hands) through one of the other holes. I tickle (can't tickle) Eva's belly, then Rachel's – she looks the lonelier of the two. Or maybe I'm projecting, but it feels that way. I gently drag my fingernails (no fingernails) on her little palm, can almost feel her as she grips.

Chapter 14

2015

Ewan must be four, although I'm finding it increasingly challenging to guess how old people are between the ages of three and six. Likewise between seven and ten, eleven and thirteen, fourteen and nineteen, twenty and ninety-two. The broad categories are easier: baby, child, teen, adult, dead.

If he's four, and even if he's not, he has a bird's nest in the back of his hair, just a bit of matting, no actual feathers or eggs, and he's yawning, his eyes slightly swollen, was probably sleeping in the car. It looks like early morning – I'm still OK at estimating the time. It's twenty past six, quarter to nine, five past eight . . . How would I know?

Rachel – would she be forty? – is on her haunches in the muddy carpark, tying Ewan's orange shoelaces. William and Gem – he'd be six or seven, she early forties – are in the car and don't seem to be getting out.

'That's you done, mate,' Rachel says to Ewan, picking up a book and a trowel. 'Let's go.'

It's wintertime, going by their clothes. It gets cold in Australia, the southern part at least, that's what Rachel has told me. You don't necessarily think it would. I thought it was warm all the time.

'Bye, William, bye, Mummy,' Ewan says, waving to both.

William ignores him, turns away. Gem waves, blows a kiss. They set off, Rachel and Ewan, she in her black coat, white hoodie and jeans, he in his green cotton trousers, blue jumper and red bodywarmer. They stroll along a dirt path, past ferns as big as Ewan that may have just metabolised carbon dioxide and released lots of oxygen because I can breathe easier, as if having no lungs wouldn't stop me lunging. The trees, I feel like I know them. Hello, trees. Have I sat on your branches? Stroked your roots? The sky through the trees, I know it too, the way it's shaped by the canopy. The mint, mulch and camphor scent . . . I can smell it. Can I smell? I've been here – it feels that way. Or maybe I know it from the photos Rachel used to send me. The trees are mountain ash, I think, impressively tall with perfect postures, their skin as smooth as freshly shaved legs, a rough brown sock around their ankles, their arms and lance-like hands too high for holding.

'Is this part of the Dandenongs?' Ewan asks.

'It's all the Dandenongs,' Rachel says.

'This tree here?' he says, pointing.

'The Dandenongs.'

'And the bushes?'

'They're the Dandenongs too.'

Rachel is walking slowly so that Ewan can keep up. There's no rush. Ewan looks up at her, back at the trees, at a bird with an ornate tail – what kind of bird was that? – taking off from behind a bush.

They leave the path and start trampling across the scrub with purpose, as if they know where they're going. Rachel, at least – Ewan is trudging by her side, the grass up to his knees.

'Here we are,' Rachel says, stopping.

They're at a tree that's maybe a eucalypt, maybe not. It's

knobblier and shorter than the others, either disappointing or distinguished by contrast. There's an opening at its base like a rudimentary church entrance, a fabric butterfly inside on a thin metal stick. In front of that, cradled by the tree's bifurcating roots, are two small bushes with yellow flowers that look like they've been planted there.

'You're looking a bit worse for wear,' Rachel says, getting onto her knees and pulling leaves and weeds from around the bushes. 'I should have taken the water bottle, we could have given them a drink.'

'They don't look thirsty,' Ewan says.

'Come here,' she says, taking his hand and pulling him into her chest, his arms still at his side, his cheeks as red as Rachel's at his age. 'I love you, mate.' And then, looking at the tree, 'I miss you, Mum. Can't believe it's been nearly a year.'

I nearly jump out of my skin (have none) but she can't see me, surely. Is she talking to the tree? Am I the tree? In a forest teeming with model-thin mountain ash, am I another type of tree, dumpier and knottier than the others? Albeit, yes, distinguished precisely for those reasons. My protuberances mean you could climb me if you wanted. I could hug you with my one crooked arm – Ewan, William, the whole family – fend off the Baobhan Sith.

'OK, let's do this,' Rachel says. 'Mum, we've brought you something to read for your birthday.' She takes the trowel from Ewan and breaks the earth just in front of the yellow bushes. It gives way easily, the earth, unstoppering – am I imagining this? – an aromatic concoction of damp moss, wet tree trunk, bluewood, beetroot, tea tree oil, warm grass, butter popcorn, liniment, redwood, citrus, softwood, toadstools, petrichor. Keep digging, Rachel. A distant, putrid base note of nondescript organics and carrion flowers. And something metallic, too – a steam iron covered in lichen, a three-bar electric fire that's been recently turned off. And behind that, maybe within it, boiled eggs, peeled, split open and abandoned.

My father took me to see *The Great Escape* when I was a teenager, after which I wanted to dig tunnels, not horizontally like a prisoner of war but down. I thought you could just keep going, at least until hitting New Zealand, but you can't – or so they say. It's all theoretical, what's down there. An iron-nickel ball encircled by a sea of molten matter wrapped in a silicon and magnesium mantle. OK. But nobody knows. Jules Verne imagined subterranean rivers, an underground ocean, petrified tree trunks, gigantic mushrooms. Why not? The world's biggest bore hole is barely eight miles deep, nearly 4,000 miles short of the bullseye. It might be empty down there. A rabbit could be running at 900 miles an hour. The core could be stuffed with leaves and rotting fruit.

The book Rachel has with her is *Frankenstein*, I can see that now, not a particularly fancy edition but the one she was reading when she visited me in Aberdeen – the revised 1831 version (I didn't know there were distinct versions until she told me). I wrote inside it at her request, not on the front pages (I'm not Mary Shelley) but the blank ones at the back, between the appendices and blurbs for other Penguin Classics. It was bland, really, the message: *Thanks for coming, dearie. It means the world to me. I love you. Mum XX.* But it was true – it meant a lot.

'Can I?' Ewan asks.

'Of course, mate, go for your life.' She takes what looks like a freezer bag from her coat pocket, lays it on the ground.

Ewan takes the trowel and starts scraping dirt from the hole, his little fingers, I can smell them, chinking the blade against stones and rock, chopping through fibrous roots that smell like a garden pot and probably belong to me, or me in tree form, the filaments of the local fungal network interrupted temporarily.

'Look, Mummy, a worm,' he says.

Rachel leans in, as do I, and yes, there's a worm, a beauty, a strand of invertebrate spaghetti wriggling and smelling of skin. Ewan picks it up by the hydrostatic skeleton and kisses it. Rachel pats Ewan's head, sits back and opens the book. She's written *Love you always* on the front inside cover. In looser handwriting – Gem's – it says: *Miss you, Margaret.* Below that, it says: *Love you, Grandma, William.* And below that: *Lov and happy borfday, Ewan X.* She slides it into the freezer bag like a salmon fillet, draws the zip-lock closed, gets back onto her knees.

'My turn,' she says, taking the trowel from Ewan, leaning one hand on the ground for support and scooping with intent, adding quickly to the mound by the side of the hole. A clunk, she's hit another stone, a sizeable one, starts digging around it.

Ewan looks at the tree and strokes the freezer bag. 'Is this so Grandma can read it without muddy pages?'

'Yeah,' Rachel says. 'We can't give her a dirty book, can we?'

'No . . .'

She pulls the rock out – it's the size of a small kitten – scoops out the loose earth left in its wake. 'Now, that looks deep enough, doesn't it?'

Ewan nods and passes her the bagged book.

'Which way should I put it in the hole?' she asks. 'Facing up or down?'

'With our names nearest the top,' he says. 'So Grandma knows it's from us, not someone else.'

She lowers it, a polyethylene and paper casket. 'Shall I put the rock on top of it?'

'Yeah,' Ewan says, animated. 'We can come back and if the rock's moved, it means Grandma's read it.'

I'd kiss him if I could, do my teeth trick, my wig trick, whatever he wants.

Rachel lays the rock on top of *Frankenstein* and starts scooping earth back into the hole. When she's done, Ewan stands on it to make sure it's flat. 'It's like a treasure,' he says. 'Can we stay a while to say things?'

'What kind of things?' Rachel asks, standing.

Ewan shrugs.

Rachel looks me square in the bark, seemingly at a loss for words. 'We've buried a book for you, Mum. I don't know why. It was William's idea, but he's in a huff because he wants icecream and he can't because it's nine in the morning, so . . .'

'Have I met Grandma in real life?' Ewan asks.

'Just once, a few years ago,' Rachel says. 'She came to visit from Scotland but couldn't stay very long. You don't remember?'

She's joking, must be.

'Hmmm . . . not really,' he says. 'I can't remember anything from when I was a baby.' He looks at the tree, says, 'I love you, Grandma, and I miss you.'

Then, with the lightness of foot of one who knows dying doesn't matter, he sets off at a run, shouting, 'Race you back to the car!'

1990

Rachel has been working at One Up Records in Belmont Street since leaving school, somehow managed to convince them she was sixteen even though she was only fourteen – and still is, I think. She knows how to lie and manipulate, we've seen it time and again, knows all there is to know about the bands of the day. The Vaselines. The Jesus and Mary Chain. The Associates. James. One week she dresses all in black, her skin deathly white, the next in brightly coloured paisley-pattern blouses and sawn-off bellbottoms. She says she doesn't smoke but I found Marlboros in her bag next to a bottle of what I'll later discover is amyl nitrite but at the time just confused me.

The more pressing mystery is the bouquet of flowers on the kitchen table.

'Maybe she sent them to herself,' Eva says.

She has a gold stud in her nose, which she wore for less than a month before I insisted she remove it, her one act of teenage rebellion. She'll nearly make the Scottish team for the World Schools Debating Championships later that year, which is far from her only act of poise and intellect.

It's only Eva and me in the kitchen. The freighted silence is punctured twice in rapid succession by the living-room door slamming (Henry) and the thud of a bedroom door (Rachel) upstairs. They're not fighting about the bouquet – if anything, it's contributed calm, although Rachel did act suspiciously when it arrived. Too happy, or too disinterested – I can't remember which, but my intuition prickled instantly, as did Eva's. The typed card says: *From a secret admirer.* Red roses would have been a more traditional gesture, but these – chrysanthemums and gerberas in peachy tones – are nice enough. Maybe a bit old-ladyish, like a potpourri bag in an underwear drawer, but who am I to judge?

They've been fighting, Rachel and Henry, about . . . Honestly, I don't remember. When were they not at each other? When were she and I not arguing? I could maybe start there instead, recall those times – don't sit down, it won't take long.

'Maybe they're from a boy she knew at school or a guy she works with,' I suggest to Eva.

'Unlikely,' she says. 'They know they're barking up the wrong tree.'

'What do you mean?' I ask, before . . . My face reddens and I can see it's coming back to me, Rachel trying to intimate something to Henry and me about her friend, Olivia, how she might be, you know, more than a friend, and both of us – Henry and me – looking genuinely perplexed before rolling up like armadillos and not unfurling until she'd left the room. It's amazing how completely you can block things out when you want or need to, and how deeply people can take this to heart. I wasn't against the idea of lesbianism, then or now, but it can still come as a shock, hearing that from your daughter. Or not even hearing it – just having it there, a guest that hasn't been properly introduced and makes everyone uncomfortable because they're standing in the corner looking nervous and hesitant. I felt ambushed – not by Rachel, and not in that moment, but by my preconceptions of her over the years, the sense that my instincts had been held repeatedly and unknowingly to ransom by my motherly myopia. I felt guilty for not seeing Rachel for what she was, blindsided and blind to my beautiful daughter.

'So you think they're from a girl?' I ask.

Eva is also beautiful – she always is, but I mean right now, her body in a tug of war between gangliness and grace.

'I honestly think she sent them to herself,' she says.

I'm waiting for the punchline even though it's unlikely to come – Eva's not the joking type. Her sincerity from thirteen onwards makes her the straight line to Rachel's screwy squiggles.

The stomping around upstairs is engineered to aggravate

Henry in the living room and will be having that effect. But I still keep my voice low, as does Eva, in case she hears us talking about her.

'Why would she send herself flowers?' I ask. 'It makes no sense.'

'She's having a bad time of it,' Eva says. 'I think she's really lonely.'

2021

'Mask on, mate,' Rachel says to William.

'Why doesn't Ewan have to?' he asks, irked and indignant.

'He's only ten.'

'So?'

'You're twelve.'

'I wasn't last week.'

'True, but you are now.'

'And?'

'I'm not doing this, mate.'

'Put it on, darling,' Gem says. 'Come on, William, you know the rules.'

They're going somewhere, I don't know where. Ewan looks happy – maybe even more so knowing he's unwittingly one-upped William.

'No,' William says. 'I don't want to wear it, masks are stupid.'

'Wear your mask,' Rachel says again, her anger an heirloom from Henry. 'William, please. It could save your life.'

1963

I'm a teenager, all limbs, and my father has just run into the house.

'Excuse me,' he says, darting past my mother and me to the kitchen sink with a hand across his face.

'Fit've ye done?' my mother asks, laughing. 'Hiv ye hurt yersel, Alec?'

'Just a little,' he says. 'That bloody soldering iron.'

'Ye wirnae wearing yer mask?' she asks, still laughing.

That was her way, the model I inherited – if in doubt, have a hoot. If you'd heard my chortling – once

upon

I

mean – you'd not have

forgotten

I slipped going down the Back Wynd Stairs as a young girl, skinned my back badly, felt like I was going to pass out. She burst into laughter, couldn't stop, her hands on her knees, falsers all but falling out, had to calm down at length before asking if I was OK.

Was my father working on his car? I can't remember. But he's clearly done something to his face. He runs cold water onto a dishcloth and holds it to his cheek. He doesn't know it yet, but the mark will take a long time to heal. I don't know it yet, but I'll sneak up to the open bathroom door in a few days and see him applying my mother's concealer to his cheek to cover it up. My father, wearing make-up. I have no problem with anyone wearing make-up, it's gendered by convention and should be worn by anyone who wants, but my father . . . wearing make-up. It's maybe not the concealer that will confuse me but the fact he wants to hide his little scar. He wasn't a vain man, that's what I thought – but maybe he actually was. Nearly a decade later, he'll come back from Spain with dual-language editions of Cervantes and copy out lines in both languages in an A6 notebook. At the top of the second page, he'll write and underline: *The knowledge of yourself will save you from vanity.*

My vanity . . . I didn't cover scars on my face but I do have a sense it caused something to happen, that I took offence to something small, so small, and it inadvertently

forgotten it

ruined everything. That's what I'm feeling – there's something big I'm concealing.

2014

Apart from my eyes, I like how I'm looking. I've dabbed them, tried not to rub off the remaining mascara. It's the shock, that's all. When the doctor sat me down, she said she wouldn't sugarcoat it, and she didn't. There was no coat, only cold. Even now, in the car, I'm shivering.

I turn on the engine, the heater, remain static in the hospital carpark. It will be lunchtime in Spain, evening in Australia. I want to tell Eva first, given Rachel had the odious honour of finding out first in Melbourne.

I look in the mirror again, pat at my eyelids with tissue – I'll be shedding more tears soon, it doesn't matter. But I want to look the best I can under the circumstances. My emerald scarf – I loved that scarf – complements my colouring, my cool winter tones, goes well with my indigo jumper. My make-up, other than the mascara and washed-out eyeliner, looks good. As does my hair. It's mine, not the wig. Why did it grow back if there was no point? Why am I still breathing if there's no point? I don't look like I'm ending. They might have made a mistake, that's what I'm thinking. They haven't – I've seen the blood work. But they might have. The partnership between brain and body has served me well but there's a clear rupture now – if the body's failing, if it's had enough, then surely the brain can live somewhere else. It's not Brain's fault Body is sick. Brain doesn't believe it's happening. Why is Body lying to Brain?

I can remember clearly wondering what it would mean for Champ, for the girls . . . but mainly for Champ – that's embarrassing, but true. He was my main dependant. The girls didn't need me in any practical sense, they were adults, but Champ . . . and Henry, of course, but he was gone already. There's a chance my news will bring us closer together and we'll see out my final days in relative harmony, cook necromantic dinners. But there's also the chance – and reality, I know now – he'll see my expedited expiry date as a series of problems for him, prompting more questions than he's asked me in years, some of which I'll answer, most of which I'll ignore and a few of which I'll want to print out and roll into a club with which to smack him around the head. What will it mean for him financially? Will he need to phone the bank? Will he have to arrange a funeral? What do I mean when I say I want to leave my body to science? Does he have to ring a scientist when I die? Can I leave the number for the scientist somewhere safe? How is he going to deal with his hospital paperwork? How will it affect his pension? Can I write down his internet password? Can I come over and show him how to use Skype and Facebook?

I bring up Eva's contact details on my phone, am clearly not looking forward to the next few minutes. But this is the worst of it – now, right now. It'll get better after this. One trill, then another, then her face.

'Hey, love,' I say, smiling.

'How did it go?' She's outside somewhere, not in the classroom, thankfully.

'Not great,' I say.

'How come?'

She knows, just knows, I can see it.

'They're stopping my treatment,' I say. 'So . . . basically that's it, dearie.'

'Oh, Mum . . .' Silence. Her eyes filling, flitting from the phone momentarily. 'I can't believe it. You were doing so well.'

'I know, dearie. I know. I'm sorry.'

'Don't say sorry, Mum.' She's crying now, me too.

'But I am,' I say. 'For everything, for getting your hopes up.'

'I'm coming over to see you,' she says. 'I can be there in a couple of days.'

'That'd be lovely,' I say. 'But there's no rush. They think I have another month or two.'

'If I came in a week, then, say, and stay a bit longer, you know, until . . .'

'If that's what you want to do. But please don't feel you have to.'

'Mum . . .'

'It'll be nice to see you, love.' My voice is vacillating – I don't even know why I'm trying to hold it together. 'I'm sorry I won't be there for you.'

'You've always been there, Mum.'

'I mean . . . you know . . .'

'You've always been there, Mum. Don't worry about me, please.'

'OK, dearie. Well, sorry to be the bearer of bad news.'

She's still crying but not as much as before. She's probably thinking about the practical steps – what she'll tell work, what she'll say to Juan, her new boyfriend, what she'll do with her apartment – while her lacrimal glands resaturate with lipids for the next sudden overflow. 'Have you told Rachel yet?'

'She's next on my list,' I say. 'I'll call her after this.'

Chapter 15

Henry and I have had more in common since I died. He sees things as being alive – not just creatures, plants and fungi but inanimate objects too. Which probably goes some way to explaining why he's lying on a hospital bed as a woman attaches what look like little clothes pegs to his forehead, another places syringes on a metal dish, and another ticks some boxes on a sheet of paper.

It's a good day for doing the washing – the world outside the window is a picture of warm summer light, golf-green grass and shrubs that look recently planted.

I'm surprised this is happening to Henry, didn't know anything about it. I maybe wasn't told. Or I'm maybe in hospital too, a mile away, taking my last breaths. Maybe I'm dead already and they're treating Henry for grief-induced insanity, his psyche under pressure from my passing to the underworld, a psychopomp rowing me through the waters of Acheron and disturbing Henry's river of pain. Or maybe that's my vanity again. Henry's brain absorbs like tissue, clogs like tissue, is made of tissue. He's sensitive to movement, detects it where others don't, but can be oblivious to the ostensibly obvious.

I think I know what the weird sisters will do to him. I've read about this, seen it in films. The pegs on his head. The wires running from his chest to a heart-rate monitor. His shirt half-unbuttoned. Electrodes on plastic handles. They're going to shoot electricity into his brain as an abusive form of control so that he ruffles fewer feathers in the cuckoo's nest. He's been unruly, inciting other patients to rebel, and Nurse Ratched wants revenge. No, that doesn't sound like Henry, and doesn't look representative either. The women look perfectly friendly. I'd have tea with any one of them, their ages . . . OK, here's my guesstimate: the doctor is fifty, the anaesthetist forty-five, the assistant late twenties. They look like kinesthesis is important to them – sweating on purpose, increasing their heart rate – as is, right now, improving how Henry's brain produces and perceives movement.

It's largely subjective, though, movement. Sobbing silently at the plane window while we sat on the runway in Australia, it was clear to me that the buildings and parked aircraft were immobile. But then the cabin shook and they started moving, slowly at first but picking up speed, until they were hurtling backwards at 150 miles an hour and downwards at 200 feet a minute – the green fields, Rachel, the houses, my grandsons, cars, Gem, the lakes, Tash and Pete, clouds . . . That's not the same as seeing demons in the wallpaper and bailing non-existent water from the kitchen floor but I still feel sympathetic . . . to a degree. I can't forgive and forget with Henry because I can't remember what I'm meant to forgive.

He'll be enjoying the attention, although three women waiting on him hand and foot is hardly a novelty. His socks look a little dirty and he's unshaven, but they don't care. Or maybe they do but don't show it.

Movement isn't the only sign of life but it's a common one,

as are its accomplices, growth and change. Air becomes trees become chairs become landfill. Oil becomes plastic becomes fish food becomes disease. Cellulose becomes paper becomes books become pulp. Minerals become stones become rocks become scree. From entoptic phenomena to the entropic universe, it's all in transit.

Henry has a plastic clip on his left index finger, cannulas in his right hand, a blood-pressure cuff around his left calf. His eyes are moving, a silicone mask across his mouth. The women look at him, at the equipment, at each other. *Quite a good scene, isn't it? One man, crazy – three very sane spectators.*

'How are you feeling there, Mr Bryce?' the doctor asks.

'Very well indeed,' Henry says, his voice muffled in the mask.

In the past they used a chemical called Metrazol to induce seizures, but the side effects caused such terror in patients that doctors and nurses had to chase them around the room to administer it. The first patient to have an electrically induced seizure was a man in 1938 who'd been found bumbling around a train station with schizophrenia. They gave him 110 volts to the head, after which he returned to his wife and job, resumed his role in the community. The voltage hasn't changed much since. Up a bit. Down a bit. The same. It's not the voltage, of course, but how you use it. Anything more than fifty volts can send a lethal current through the body. If it flows between the arms, that's bad, between the toes, not so much. The wires Henry snipped under a floorboard in Mastrick were 230 volts, a static shock is 500 volts, a Taser gun 50,000 volts, lightning 300 million volts. Surviving or succumbing depends largely on the circuit that's formed and the amperage. Get it right and you can *cure* gay people – that's what they used to think, imagine that. Get it wrong and you crack the skull and cook the brain.

'We're just going to jab your hand a couple of times with these little needles,' the anaesthetist says. 'You should drift off nice and quickly to the Land of Nod.' She feeds one of the syringes into the cannula, drops the plunger. 'This one's your general anaesthetic. And this one . . .' She removes the first needle, lays it down on a tray, takes another, pokes it into the second cannula. 'This one's just a little muscle relaxant called Suxamethonium.'

She's babying him but it's probably appropriate. It must be hard being an anaesthetist, stopping all those pain signals reaching other people's brains while your own stays conscious to the sawing and slicing.

He's unconscious already, his hands twitching.

'Light fasciculations,' the assistant says. 'Noted,' the doctor says.

The assistant slides a rubber mouthguard between Henry's teeth, adjusts it, pulls his lower jaw closed.

The doctor dips two hand-held electrodes into a tray with pink liquid, turns and stands behind Henry's head, cackling maniacally as thunder booms and successive forks of lightning streak the sky . . . I'm joking, it's still sunny outside. She presses them into Henry's temples and nods at the assistant, who lurches to the wall and pulls down a metallic throw switch . . . Joking. I must be nervous. She presses a small orange button on a machine that looks like a DVD player, and—

Oh

Henry's forearms shoot up, eyelids gripping tight, jaws clamping like when . . . I shouldn't say this . . . like when he's having, used to have, an orgasm, as if it feels really good but also, I don't know, painful in some way, a little death as his sperm charge forth to forge new life or die for queen and country.

The heart monitor is bleeping faster, a continuous line of

paper juddering out of the DVD player. The doctor has removed the electrodes from Henry's temples but he's still in seizure, his forearms like a kangaroo, his legs moving as if he's shuffling quickly on the spot. The women watch him and glance at one another without concern, and I can't say I'm worried either. There's no jeopardy. I know Henry gets through this because I sometimes watch TV with him in his flat. He's fine, has years ahead of him . . . I think.

The bleeps are slowing, the body shock abating.

'Blood pressure a little low,' the anaesthetist says, removing the mouthguard and replacing the oxygen mask.

'ECG also low,' the doctor says.

She and the anaesthetist take Henry's forearms down to his sides and hold them in place for a few seconds. It's tender, humane.

'Heart rate slowing,' the doctor says.

Mine must be slowing too, a mile away, today, some other day, I don't know. They say it goes last, the heart, but mine has been gone for ages. It's quarter past ten in the morning according to the clock in Henry's room, which is roughly when my lungs take a permanent breather. Not that I was clockwatching at the time – I was too busy letting my eyelids relax and my jaw fall open – but they say it while they're pressing a finger into your carotid artery. Ten twenty-three. I wasn't alone, though, that was the best bit. Rachel – not her fault – was back in Australia. How could she have known? I could have held on for weeks yet. She had a family to look after. But Eva had changed her ticket, just in case, and it paid off, palliatively speaking. For me. For her too. She was with me at the end, holding my hand. Thank you, I wanted to say. Thanks for holding my hand. But I couldn't. I felt so distant. Patients sometimes get a burst of energy right before death, sit up, say they're famished, ask if they can get dressed and go home, maybe swing by the drive-through McDonald's, but I didn't. I knew my body was shutting down, turning off non-essential functions, and I directed what juice I had left to feeling Eva's hand around mine. I heard her saying she loved me and said – or tried – I love you too, while gripping – or trying to – her fingers. The monitors around me were noisy, as those around Henry have suddenly become too.

Apprehension flits across the women's faces.

'Fifty-six,' the assistant says.

In some ways it's lovely – I've never seen Henry this relaxed.

'Fifty-two,' the assistant says. 'Still dropping.'

A second alarm sounds and it looks like Henry is coming to, probably thinks he's slept in for work, has forgotten he's retired, who he is. His eyes open briefly, dun white, close again, and his legs start kicking, the left one pulling at the cuff – easy Henry, relax. Another sustained alarm.

'Patient going into cardiac arrest,' the assistant says.

'Prep the defibrillator, please,' the doctor says.

The assistant presses buttons on a machine, either checking or setting an electric charge. She squirts gel onto a couple of metal paddles while the anaesthetist helps the doctor open Henry's shirt all the way.

The monitors are in a fluster, as are Henry's legs. But there's movement and he'll be fine – Henry always is.

2014

Rachel's handbag is on the sofa but she's not here with us in the living room – she might be out walking Champ or preparing a meal, I don't know. And me, I forget

forget it

I've had enough

Eva is sitting on the carpet, massaging her feet, hopefully as a prelude to massaging mine. My toes wiggle like Champ's lower half when he wants a biscuit.

'I do agree with Rachel about *Frankenstein*, mostly, but I think there are other aspects that need to be considered – contingencies and so forth.'

Here we go. My teacher Carol, the year I did a night class, was the warmest woman, not a hint of pretension. She opened books as if she was holding a church door ajar for you to go in and look around. Please don't touch anything? You could touch whatever you wanted. The church was as robust as it was broad, as welcoming as it was, at times, intimidating. It only exists with you, she used to tell us. Never forget that. There's no book without the reader – you have all the power. You can walk away, get better acquainted or fall head over heels in love.

'Just take Robert Walton,' Eva says.

'Sorry, dearie, remind me . . .'

'The whole Frankenstein story is told by him – it's an epistolary novel. What we're reading are the letters he's written to his sister. He tells her about the sea voyage he wants to undertake, how excited he is at the prospect of discovering the Northwest Passage, near the North Pole. Letters in which he also reports that he's of depressed spirits because he has no friends, and that he bitterly wants a friend of noble mind. He calls it the *most severe evil*, this lack of friends, how it makes him feel about himself. But it's useless complaining, he's at sea. His crew – none of them are of noble mind. Where is he going to find the noble-minded friend he so desperately craves at sea?'

'So he's a bit lonely,' I say.

'Precisely that,' Eva says. 'Precisely. Robert Walton is a

lonely man. His only contact is his beloved sister, to whom he sends off three letters, with no response, before things go awry and his isolation intensifies. The ship is surrounded by ice, *scarcely leaving her the searoom in which she floated*. He continues writing letters, aware they can't be sent, in which he relays – or maybe concocts – a long and fanciful story. A wild-eyed, hypothermic man who comes on board. A monster travelling by sledge across a frozen sea. And we're supposed to take him at his word.'

'I have something to say about that,' I say. 'But also, my foot's gone numb, hang on.' I lean forward in my brown chair – it's not easy – rub my left foot as best I can. 'It's so tense, the muscle there.'

'You want a foot rub, Mum?'

'I wasn't hinting.'

'It's not a problem. I'd love to.'

'Well, if you're sure, dearie.'

She pulls her socks on and comes forward on her knees. A light crash and thud in the kitchen. Rachel's there – must be cooking. Champ must be with her.

The ball of my left foot curls contentedly in Eva's creamy hands, her fingers squelching between my toes. Judging by my face, it feels good. More than good. 'What I was going to say is . . . It doesn't matter, dearie. Tell me what's on your mind.' It's funny, the need to communicate, to have someone to communicate to. A god listening even as you laugh at the godless universe. Someone waiting near the wings at the theatre, dressed head to toe in black, not seen by the audience but there all the same, listening to the voice on stage. I'm wiping my feet on the welcome mat at death's door, malleable on morphine tablets, and yet Eva needs to tell me something about a book written by an eighteen-year-old nearly two hundred years ago.

190

It's important that I know – important that I know that she knows. But I also have wisdom to impart before I depart, and it is this: just listen, or pretend to – it means more to your loved ones than you could ever know.

'Just having someone to listen to him,' Eva says. 'An audience, if you will. Up until then, he's had his sister. But now he's cut off from her, cut off – through his superiority complex – from his burly crew. And cut off geographically from everything and everyone else in the world. What was perilous water is now treacherous ice. What was it that Kafka said? *A book must be the axe for the frozen sea within us* . . . Well, there's no axe for what Robert needs. Unless it arrives in the form of . . . an imaginary friend.'

I open my eyes and smile, responding to Eva's intonation. She's said something profound, and if my shoulders are anything to go by, I'm receiving profound pleasure from what she's doing to my feet. 'That's really something,' I say.

'I mean, Rachel's better at this stuff, naturally. The psychology, I mean. But could Robert's deep loneliness have augmented his depression and anxiety? Could this in turn have kickstarted a state of delusion in which he sees, or thinks he does, a monster and then a man? And not just any man, of course. A noble creature with a noble mind, by whom he would happily be led . . . a *divine wanderer*, no less.'

2014

I'm delighted the box I'm in is eco-friendly, but I can't say I'm looking forward to the fire.

More mourners would have been lovely. But I told the girls I didn't want a big funeral – or any, ideally – so I've only myself to blame. Barb and Des are here – Des in a black suit, white shirt, black tie, Barb in a black dress she might have bought for the occasion. She's an elegant woman, always was. I miss you, Barb. It's nice to see you. I'm glad you came.

Henry (I'm guessing) is in an acute psychiatric ward, scratching his name into the walls or sedated into somnambulance, unsure, as he used to joke about people in Cornhill, if it's New York or New Year. Rachel . . . She's here, virtually. She's on a tablet screen on the chair between Barb and Eva. It's tempting to make a joke about her being late for her own funeral, but it's my funeral, not hers, and she wouldn't hear me anyway. She still looks jet-lagged, has been back in Australia for a week or so. Or maybe it's her sadness I'm seeing. There's plenty of that. Des, bless him – his head is down. He's maybe thinking about his son, Michael. Barb is sniffling already, a tissue at hand. Do you remember how we laughed, Barb? How good it felt, all that laughing?

Some people have a gift for making others cackle
but my special talent
was chortling and

Eva is in black too – that's just the way, isn't it, a touch of eyeliner but otherwise pasty with loss and exhaustion.

I've asked the celebrant, Angela, to read aloud a letter I wrote because I thought the girls would be too upset. There's nothing worse than crying when you're speaking publicly. For the person crying, I mean. As an audience member, it's pretty much the best thing ever. All that apologising and wiping their nose and trying to hide their face. There's nothing more endearing than that type of vulnerability. I've been at funerals where nobody cried and I felt robbed. Even if it's the
choking

Sorry, I feel weird, nauseous somehow, the opening of a supermarket, you want some tears – a rebellious release that says, through the shorthand of tears: I've been up all night because this means so much to me and now that it's happening, oh, I'm sorry, excuse me, please. Just cry. Yes, you look ugly, but we all do, that's the nature of crying. It's good for you, prolactin, even some potassium, like a banana.

Rachel helped me find Angela before abandoning – leaving – me for Australia. Her website had a muted colour scheme, custom font and nice testimonials about her professionalism and warmth. And that's how she seemed to me when she came over to the house – proficient and full of laughter. She looks suitably sombre now, but smiles as she approaches the front of the . . . I can't really call it a congregation, just a few special souls.

She stands next to the microphone, doesn't need it. 'I'm going to read something Margaret wrote.' She smiles again, clears her throat, choking. *'Thank you all for coming today. I suppose, if you're hearing this, it means they haven't accepted my body for medical research. That's OK. It's not the first time I've offered my body to someone and they've refused.'*

Barb smiles and sniffles. Eva has her head down, her hands on her lap, looks too sad to smile. That's a shame – it was a good joke. Her hair – I like the way she has it today, tied back like that, showing off her forlorn face.

'Sorry, can you pick me up, please? Hello?'

Oh no – that's Rachel's voice. She must be looking at the ceiling, disembodied

Like me

So woozy and

wobbly and

Barb glances at Eva, who remains motionless, gives a cursory wave to Rachel, holds the tablet so that it's facing

Angela and the cardboard box in which I'm resting. Thanks, Barb.

'*I've been reflecting on what a privilege it is to know you're dying. Don't get me wrong, I'd rather I wasn't . . .*'

No laughter.

Barb now seems as worried about the iPad as she does about the fact I'm dead.

'*But it's better this way than just suddenly popping your clogs without any chance to reflect on your life and what mattered to you most. In my case, that's been friends, some of whom may even be here today.*'

Nicely vague – I'm content with that. My last phone call with Barb, maybe a month earlier . . . I'd told her it was game over. She'd come to the house, taken me and Champ to the Gramps, and we'd sat at the picnic table at the lookout spot and cried. Her looking out across the city – her Michael, her life. Me looking out across the city too, wondering which roads I'd travelled on most, whether I was still down there on a pavement somehow, running with my satchel and scraped knees, in a hot rush to tell my father about a mouse.

'*And, of course, my family. I feel incredibly lucky to have been chosen as Eva and Rachel's mother. I don't mean that in a hippy-dippy New Age way.*'

No laughter – Eva is sobbing quietly and Barb and Des are, awkwardly, quite fond of New Age mysticism.

'*But they had the choice, my girls – we all do at a certain age – whether to accept or reject me, and despite everything, they chose to accept me. Not that we didn't have bad times . . . I could tell you about those. How long do we have before the next cremation?*'

Nothing – it's a tough crowd. Even Rachel, on the tablet, she just looks miserable.

'*But that's all part of life, isn't it. More than anything else, I'm proud of my girls.*'

Eva's head remains down. I wish I could put an arm around her – both arms. Barb's still holding up the tablet for Rachel. She wipes her nose with the tissue in her other hand.

Rachel . . . Are Gem and the boys with her? I hope so. It must be hard not being here.

I went to see my mother but not my father in the funeral home, and not visiting him was a momentous mistake. At the time, it felt like not seeing him would stop him from being dead, but that was exactly the problem. That's how complicated grief works – the wound festers and breeds disorders if you can't see those you've lost, or just don't want to. Maybe because you already shared a meaningful goodbye when they were alive, said I love you and hugged as if you knew it was the last time. Or maybe you just said a normal goodbye because, clearly, they were alive and well, or even alive and unwell, or alive and, look, it's not their fault but you were in a foul mood the last time you saw them and you simply needed some time away from them, some time with them away from you, and you never knew, never. You grieve nobody when you see no body, mourn no one because for you they're still alive. That's the trick the mind plays – an invitation to magical thinking in which your denial . . . What denial? There's no denial, none at all, because there's nothing to deny.

Eva saw me in the moment and immediate aftermath of death, but did Rachel? Did Eva take some photos of me like a Victorian corpse? I hope so, for Rachel's sake.

'And this song from Dirty Dancing *says it all. It's the one they dance to at the finale, "The Time of My Life" – a bit cheesy, I know. But I loved that film and cherished watching it with my girls. I would have happily offered my body to Patrick Swayze. And, of course, on a literal level it's true: I've had the time of my life, it's done. Thanks again for coming today.'*

Eva's shoulders are raised. She's unburdening herself, properly weeping – good girl, let it out. I hope I haven't ruined *Dirty Dancing* for her and Rachel.

Angela raises her phone and puts the song on through the crematorium speakers and . . . well, it could be louder, much louder, like it was in the cinema or when we watched it at home, loud enough to make you get up and dance, to feel, really feel, you were there at Kellerman's in the summer of 1963, your body grinding up against Johnny's. That's not a criticism of Angela, by the way, or maybe it is. If she wants a five-star rating from me on her website, she should crank up the volume, live a little. It was meant to come across as joyous, but everyone just looks depressed.

At least I'm moving – but just on a conveyor belt. I'm heading through little doors, to be thrown into a furnace by the two people whose job it is to feed the famished flames. Like Joan of Arc or the thousands of women sent to burn by panicky King James, convinced that witches tried to sink his ship and drown him in the North Sea, a paranoid man prone to psychosis informed, no doubt, by trauma. His mother's head, chopped off because she was a Catholic, a close shave in which Guy Fawkes and friends tried to restore Catholicism by flaming James and his cronies alive, the foiling of which would see effigies of Fawkes burnt on bonfires every year for centuries.

Do the girls know I'll meet the furnace head-first, a molecular martyr, that my skull will disintegrate before my feet are even in flames? In my end is my beginning.

Chapter 16

2014

I'm lying in bed, watching the curtains glow at what the clock says is four a.m., warm light pushing at the white fabric, the cream wallpaper rendered a wet yellow that might smear if I leant against it.

Gulls lead the morning chorus, a requiem to hot chips they have known, a fried haddock that got away. Two orange bottles with tablets wait patiently on my bedside table, my stomach pump leans back casually on the carpet. My midriff is a reservoir of retained fluid. If I pressed at my swollen shins, the indent would remain for sixty seconds or more before slowly rebounding. But I can't see them properly, legs or tumid tummy, they're beneath the covers.

I'd like to speak to myself – just a few words. Hi, Living Margaret, it's me, Dead Margaret, how are you feeling today? So-so, Dead Margaret, thanks for asking. How about you? Are things OK over there in the . . . sorry, where are you exactly? I could keep my own counsel, offer myself a second opinion, have my back. I could . . .

I'm sick, then and now. Sick of being here still, my eyes (none) prised open against my will.

The girls . . . they're in their old rooms, sleeping. I can sense them, almost smell their souring scents. I had a soft spot for the bacterial bouquet of my own underarms, the girls' odour too, like acrid straw; the way we slept together when they were kids, when they were scared, how their heads smelt, their necks and shoulders, the way I'd lie with them now if I could, spoon right up and hold them close, even as adults . . .

It's night but it's not. The midsummer light in north-east Scotland offers quantity over quality, the days delineated, if at all, by a smooth crepuscular crescendo. In winter, of course, it's the opposite – the sun meek, showing once a week. I knew people who suffered from seasonal affective disorder, became as gloomy as the waning moon. I tried to convince Henry to go to the doctor one January, pictured myself co-opting the light therapy box he'd surely be prescribed, letting 10,000 lux go radge on my visage with none of the SAD stigma. But he refused, could hide his depression like broccoli under a lettuce leaf until, quite spectacularly, he couldn't.

I was sixty, visiting Eva in Spain, before I realised not everywhere left the light on through spring and summer. We were outside a noisy bar eating tapas at eight-thirty in the evening when, bam, the night fell like the backdrop in an am-dram theatre production. In Australia . . . I wasn't focusing much on the diurnal cycle there, to be honest. The ultraviolet radiation beaming through the ragged craw of the ozone layer with its electromagnetic charm – I didn't pay that much heed either.

Champ must be in the kitchen. I could tiptoe downstairs, get his lead and drive him up to the Gramps – it's a good night-slash-morning for it. Or, evidently, I can just lie in bed staring at the wallpaper. If it moves, it's because the woman behind shakes it.

I don't know how long I've been watching myself – now or in sum – but I don't think it's good for me to be stuck with an evolved selective attention system now that I've evolved beyond the theory of evolution. I'm in thrall to stories I've already lived through, the main difference being I can see myself from the outside, and inside (no insides) and yet

feeling one surge, another, like

it's going to end badly and that

something's coming

of course it is of course of course of wet and

the water vapour and frigid air condensing swathes of sea, if the sea can be swathes, into low cloud, leaving me mostly moistly

foggy, my boat still trapped in ice, my body still incinerated, my mind (no mind) overstimulated

I'm meant to be with other people, need a friend, at least one, of noble mind. I miss depending. I need not only a parachute but someone to check and fold it. If it doesn't open, I want someone to have checked and folded the reserve. And if the reserve fails, or I've passed out, I want the automated activation device to have been checked and tested, and to deploy at its earliest convenience. I doubt there was a plan B for Grandad Duncan as he plummeted from a plane over Würzburg, hitting the lake surface hard before being wrenched ever deeper. I hope he was unconscious. It would be far worse holding your breath until the hypoxic convulsions overwhelmed, the torrent of electrical activity in your brain forcing you to breathe, just, glug, the water breaching your gullet, flooding your insides like Ophelia, breathe, in a brook, a poem, breathe, in a book.

Three times, 'tis said, a sinking man
Comes up to face the skies,
And then declines forever

Who wrote that? Shakespeare? Emily Dickinson? My mind although I do recall certain things, weird things.

A public information film on TV in the 1970s, for instance. *I am the spirit of dark and lonely water, ready to trap the unwary, the show-off, the fool.* Images of children falling into rivers, holding rotting branches while trying to fish out a football, slipping down muddy embankments with cockney accents. *It's the perfect place for an accident.* My girls – it gave me the heebie-jeebies, that ad. The girls. They're OK. Waking up, sweating. The girls. *Under the water there are traps.* The Grim Reaper in a hooded cloak. It was just an ad, child actors playing the unwary, the show-off, the fool. But so much water. In the lungs. My girls.

1978

I wet Rachel's armbands under the shower, pull them up onto her arms, do the same for Eva. It makes it easier to get them on that way. I take each girl by a hand as we toddle from the women's changing room.

The footbath – yuk – we have to walk through it.

'I don't want to,' Eva says.

'Me too,' Rachel says.

'We have to,' I say, pulling at my swimsuit to better cover my behind. It looks good – the swimsuit, and my behind. 'It's for verrucas and warts, things like that.'

They dip their toes in, pull them out again quickly. I can't blame them. I feel nausea (have no stomach) watching us now. They were always so cold, those footbaths. So bleachy. So warty.

'OK, let's count to three,' I say, 'then we can run through it quickly.'

'One,' Eva says.

'Two,' Rachel says.

'Three,' I say, splashing through the liquid, pulling them along with me.

I can't remember noticing at the time, but we look like traffic lights, my burnished orange swimsuit, Rachel in tomato red, Eva in forest green. It's noisy in the pool, must be the weekend. Voices echo off the walls, windows, tiles and arched ceiling, the cavernous space a garbled riot of shouting, splashing and happy screaming. Henry . . . it takes a while to locate him, but there he is, doing laps.

I help the girls put on their goggles, sit with them at the pool's edge, green, orange, red, our feet in the water. A whistle, the lifeguard – someone has done something they shouldn't have on the lowest of the five diving platforms. Someone else shouts and waves at their friends from the highest, adjusts his trunks, dives. A man lost his life diving from the highest platform the year the pool opened, a day after the city was bombed in the Second World War. Dozens of people died in the raid, but this man outdid them all in infamy, his flamboyant ten-metre leap in defiance of the Nazis going wrong and becoming a fatal bellyflop. Was it true? I heard that story so many times, everyone did. I don't know.

'Hello, hello, hello,' Henry says, emerging from the water, a friendly alligator, right in front of us.

The girls laugh, as do I. If he splashes me like he sometimes does before I've grown accustomed to the water temperature, I'll . . . I have no say now, no legs with which to kick him. But if he does . . . He doesn't.

'Taxi for two,' he says, reaching out for the girls, who slink carefully into the water, grab his toned arms.

'S'cold, Mummy,' Rachel says.

'You'll warm up in no time,' Henry says. 'Now, all aboard?'

'All aboard,' Eva says.

He positions them so he can swim backwards with a neck nestled in each armpit, pushes off with his feet. He doesn't need to do much with his arms, can propel himself through the water with his legs and torso. I can't, but then again, I'm not the strongest swimmer. Henry tried to show me how to rescue someone once, played the person in need of salvation, showed me the special strokes, the release and evade techniques. I couldn't do it, kept going under the water, seemed in greater need of rescuing than him. Same now, really.

They're halfway down the lane, still going backwards. It looks like I don't want to get in, but it's always better just to get it over with, isn't it. Get in, Margaret. Go on. I slide in from the side, my body – not head – ducking under. That's the worst part, the initial shock, and now I look fine. I've slipped from the lily pad of my own despair and am sloshing, sloppy and brackish.

I swim breaststroke nearly all the way to the deep end before stopping and holding onto the gutters, the back of my head against the tiles, kick my legs out . . . It looks relaxing, sounds incredibly noisy. The seating banks are nearly empty, always are.

Henry and the girls are on their third lap, their eyes to the ceiling. People continue to leap and dive from the boards, some faces in the pool strain in a way that makes me think they're peeing. Kids and teenagers run along the side and get whistled at by the lifeguard, who also looks like a teen. There's a sign on the wall with drawings of a man – patrons are kindly requested to refrain from running, pushing, acrobatics or gymnastics, shouting, ducking, petting, bombing, swimming in the diving area, smoking. Did people ever smoke at the public baths? Presumably they did. And petting – I never understood that one. Isn't that what you did to dogs?

Here they come, Henry and the girls.

'Hi, Mummy, armband,' Eva says, holding her little arm out, the band at her wrist.

'OK, hold on here,' I say, gliding her to the gutter and adjusting it.

'Will you be OK here for a bit?' Henry asks, moving Rachel towards me.

'Yeah, where you going?'

'Just a few laps,' he says, pulling his goggles back over his eyes, his shoulders and chest every inch the swimmer's body. He does a double thumbs-up to the girls, sinks comically under the water – they love it, and so do I. He's funny sometimes. Lots of times, actually. He's a good dad, a good laugh.

We watch him swim away, freestyle. 'Monkeys,' Eva says.

'You want to do monkey crawls?'

'You first,' Rachel says.

We start pulling ourselves along the side of the pool, holding the gutters. People have to move out of the way when they see us coming but they do so happily because of the girls, not me, although now I have actual hindsight, I can see that some of the men, even the good-looking ones, are watching me as we pass. And why wouldn't they? I'm not even thirty. My hair, tied up, looks amazing, as does my neck, my unblemished shoulders. Why didn't I know this at the time? Even if someone had said so, I'd have laughed, made a joke to put myself down. You had to get in first, that was the rule.

'Look, Mummy,' Eva says.

I follow her wrinkly water-baby finger, see Henry. He's standing on the highest diving platform, waving at us. I went up there only once, my legs shaking on the ladder, my teeth chattering at the top, edging to the ledge before retreating quickly with vertigo.

'Daddy, jump,' Eva says, to me, not to Henry.

He'll be OK. I know that now, but not then. My face, I can see what I must be thinking. He could slip, become the second – if the first was true – bellyflop death at the Bon Accord Baths, living on only as a warning for future generations.

'Be safe, Henry,' I say under my breath.

He waves again, readies himself and leaps, arms out ahead, his hands leading him into the water with scarcely a splash.

1986

The girls have clearly just turned eleven – there are two golden candles in the shape of number ones on a paper plate smeared with marzipan and bits of sponge, a flock of birthday cards with glittery elevens. The cake itself has gone and the plastic plates on the table suggest ten people at least had a slice, maybe more going by the mess elsewhere in the kitchen. My parents, maybe, Barb, Des and Michael, Rachel's friend Barry, Eva's friend Keely . . . There are torn and intact streamers from party poppers, half-eaten oven croquettes, an encrusted quiche tray, a trampled-on tail from Pin the Tail on the Donkey, plastic cups, shrivelling balloons, shiny cardboard hats, sticky spills on the linoleum.

At least you get it over with in one go with twins. My mother wouldn't have had any cake because she thought it was bad for the teeth, even plastic ones. Who else would we have invited? I can't remember, my mind (don't even have one) is not what it was. Is this how it was for Nana Jean, her recollections a crumbly crayon set that increasingly drew blanks? She used to say that old age didn't come alone. She meant it brought complaints like arthritis, I think – I didn't ever ask. Lacunae, that's what they're called, I remember that much – the gaps in your memory. Lagoons of the mind, the water as cloudy as cataracts, the fish edible, maybe, the sandbars eroding steadily, three lagoons becoming two, and then one. Ignore the calcifying coral and make a splash while you still can. Lacuna matata.

'A little more aqua for the eyes,' Eva whispers.

'Here, take this,' Rachel whispers, passing her a shadow brush.

They're applying make-up to Henry, who's like the ogre from *Jack and the Beanstalk*, snoring thunder, sending vibrations through the kitchen chair. His head is hanging back, his mouth open, and it's hard to believe he's not waking up. Was he drinking at the party? Probably. But a can or two at most. He generally kept his head above water in those days, would go off the deep end a couple of years later. The girls are sitting either side of him, their chairs pulled in close, their hands gently working on his shuddering skin. I'm nowhere to be seen, might be in the bathroom having a sneaky cigarette out the window or out walking Sam.

'And this heather colour here?' Eva whispers.

'Yes, lovely, darling,' Rachel whispers.

I love to see them getting along like this – am glad, then and now, that their new make-up palettes are being put to creative use. Henry's lips are frosty pink, his cheekbones a blaze of rouge. If you squint your eyes, if I had eyes to squint, he'd look like . . . he'd probably look like a thirty-nine-year-old man who's wiped out from the week and is now being prepped for a Culture Club video. I must be working on reception with him by this point, his hedgerow of handymen growing stronger and leafier.

Rachel pulls her chair in a little closer, contorts her face, apologises silently to Eva for the scraping noise, but Henry merely stirs, doesn't wake. If I was to sneak up alongside them all now and shout *Husband, husband, what have you done with my golden goose?* it would make no difference.

Wake up, you grotesque gype. Open your watery eyes – and mine – to what you've done, or what you're going to do, or what you're not going to do, you glaikit guff-muncher. Maybe that's it, Henry, what you're not going to do – your abjectly abortive attempt to attend to my golden geese. Wake up, you bucket of Brobdingnagian ball sweat, or god help me I'll smite your beanstalk, watch you faceplant the ground and make bread from your bones.

See – still snoring.

'I'll do the brows,' Eva whispers, taking a brush from the palette.

As well as the make-up sets, they've been given some new books – a *Guinness Book of Records* for Rachel, a *Teach Yourself Spanish* for Eva. My father got her that one, has already taught her dozens of phrases.

¿Cómo estás, nieta?

Muy bien, abuelo.

Before long she'll be trying to teach me and I'll be trying to learn, but it won't sink in. That's my fault, my lacuna, not hers. She presses the thin brush into navy, nearly black eye shadow, pulls it back and forth gently across one of Henry's brows. He looks like a marionette, will become a puppet to his addiction, on permanent lookout for a gottle of geer.

Both pull away quickly as he stirs again, snores in one big snort, settles. They glance at each other, at him, at me (I wish), start giggling.

'Shhh,' Eva whispers.

'I can't help it,' Rachel whispers, holding her mouth. 'Look at him, Eva.'

206

'I know,' Eva says, covering her mouth. I see them clearly, see it all clearly, but can't shake the sense I'm missing something.

The eye has a blind spot, a rotunda in the retina with no cells to see the light, a permanently restricted view thanks to the pillar of the optic nerve, a design flaw in all vertebrates. The nerve cable bundles the big picture to the brain while the occipital lobe fills the gap with something plausible – a splash of red here, the edge of an elbow there. It's easy to prove. Imagine R is Rachel and E is Eva.

R   E

Cover one eye and pick a letter. Move your head closer and further from that letter slowly until the other girl disappears. That's your blind spot. Who were you focusing on, Rachel or Eva? Who's still there? Who disappeared?

Chapter 17

2007

There are shoeboxes on the floor, photos spread across the carpet. I'm in Aviemore, or close by, can see the ... No, I'm at home, and I'm crying, just a little, Eva and Rachel too. Henry, he's dry-eyed and watching TV, holding the edge of the remote against his chin, looking glum. Champ's sleeping in front of the gas fire, his legs twitching.

We're in our new house in Kincorth ... only, it's not new anymore. It must be twenty years since we came up in the world, or down as the sparrow flies, six miles south of the scheme. We made a profit on our former council house, even though it was cracked and crumbling. This one, too, now that I look, hairline fissures, its kneecaps starting to yield – that's just what buildings do. Turn your back on them and the land will take over, the weeds, shrubs and trees getting their claws up through the concrete and pulling it apart, reclaiming the wood as kin, absorbing the plastic, glass and plasterboard, yanking gutters from their spikes and ferrules – a stately procession of ecological succession.

My mother is dead. I think that's what's happening – seventy-five and no longer alive. The locket she'd inherited from Nana Jean hangs round my neck now, a different chain, the one I got for my eighteenth birthday, but the same old eternity knot.

Most of the pictures on the carpet are of her, or include her – black and whites, Polaroids, washed-out colour prints. My father is in lots of them too, an unknowing widower in waiting.

'God, check her out there,' Eva says. 'Those stockings.'

We laugh, the three of us. It's not particularly humorous – she's wearing a shorter skirt than we're used to, nylon, maybe even silk, stockings – but we need it, the release, even as we sniffle.

'She was such a good gran,' Eva says.

It's wrung them out a little. Me too. Death is disappointing. But it has perks. The girls haven't seen each other for years – I can't even remember how many. We were together for the turning of the millennium, the girls, me and Henry, Thom and Gem, my parents. I felt hopeful, couldn't help it – Rachel had just started her Gestalt therapy training, Eva was doing her teaching postdoc, Henry was pickled but still productive, the Y2K bug had retreated without really biting. The century ahead looked welcoming enough, might even be better. But after that, I don't know. Maybe this is the first time we've been together since then. That seems improbable, but maybe it's true.

They'll continue to visit individually and with their partners, will keep tabs on each other – albeit dismissively – through my regular phone calls and occasional visits, but I don't think we'll assemble again until my grand finale. For now, it's my mother who's inadvertently brokered the truce.

Both girls met Henry's mother, but she exited at fifty-six with an aneurysm. The girls were just four – old enough to have an impression but too young to worry about it waning.

Henry's father bailed the year before they were born, at fifty-one. Going by those numbers, Henry must have struggled to imagine himself surviving to sixty – the fact he's done so and keeps going even now is testament to something, I don't know what. He got their better genes, maybe leached their lifeblood. Not that he had a choice in the matter, so I shouldn't be mean. It's because he's watching TV while the three of us are sitting on the floor feeling happy-sad looking at pictures. He should be actively grieving with us, but he won't. When his mother died, he locked himself in the bathroom for eleven hours – the girls and I had to pee in the mop bucket. I know he feels things deeply, that he loved my mother as much as she loved him, but he's making it look like the TV's more important. An advert announces that *Last of the Summer Wine* is about to come on and, actually, I'd quite like to watch that with him, even though it's been declining in quality since the mid-eighties. I could pull up a chair (have no arms), sit on my bahookie (no bahookie). It was one of many shows we enjoyed watching together. *The Thorn Birds* was another. *EastEnders*, of course, *Brookie, Corrie, Casualty, The Flying Doctors, Neighbours, Randall and Hopkirk (Deceased)*. We watched some top TV in our time together, some shows Henry liked and I didn't (*Spitting Image, The Weakest Link*), some I liked and he didn't (*Ab Fab, Who Wants to Be a Millionaire?*). *Morecambe & Wise, Only Fools and Horses* – we both loved those.

Next to the shoeboxes are albums with bobbled cellophane pages that have long since trapped hair, eyelashes and lint. My mother, still young. My mother becoming a mother. My mother, now gone. She nursed briefly after the war, raised me, worked as a dinner lady, had – like me – a hysterectomy. Pictures of her with the girls as babies, with her father, Duncan, by a loch, with Nana Jean, her mother.

'She's never smiling in the early ones,' Eva says.

'Was she depressed as a young woman?' Rachel asks.

A black and white of my mother in her nurse uniform – she must have been sixteen, seventeen.

'It's because of her teeth,' I say. 'When she got her falsers, you couldn't keep her gob shut.'

They laugh again. Me too. Another photo is a case in point. She's wearing a black hat and standing with my father and Henry's mother. The other two are frowning – it must be Henry's father's funeral, it's dated 1974 – but my mother is all smiles.

'Are we picking Grandad up tomorrow?' Rachel asks.

'I think we're meeting him at the crem,' I say. 'I'll phone him a bit later.'

For the most part, the photos are unimpressive – especially night shots, the flash rebounding from blood-filled choroids and making everyone's eyes red. There's an order to the albums – 1975, 1967 – but not the images in the shoeboxes. They've been shuffled like cards from different decks, some inherited, some our own, taken out slowly and put back hastily at Christmas or when someone in the family dies, like now.

It's good to have them in one place, though, or a few places but stored in one location. The cloud . . . that's not a concept yet, in the modern sense. Strati exist. Cumulonimbi exist. I don't exist, not anymore, wander lonely as a cloud *in the bliss* – it's actually misery – *of solitude*. The notion of having round-the-clock access to tens of thousands of your own photos and a practically infinite number of other people's on a device not much bigger than a packet of Silk Cut via a cloud you can't see – we'd have laughed that nonsense out of the room. At a guess, there are six hundred photos in total in the shoeboxes and albums, a decent cache for the era, and even the bad ones (most of them) have a serendipity that wouldn't exist now. Or rather, it would exist – it always does – but those images wouldn't be printed. Even the good ones rarely get that honour. Rachel will send me some prints of my grandchildren, mind you, and I'll frame those, my sweethearts. But the one that accidentally

212

catches Uncle Archie sneaking past with a tray of drinks during the best man's speech – that probably wouldn't get printed. Nor the one where the lampshade behind Auntie Morag's head makes it look like she's wearing a bearskin hat. They'd languish on the phone, or on a server in the States somewhere. I've never been there in the flesh, but my likeness is an inhabitant of the great American cloud.

Last of the Summer Wine is on now, its maudlin theme music at least. The girls never liked the show, thought it was boring, and Living Margaret can't watch it because it's a special occasion, a crying circle, or teary triad, although the water works have stopped for now.

'Oh wow,' Rachel says, holding up a thick sepia picture. 'Who's that?' Eva asks.

'That's Nana Jean's grandparents,' I say. 'So, hang on . . . your great-great-great grandparents, Violet and Malcolm Bullimore.'

It's dated 1892. They're standing in their wedding clothes in a studio, arms hanging stiffly by their sides, Violet's left hand in Malcolm's right, Malcolm's kilt a little high on the knee, his sporran sporting what looks like a fox's head. They're staring down the lens, would have been told to stay still and watch the birdie. They've done well, their eyes are clear, the image sharp. It always made me sad to see old photos in which one person got an itch before the exposure was complete, their face, but nobody else's, a splodge, blowing what might have been their only chance to be remembered as they were by future generations who'd never met them and couldn't give a rat's arse anyway.

'His moustache looks so tickly,' Rachel says.

'I love Violet's veil,' Eva says. 'I want a veil when I get married.'

'Malcolm's got bandy legs,' Rachel says. 'Was he a cowboy or something?'

Eva laughs, me too.

'Mind if I turn the sound up a bit?' Henry asks. He's displeased, there's a peevishness to his voice.

'Feel free,' I say. He can't begrudge me grief, even with laughter. And if memory serves, he'll hold me tight later that same night when we're in bed, let me cry, won't complain.

'How long did they have to stand still for?' Rachel asks.

'I've no idea,' I say. 'A few seconds, maybe more. They look petrified in more ways than one.'

I once read about a trend for hidden mothers in Victorian-era child photography, whereby the women were disguised as a chair or bound in cloth so they could surreptitiously stop their sprogs from squirming and spoiling the image. But you could still see them there, the mothers, wrapped head to toe in sheets like a corpse on a Hindu pyre, their remains destined to be dropped in the Ganges. Some photographers almost managed to meld the matriarchs with the mise en scène – a caliginous carapace against an inky black background – but in most they were obvious, their otherworldliness commanding more attention than their rictus-faced children. Which raised a number of questions. Why not just have everyone in the picture? Why wrap mummies like mummies? Why would anyone be a mother?

'You know, Gem and I are trying for a baby,' Rachel says.

'Good luck with that,' Eva says, laughing.

'That'll be fun for future generations,' Rachel says, ignoring Eva, looking at me. 'Imagine – here's a photo of your great-great-grandmothers, Gem and Rachel. They married eventually, when the UK and Australian governments decided same-sex couples could wed without the world imploding.'

'How very modern,' Eva says.

She's jealous, doesn't even know she's pregnant yet, that her second foetus, like the first, will jump ship.

Henry contributes to the conversation by saying nothing, doing nothing, watching *Last of the Summer Wine* – he's listening, though, I know he is.

'Hey, look at this,' I say, holding up a picture of him at eighteen, receiving a rowing medal.

'Ah yeah,' he says, nodding, barely looking, returning his gaze to the screen.

We're maybe not meant to see ourselves, would have developed revolving eyes on stalks if we were. We upload more photos every month than the number of humans that have ever existed, more every couple of minutes than the sum total of images in the world when Violet and Malcolm married. The bulk of humankind has persisted, if at all, in short-lived and barely shared stories, silent vigils, ephemeral griefs. We fade more quickly than we might want, our loved ones too.

1990

It's going to be OK. Believe me, Living Margaret, Rachel's going to be fine. I can't hear myself, of course.

'She'll be OK,' Henry says.

'How the hell do you know?' I snap.

He shoots a glance at me, turns away. 'I don't.'

His head drops, his hands squeeze his thighs. He's weak with worry, me too.

I feel confused

all out of puff

His hair is greasy and he's still in his work clothes. There's dried gunk of some sort on his trousers and jacket. It doesn't matter. My jeans . . . neither of us are in our best attire, wouldn't have been banking on a night out.

'I hope she'll be OK,' he says. 'That's what I meant to say before.'

He was right the first time – she'll be fine. But we're at Accident and Emergency on a Friday evening and don't know that yet. They've taken Rachel away on a bed with wheels. Any allergies? No. Existing health problems? No. Can we go in with her, please? She's only fourteen. I'm sorry – we'll come and fetch you as soon as we can, it shouldn't be too long.

They'll use activated charcoal for what the paperwork will call 'gastrointestinal decontamination'. I don't know that yet. As far as I know, I don't know . . . My Rachel. My darling girl. Eva's not with us. She's . . . where is she? At a friend's house playing Dungeons & Dragons probably, being our lawful good, with no nausea or chest pains, no palpitations or dizziness, no agitation or paranoia.

In the ambulance, I didn't think Rachel would hear me, but she did. I said it under my breath, didn't mean to, it was a stress response. 'Why can't you be more like your sister?'

'Maybe that's what I was trying,' she said, her eyes opening, only the whites, closing again.

What did she mean by that? Eva hasn't ever taken drugs, as far as I know. Hasn't, to my knowledge, drunk, sniffed, injected or tripped herself into a state requiring hospitalisation. And certainly not twice – soon to be three times – in a year.

'I'm sorry,' I say to Henry. 'I didn't mean to . . .'

He puts his hand on my leg, just above the knee – if he gives me a horsey bite I'll elbow him in the mouth. He won't, though, because he's being nice. He followed the ambulance in his van, is probably half-cut. He employs ten people now, sometimes drinks openly but mostly not, buries empty vodka and whisky bottles in the outside bin. Was it me? Was he unhappy with me? If I could ask him now – what gives, Henry, why the constant libations? – but I can't, and I didn't want to at the time, or I did but didn't want to hear the answer. Things will get worse for him – for both of us, to be fair – but for now, on the whole, I'm happy, or content, or not unhappy, or not always unhappy, or consciously trying to look like I'm not drowning in desperation thanks to Rachel's recklessness. Her safety and state of mind is a shared concern, but I'm in my own private hell and Henry in his, a place of . . . I don't know, because it's private.

But I do know the image of Hell we're most familiar with came from the Apocalypse of Paul, composed at a communal monastery in Egypt nearly four hundred years after Saint Paul's death – a psychogeographical account of Heaven and Hell that was apocryphal, of course, but also taken as gospel. Heaven is upwards, with rivers of milk and honey. Hell is downwards, with rivers of fire and ice. I suppose a different hallucinatory trance could have put Heaven in the basement and Hell in the attic, the goodies enjoying an icy dip, the baddies unable to move, stuck to their sins and swarmed by bees in rivers of cloying honey. That's maybe closer to Henry's hell and mine. Rivers of alcohol. Rivers of regret. Rivers.

1987

There are many things you're not supposed to do in the River Spey – salmon fishing without a permit, swimming where the signs tell you not to, or, in my view, going into it at all. It's not warm. The snow on the nearby mountains, even now in summer, is a dead giveaway.

Henry's in there, though, no wetsuit – just his trunks. I recall him doing it as soon as we reached the campsite, pulling his trunks on quickly, Scotland's fastest changing man rushing out to meet its fastest flowing river.

The whisky . . . it makes for good whiskies, the Spey. Its name comes from the early Celtic word for thorn – that's what the leaflet said in the tourist information centre, and that's how the whiskies taste, the ones of Henry's I've tried at least, just little sips at Hogmanay: spiky and sharp. I'm sitting on the shore among the trees – he's downstream, treading water. Rachel and Eva – are they eleven? – are half-in, half-out, their lips already turning blue. I have towels and sandwiches at the ready, am on the bank, on my lily pad

but if you'd heard it, my chortling, once upon

'Come on, slow pokes,' Henry shouts. 'The quicker you get it over with, the better.'

Both girls are wearing rubber sandals; I would have made sure of that, always did. You can't see the bottom but it's a safe bet the rocks will be sharp and slippery with moss.

Eva lets herself fall forward, screeches and laughs, is carried quickly in Henry's direction.

Rachel is still standing waist-deep at the edge, high shoulders, arms out of the water, shivering. 'Can you come a bit closer?' she calls. 'It's scary, Dad. The water's too fast.'

'Don't just leave her there,' I shout. 'I can see her goosebumps from here.'

'Float down to me,' he says. 'Come on, just come out a bit and let the current take you.'

Eva is already next to him, holding his arm, treading water, her teeth chattering. Rachel falls forward, screams, laughs, immediately starts floating downstream, the branches green, the wind green.

William and Ewan are in the bath with lots of bubbles, looking cute and . . . so what? It's nice seeing them like this, don't get me wrong – the way they're sitting, William holding Ewan against his soapy belly. He's tender with him, it's gorgeous to see. And Ewan, at maybe thirteen or fourteen months, is about as tender as he'll ever be. If he was done right, low and slow, with ample salt and pepper . . . I'd eat his cheeks first, rip off the tops of those arms, sink my teeth into those chubby thighs.

Give it a decade – I have – and it won't be the same. There will be far less affection from William to Ewan, although Ewan will still idolise his big brother – they can't help it, the younger siblings. Like Rachel with Eva, her senior by a matter of seconds.

'Good boy, Will,' Gem says. 'Just be careful with Ewan's neck, that's it, good boy.'

Rachel is kneeling next to Gem at the edge of the bath, in a vest top and tracksuit pants, filming on her phone. Her tattoos – William, Ewan, Eva.

Eva?

She has Eva's name on her upper arm – I've never seen that one.

I'd not have

'Just look this way, darling,' she says. 'That's it. And Ewan. Ewan. Ewan. Hello, Ewan.'

Ewan smiles gummily, is still largely pre-verbal, although he has a few good words. Ball – he knows that one. Mum – he likes saying that. It's so mellifluous with those marvellously bilabial emmms, like a hoover's *hmmm*, an underwater *ummm*, a milky meal from mummy's mammary glands.

I had a girl on each breast simultaneously, was relieved to let rip with the let-down reflex after their time in the incubator. *Mmm.*

'Mum,' Ewan says.

The pre-verbal months are magical. As Henry rightly observed once, parents spend so long waiting for their kids to walk and talk, then tell them to sit down and shut up. He babbles, Ewan (and Henry), can communicate perfectly well in his own way, mostly cooing, laughter and tears. Pointing at things. Biting. Squeezing. His grisly face. Entranced face. Distressed face. Bored face. Angry face. Fear face. Happy face. *Mummm.*

William must be two, nearly three, which means I've not been to Australia yet and am still unaware of what's ahead, the world my oyster to be opened with a rusting sword, its shell bearded and stiff, its flesh dry and withered.

Some moments – like these – are precious. I'd cry with joy if I had eyes, but I just don't know to what end it's occurring. Or if there needs to be an end, a teleo . . . teleolog . . . I've forgotten the word. All words. The world. All of it is fading. That's how it feels some days, they're not even . . . What's the . . .?

Why am I here, right now, in a Melbourne bathroom? If there's no inherent meaning to life then there's no inherent meaning to death, which means there is doubly, triply, no inherent argument for lingering invisibly and interminably after death – *discuss.* Eva's essay questions at university were always like that, as were the sample papers Carol gave us in our night class: a contentious statement followed by a bossy invitation. Madame Bovary was betrayed by an ovary – *discuss.*

'OK, splash for Mummy,' Gem says.

William smacks the water and laughs. Ewan too. Splish, splash, sleepy splosh.

> . . . *as the Turks say, 'Water sleeps, and the enemy is sleepless'*
> water induces sleep when the enemy is asleep
> the enemy is water and I can't sleep –
> *discuss.*

'Oh, hang on.' Rachel moves backwards on her knees, lifts her phone away from the water that's otherwise spraying her, drenching Gem, soaking me . . . look at me, oh no, my frock, my tights, poor Grandma. I'm just behind Rachel and her phone, my whole body wet, they've soaked me to the skin – William, how could you? Ewan, you naughty boy, Grandma is saturated even though she has no body no body no body so she can't be wet or dry or warm or cold and in time you'll have no body either, little pumpkins, regardless of how vital you seem and the hope you seed just by existing, so what's the point what's the bloody . . .

I'd like to splash the water, just once, smack both palms against the surface, see everyone's faces, their shock. Who did that? Who was it?

William looks at Rachel's phone, and by extension at me – where I'd be standing if I had legs and a torso and arms and a head. *Hello, darling. Grandma loves you.*

'Love you, Will,' Rachel says.

'Love you,' he says, looking at the phone, at me.

'Who are we sending this film to?' Rachel asks in her babyish voice. It's funny hearing that voice. She's mirroring the preferred communication style of an imagined baby to promote feelings of positivity and further develop a sense of attachment. But it makes me remember, I can't help it, all the pain she put me through as a teenager and young adult, saying I was treating her like a baby, the negative feelings she

221

engendered, the happiness surrendered. 'Who are we sending it to?' she asks again.

'Grandma,' William says.

'Ramma,' Ewan says, clapping his wet hands, looking at the phone, at me.

'OK, great,' Rachel says, stopping the video, lowering her phone.

'Ramma,' Ewan says again, still staring directly at me.

Chapter 18

2014

'I don't want your money,' Rachel says. 'Put it away.' Her eyes pinball round the restaurant.

Nobody's going to rob us here. I'm sitting opposite her, Eva right next to her – it's fine.

'Just take it,' I say. The roll is thick in my hand, fifty-pound notes bound with elastic. They're the Bank of England variety, not Bank of Scotland – I made sure of that so she'd have no trouble changing them over in Australia. It always amazed me when people refused Scottish money – it's legal tender, look, it says STERLING in capital letters. You could make a plea to the obvious and, if that failed, to people's better natures, but it didn't always work. They thought you were trying to diddle them, didn't realise they were cheating you. Even in Heathrow, at the café, on our way to Australia, the woman was suspicious of our spondulicks. *Who's that geezer on the front? Is he meant to be the king or summink?* That's Walter Scott, young lady, *Sir* Walter Scott to you and me, author of *The Lady of the Lake* and *Old Mortality*, who campaigned successfully under the pseudonym Malachi Malagrowther to ensure Scottish banks would continue to print their own paper currency.

'Please, love, just take it,' I say to Rachel. 'It's for you. For the boys. You and Gem. Whatever you want. Get yourself some clothes. Something nice.'

I have another bundle for Eva in my handbag, was worried about leaving it at home even though Champ is there and would lick any burglars into a stupor. It will be theirs soon enough anyway. Henry has his stash, I have mine.

'I appreciate it, Mum. But you might still need it. Maybe, I mean, if the worst happens . . .'

'It's not *if*, Rachel, it's not . . . It's really not.'

She looks away. Eva is doing her best to focus on the anointed victuals of our Last Supper, or last all-you-can-eat buffet. In my case, so far, that hasn't been much. I've steered a few vegetables around my plate, stuck my fork through an oily parsnip. I'm hungry, want to eat, am being eaten.

Rachel leaves early tomorrow morning, Eva in a week, all going to plan – it will be more than two in reality. I'd have preferred we went to Jimmy Chung's at the beach, my buffet of choice, but it was razed to the ground a few months earlier despite the efforts of more than fifty firefighters working through the night. This one is closer to the house anyway, and the parking means it's a short stroll from car to food bar. It was always a shock after driving to remember how hard it was to walk. I'll drive Rachel to the airport tomorrow, blow her a kiss, watch her not wanting to look away, nearly crash as I pull back onto the A96 because I'm crying so much. I'll be dead in a week in any case, a mound of pulverised bone fragments within a fortnight.

'Maybe you should just take the cash,' Eva says.

Rachel says nothing, looks at her plate. I'm still holding the bundle of notes, but closer to my body. It might look conspicuous, if the other patrons were focusing on us and not what the menu says are pan-Asian cooking stations and global banquet options . . .

'I think it would make Mum happy if you took it,' Eva says. 'She wants you to have it.'

Rachel shakes her head slightly, sighs.

'I'm really going to miss you,' I say. 'And the boys and Gem.'

'You might not believe this, but I'll miss you too,' Eva says. 'It's been so special having this time together.'

Rachel pulls her arms off the table, tuts. It looks like she's going to get up and buy time by dithering over which dessert to try from the global banquet options. I can't even imagine what the choices might be. Chicken legs in chocolate mousse. A stag's head in strawberry icecream. She plants her elbows on the table again, rubs her face.

It's a lot. But they've not argued, the girls, not once, and that's been nice. We've been nice. We could have been nice all along, our whole lives, without the gaps, the lacunae. But gaps are better than endings – our lagoons have been bridged, our choppy waters disgorged.

Walking in here, hand in hand, the three of us, that was a bridging too. It must have looked odd. What were we, kids or something? Or maybe it's obvious that I'm sick. Maybe everyone sees it. My make-up goes only so far. But the combination of gauntness, eye shadow and mascara is doing wonders for me – my eyes are like pitchy plunge pools and my cheekbones could cut cheddar cheese. We'll hold hands if we want, thank you very much.

But I can't keep advertising the cash. I hold it under the table, could donate it to charity, give it all to Eva, or – why would I even consider this? – the church. For their Last Supper, Jesus and his disciples had a bean stew, lamb, olives, dates, unleavened bread, aromatised wine. Rachel went straight for the sweet and sour pork. Eva is still working her way through a small mountain of roast potatoes.

She swallows heavily, should have chewed more. 'You know, one way to look at it is, you're doing Mum a favour. And it's better this way – it means there's no tax or paperwork, just the dough . . .'

'I don't like thinking about the worst happening,' Rachel says, looking at me, not Eva. 'I feel so bad for you, Mum. I feel . . . If you really do die . . .'

'It's not *if*,' I say, reaching over and taking her hand, squeezing. 'Dearie, it's not *if* anymore. You know I'd stick around if I could. I have lots to live for.'

As did the apostles. Andrew and Matthew were crucified; James the Elder and Paul were beheaded; James the Younger was thrown from a temple and clubbed; Judas hanged himself; Philip was hanged by others; Thaddeus was shot with arrows; Nathanael was flayed alive and beheaded; Peter was crucified upside down; Thomas took a lance through the body; John died of extreme old age in Ephesus.

Rachel's tears are welling, spilling over. 'I fucked everything up.'

'You didn't fuck anything up,' I say. 'What are you even talking about?'

'It just, it all went wrong, it all went so wrong, I can't . . .'

A man who looks like the manager approaches, primed to regale us with anecdotes and rehearsed happiness, sees we're having a moment and walks past.

'Look at me, Rachel.' I squeeze her hand again, she looks. 'I love you. OK? Everything about you. There's nothing I would change. Nothing. I'm so proud of you and everything you've achieved.'

'Me too,' Eva says, laying down her fork and hooking an arm around Rachel's shoulders. 'I love you, sis. I'm always here for you, we're twins.'

'I just need a minute,' Rachel says, her head down, wiping her nose with a napkin. I slide my other hand forward, push the wad into hers, cup her fingers with both of my hands.

'It means a lot to me that you're OK,' I say. 'That's what will make me happy. And Eva too, I'm sure. That's right, isn't it, Eva, you want Rachel to be happy?'

'Of course,' Eva says, her arm still cradling Rachel's shoulders.

'Your sister loves you. I love you.'

'I can't do this,' Rachel says, screeching her chair back, standing, leaving the money on the table. 'I can't. I'm sorry, Mum. Not now. I can't. I'm sorry.'

1982

We're at Hazlehead Park, in the maze. It's the oldest in Scotland and, like all mazes, doesn't particularly look like one when you're inside it. They had an aerial shot in the *Evening Express* once so you could see exactly how it looked and where the middle was – which wasn't even in the middle, it transpired, but off to one side. At the moment, it's just a big hedge on one side, a big hedge on the other, the option every ten steps or so to go left, right, or both.

I have no memory of this, but it must be the school holidays. It's clearly summer. I'm in a T-shirt and jeans, my hair cropped as it was when I was working at Fusion, the girls in play dresses and plastic sandals, their hair – my fault – unflattering. I don't know how we've got here. By bus from our old house – that seems implausible. Henry will be using his van for work but maybe he dropped us here on the way to fixing someone's something-or-other. I don't know. The bus seems more likely, but it would have taken an age . . . I give up.

227

Rachel's holding her doll, Mindy, and Eva her teddy, Sooty. Sam must be tied up outside, maybe they don't let dogs into the maze. Who knows? I can't see him, can't see anything but us, the leaves, the mossy path, the blotchy blue sky.

The maze was gifted to the city by Sir Henry Alexander, the Lord Provost, and opened by his children in 1935. I remember that, or maybe I'm making it up. How much did it cost to get in? Fifty pence? That seems so cheap now.

'Let's go left, Mummy,' Eva says, pointing ahead and to the left.

'Sounds good to me,' I say.

'No, the other left,' Rachel says, pointing to the right.

'That's not left,' I say. 'That's right.'

You can get out of most mazes by holding a hand against the hedge and maintaining contact until you reach the exit, although I don't know that I've ever tried it. But I can leave us now – we'll find our way out. Living Margaret wants to get to the middle, will probably enjoy looking at the rose garden afterwards, licking icecream with the girls and reading how the land the park sits on was part of the great hunting forests of Stocket but was gifted to the city by Robert the Bruce as a gesture of thanks after the Battle of Bannockburn. Dead Margaret can't be bothered with that, just wants to sleep, perchance to sleep.

Rachel walks to the leafy intersection, turns to face Eva and me, stamps her foot playfully. 'This is left,' she says, pointing in the same direction as before.

'Yeah, now it is,' I say. 'It changes depending on which way you're facing.'

'My left,' Eva says.

'No, mine,' Rachel says, stamping her foot again.

1960

I'm at Rubislaw Quarry, a gigantic, scooped-out cavity in Aberdeen's posh west end. It must be 150 metres deep, another 120 across. I'm on my own, can't be more than ten or eleven years old.

The quarry's been operational since the mid-eighteenth century and was once the biggest man-made hole in Europe. I liked it for that reason, wanted them to keep digging deeper to see what was there.

Ant-men climb up and down the ladders and walkways zig-zagging its internal walls. They take a long time to reach the bottom, much longer to come back up. Others descend and ascend in a basket that looks terrifying to me as a child, even more so now, the men crammed into it with their elbows on the side, smoking and having a laugh. The immense pit is skirted by trees, bushes and bracken that hide it – and me – from prying eyes. There's a gap in the outer fence, too small for an adult but fine for skinny little me. The gorse flowers blaze yellow, always do. There's even a saying: *When the gorse is out of bloom, kissing's out of season.*

My parents must be at Nana Jean's house nearby – that's the only time I can come. She lives in a Victorian building, smaller than those surrounding it but still impressive. She'll sell up and move to Northfield, much closer to Henry and me, the year the girls are born.

The lengthy steel cables drawn across the vast quarry mouth were named after a famous tightrope walker, Blondin, Blondie, Blondman – I forget his name. Did he ever walk across it? I don't think so, but he crossed Niagara Falls on a rope many times. The cables bearing his name support the lifting of granite from the quarry bed.

Sometimes there are explosions, and that's my favourite thing, the noise especially. The pit acts like a speaker, amplifying everything – swearwords, hammering, the pumps clearing water that seeps in constantly from the sides and comes up through the ground.

The granite used for almost all of Aberdeen's older streets and buildings has been taken from this hole, as has that for the Portsmouth and Southampton docks, Waterloo Bridge, the Paris Opera House, the Texas State Capitol and the parliament of New Delhi.

My knees are muddy, socks at different heights, cheeks filthy. I look like more of a tomboy than I remember. But I like it here. The squawk of gulls and clatter of industry.

The granite contains quartz that sparkles when – if – there's sunlight, but it gets tarnished over time. It's filled with an invisible radioactive gas called radon that escapes when there are cracks.

A couple of the men are singing 'Living Doll' as they smack metal plugs into the stone to make it easier to split apart.

Am I the only spy? That's how it feels. But maybe there are others like me, hiding, watching, alive, dead.

The quarry will close in a decade, its workers either retiring or turning their hands to the oil and associated industries. When the pumps are switched off, the cavity will start filling with rain and groundwater, swelling year by year until it holds 200 million cubic metres – an urban lake, fenced off and hidden by flora, that's deeper than Loch Ness. It's the perfect place for an accident. If you were to slip into it, that is, the spirit of dark and lonely water ready to trap the unwary, the show-off, the fool.

Eva and Rachel are standing on a chair at the kitchen sink, their little school uniform sleeves rolled up, playing with the basin while I prepare their lunch. They're at Marchburn Infant School, a short distance from the house, and can come home to eat as long as they hold hands and cross Provost Rust Drive with Mrs Rollo, the lollipop lady – or school crossing patrol person, as they're called now. But she's more of a lollipop lady, Mrs Rollo, her big yellow and red lolly – STOP | CHILDREN – as enticing as anything the culinary witch might cook up in 'Hansel and Gretel'.

The TV's on, a portable black and white Binatone with a five-inch screen and much bigger casing. My parents gave it to us for Christmas and, despite my initial reluctance, I watch it every day when I'm working in the kitchen. BBC 1, mostly – it has a dial if you want to change channels.

Sam's at my feet, wagging his tail, looking eagerly up at me in the hope I'll give him food or knock morsels from the worktop by accident.

I'm making the girls some toast and tuna, a boiled egg each – a cheap meal, but a healthy one provided there's not too much mercury in the tuna. They get free milk at school during the morning break, even though kids in England have had theirs cut by Thatcher the Milk Snatcher. We leave plastic cups at the door for our milkman to put on top of the two bottles he delivers daily, to stop the crows pecking through the silver foil. The necks on those bottles, their delicious plug of fatty cream – fine.

'Oh, it's Charley,' Eva says, turning round from the sink. On the TV, an illustrated cat called Charley and a boy called Tony. It's a Central Office of Information ad, part of a series that's been running for about a decade already – although this one is being shown as part of a broader retrospective.

Charley and Tony have been invited to join Tony's father on a fishing trip and have wandered off to play by themselves in puddles. But Charley jumps right past Tony and into the water.

The eggs . . . 'Excuse me,' I say. 'Coming through.' I ferry the pan to the sink, its edges hissing, empty the boiling water into the gap between basin and metal. 'What're you doing, girls? Why's there mud in my basin?'

'We're making a rock,' Rachel says.

'We're rock twins,' Eva says. 'We're going to share it so we're never apart. One rock. One heart.'

'Right . . .' I put the pan down, search for the eggcups. Charley nearly drowned but has luckily caught Tony's father's fishing line. He miaows, shaking water from his head in front of a roaring fire. *Miaowwwww*. He's voiced by the comedian Kenny Everett, who has a popular TV sketch show with characters called Sid Snot and General Cheeseburger. He'll die of an AIDS-related illness, like Michael but with way more publicity.

Miaow . . . Charley wants Tony to know they should stay by Dad's side the next time they go fishing.

Eggs in their cups, toast and tuna on the plate.

'You shake the water round like this,' Rachel says, tilting the basin up and down, left and right. 'Mrs Reid said that's how rocks are made. Water and movement and sedatives.'

'It's movement and *cement*,' Eva says, tutting.

'Sediment,' I say. *Miaowww*. Charley hopes you'll stay close to a grown-up if you're ever near the water too.

'Oh yeah, and time,' Rachel says. 'It takes time.'

'Did she say how long?' I ask. 'You know school goes back in twenty minutes?'

Barb, my friend Barb. I love her hair – she has it pinned up like she did at my funeral, post-middle-age Kathleen Turner . . . or is it Lauren Bacall? But she looks sad.

What's she doing with Champ? Am I hallucinating? I don't think so.

Why's Champ with Barb? He's lying on a table, his front paws out in front of him. I don't want to see this. A man – a vet – with a blue shirt pats his head. Barb is sniffling, her cheeks red.

Why is she with him? I don't need this.

I convinced Eva that Champ wouldn't settle with a new owner, that he was too old, and that if – when – the worst happened to me, the most compassionate thing would be to take him to get put down, assuming she wasn't already back in Spain – which she wasn't, I know now, because she extended her stay and was at my funeral. Would he really not have settled with someone new? I think that might have been the morphine talking, or my vanity . . . He was ten, a couple of years older than Sam was when I had him euthanised, but in Sam's case his back legs were gone. I was convinced, though, and thought Eva would be the one to do it.

She wanted to take him to Madrid with her but it was impractical – he'd probably not survive the journey. That was me being pessimistic again. But could Henry not have cared for him? We laughed at that idea. Henry. Ha. It wasn't funny.

'I'm sorry,' Barb says to the vet, wiping her nose. 'It's just so sad.'

'Crying's normal,' the vet says. 'Please don't apologise. He looks like a really good dog.'

He takes Champ's front right paw in his hand – good boy – shaves a patch of fur from his leg. Champ looks fine, as if he's getting a haircut. The man cleans the shaved area, inserts a cannula – good boy, Champ. In goes the needle, the plunger squeezed, but Champ's not bothered. He has his head down on the table, looks as if he might sleep, doesn't even flinch, maybe doesn't feel it.

'You can hold him if you want,' the vet says.

'Thank you, that's very kind,' Barb says, her hello-girl voice, like mine, still very much intact.

She comes closer to the table and strokes Champ's back. He looks relaxed, sniffs at the clippers, still on the table, can smell himself – that smells good, doesn't it, Champ. Henry would do the same, sniff the back of his hand while he was watching TV, an animal engaging in a spot of olfactory investigation. I did it too, though less obviously, I think, we all do – basking momentarily in that unconscious reflection of the self, a perfunctory perfumatory reassurance that we exist.

Barb continues to stroke Champ as the vet moves him into the recovery position. Only, he won't recover. His lungs are still filling, deflating. Let me go now, I want to remember him alive, let me go.

Chapter 19

2012

I give my name to the receptionist, return to the waiting area, sit between Rachel and Henry. There are leaflets in a plastic rack – *Living with diabetes?* (I wish) – magazines on the table. I've done my hair and make-up for my big day out in Melbourne.

A man with poor English tries to communicate his needs to the receptionist. We steal glances at other waiting faces. It's easy to separate those left high and dry from those, like me, in hot water. *When now the heroes through the vast profound, reach the dire straits with rocks encompass'd round.* What?

'Mrs Bryce.'

We stand, the three of us as one, walk to the open door of what looks like an office-cum-examination room. 'I'm Colin,' the man says. 'I'm your doctor today.'

Colin. Maybe that's how they do it in Australia, no Mr, Mrs, Miss, Ms, Mx. First names only. Unless his surname is Colin, which seems unlikely.

'I'm Margaret,' I say, pointing at myself. 'This is my daughter, Rachel, and my husband, Henry.'

Colin smiles, motions for us to come in. 'This is Siddharth,' he says, gesturing to a young man in a chair. 'A student of mine. He'll just be watching, if that's OK?'

I nod and smile at Siddharth, sit on a plastic chair. Henry sits on another. Rachel sits on the edge of the examination bed, watches over us.

'So, you found us easily enough?' Colin asks.

'Yes, we arrived a touch early, to give us ample time,' I say in my hello-girl voice, as if that's going to help me. Your larynx doesn't matter anymore, Margaret. None of it does.

'It's like a maze in here,' Colin says. 'But it's not too bad once you get used to it.'

He's foreign, sounds East European. I'm foreign too, of course, Northern European. And yet here we are, exchanging niceties on the bottom of the world. Or the top. Or the side. It depends how you look at it, your political mindset, where you are in the universe.

I like Colin, then and now. He's kind. I can see it, feel it. Siddharth the student doctor . . . well, he's practically a child, may or may not turn out to be a kind man. I hope he does. For now, he mostly looks embarrassed. Me too.

I glance at Henry as Colin brings my information up on the computer, pulls his glasses on. Henry looks depressed, doesn't even make eye contact. I look compressed, my body prepared to absorb a knockout blow as best it can. I glance at Rachel, who looks concerned but smiles and winks.

Some data appears on Colin's screen, signalling . . . well, nothing to me. He examines it quickly, his face up close to the monitor, coughs.

My mouth is tight, my face still trying to emit politeness – I'm dreadfully sorry, but I'm not sure I would like to be diagnosed with anything life-threatening today, thank you very much.

Colin coughs again – I hope he's not ill – turns to face me. 'So, yes, it's what we expected,' he says.

My eyes, the hope I didn't even know I had, dwindling. My heart dropping through a murder hole into a pit of icy slush. Rachel shuddering with an algid aorta. Henry – I don't know what his heart's doing but his body's slumping further into his chair. My hero.

Colin's posture is good, his bearing empathetic. 'I wish I was Harry Potter,' he says. 'So I could *expelliarmus* the illness with a wave of my wand.'

Is that a line he uses often? Is he a Harry Potter fan? I've never read them but know – who doesn't? – that Harry has a wand and gets saved repeatedly by a girl called Hermione.

'How long can I expect?' I ask.

Colin nods. 'Everyone asks that,' he says. 'But it's not like in the movies. The truth is, nobody really knows.'

'Not even a rough idea?' Rachel asks. The poor thing. Her flushed cheeks, her milky white arms and legs, her tattoos – why did she ever get those? The Eva one. Is it a know-thy-enemy Sun Tzu affectation? A time-honoured stratagem in the body art of war?

'It would be a guess,' Colin says. 'We don't like to do that. It's just guessing.'

I don't know what to ask, there's so much, and hardly anything, I want to know. 'What will happen if I don't have treatment?'

'Please don't go down that road,' he says. 'The next thing to do is have a scan, which I think you're booked in for after this, is that right?'

'Yeah,' Rachel says. 'At quarter past.'

'After that, we'd want you to start treatment quickly, in the next few days. And then we'd be looking at an operation.'

'We don't actually live here,' I say apologetically. 'I told them that the other night. I don't know if my travel insurance will cover it.'

Colin nods, peers at Henry, at Rachel.

'I live here,' Rachel says. 'My parents have just arrived on holiday. We've been wondering if Medicare might cover the cost of treatment, if there's some kind of agreement in place with the NHS.'

'We'll have to investigate that,' Colin says, looking at Siddharth.

'What if I start the treatment here then fly back to Scotland for the operation?'

Colin nods, Siddharth scribbles something on his pad – maybe *buy cat food, defrost freezer*. 'My preference would be for you to have the operation here if you begin the treatment here. You're going to be very weak. And the operation will be big. I think maybe sixteen hours. That's a long time. And if you're weak . . . If you want to go back home to start the treatment there, I'd advise you to do that quickly. We need to move fast. Would that be the best course of action?'

He looks at me, sitting there with my hand over my mouth trying to stop myself from laughing, crying, screaming, looks at Rachel, holds her gaze.

'I'm sorry,' Henry says, sitting up, leaning forward limply. 'I don't mean to be rude. But that's my daughter.' He points at Rachel. 'I'm Margaret's husband. You should be asking me, not my daughter.'

Siddharth looks mortified. Me too. But Colin's a professional. He wheels his chair towards Henry, lays a hand on his shoulder. 'I know,' he says. 'You're going to have a lot to deal with. I know that. You have many things to do and think about.'

Can he tell Henry's in a bad way, his anxiety a tin opener hooked onto the lip of his psychosis and cutting circles through his meds? Of course he can.

Henry looks at him, through him, falls back into a state of silence.

238

'You can call me any time,' Colin says, handing me a card with his number. 'You'll have questions. Day or night, it's fine.'

2021

Rachel, Gem and the boys are ambling through a park with a dog – a puppy. Have they bought a puppy? Is it someone else's? It's gorgeous – a golden retriever. I'd love to pet it.

William's wearing a face mask again, as are Rachel and Gem. Ewan isn't, and I still don't know why. Is he immune? Is he the contagion? Two children, both alike in dignity, but only one with the power to kill.

This will sound nasty, I know, but they've all put on weight since I saw them last. Not an incredible amount, but it's noticeable. They look softer, rounder. I suppose there's nothing wrong with that – these are matters of the flesh, and the flesh barely matters in the end. To its fleeing tenant, I mean. Others will find ample use for the breast that no longer trembles, the unquivering loin. Flesh feeds flesh and furnishes microorganisms that make a miasma minging enough to intimidate other munchers or spur them to spew. Salmonella, *E. coli*, necrotising fasciitis – trillions of bacteria, viruses and fungi that live in and on us. We are their hosts, the subject of their favourite toasts.

Bottlebrush trees – I remember those. The birds, I think, are rosellas. There's a rusting artillery gun that looks like it hasn't been fired for many years, which is probably for the best in a public park. Swings and a see-saw – the boys ignore those now, must be twelvish, tenish, elvish, play tennis. In any case, the play park has yellow and black tape around it like a crime scene and a sign that says: *No Entry*.

239

Most of the other park visitors are wearing masks too, disposable ones, mostly, but some that look flashier. I don't think Earth's atmosphere has collapsed – they'd all be dead like me. There may have been a leak at a chemical plant, although the masks look a little flimsy for that. Or the country could be on fire again. Nearly 3 billion mammals, reptiles, birds and amphibians were killed or displaced in a recent conflagration, caught in the flames, suffocated by the smoke, or starved and dehydrated, their habitats destroyed, their predators emboldened. Or did I dream that? Do I even dream? And if I do, would I have had such a nightmare? Charred native birds washed up on hazy beaches, burnt koalas drinking from plastic water bottles, road-sides littered with mammalian carcasses, skinks scurrying across smoking charcoal, kangaroos silhouetted against white-hot flora, frogs frying, 80-million-year-old rainforests dying, a eucalypt inferno ripping through a landmass bigger than Scotland and releasing 700 million tonnes of carbon dioxide.

But I would expect the sky to be smokier, and even then, why are the youngest children not being protected? Is it a pagan sacrifice – give up the young, placate the sun?

'We could sit for a bit,' Rachel says.

The exercise, it's maybe too much for them. Maybe that's part of the malady – it stops them moving, makes them want to stay home and eat crisps and chocolate all day.

'Maybe here,' Ewan says, sitting down on the grass without waiting for a consensus, holding the puppy by the lead.

The others sit too, Rachel loosening the button on her jeans discreetly – I can see it – before getting down.

'Well, this is nice, being out of the house,' she says.

'I suppose,' William says.

They all look bored, oxygen depleted, vitamin D deprived, but especially William. He seems completely over it.

A man kicks a football – one of those funny Australian ones shaped like a pig's bladder – to his daughter. It might not be his daughter, I'm just guessing. He's wearing a face mask but the girl – she'd only be six or so – isn't. Let her die, protect our crops.

'We should have brought some food,' Gem says.

'Can we go home now?' William asks.

'You can let Sadie off the lead for a minute,' Rachel says to Ewan.

Sadie – little Sadie.

Ewan unclips Sadie and she runs a short distance, her golden ears flapping, turns, bounds back, sniffs the ground, scratches at it. What's there? What's under there? Good girl, Sadie. She rubs her back on the grass. That feels good, doesn't it. Good girl.

'It's my mum's anniversary tomorrow,' Rachel says.

'Shit, that's right,' Gem says. 'How you feeling?'

'Oh, you know,' Rachel says. Her tone makes it sound like she's upset about it, even though I've been dead for – how long? – seven or eight years. I'm glad, in a way, that she still marks the date. I was always good with people's birthdays, bad with their deathdays. My father, the twelfth of November. My mother, the fifteenth of February. But anyone else, who knows . . .

'Does that mean we're going to the Dandenongs tomorrow?' Ewan asks.

'We can't, you idiot,' William says.

'Hey, enough,' Gem snaps.

'I'm just saying. We're not allowed to go that far.'

'OK, just calm down,' Rachel says. 'We're all a bit tired, that's all.'

They should rest, let Sadie dig some holes for them to lie in, feel the worms squirming up their nose, the larvae lounging in their ears, the pupae cocooning on their pupils. I'd give anything to sleep but have nothing to give. If you'd seen me sleeping, before I mean, chortling in my sleep, sleeping in my chortles.

I'd forgive

you'd not forget

Or if not to sleep, to be less awake, less compos mentis, even though I've literally and figuratively lost my mind. Something's not right. I have the logical and comparative skills of . . . I don't know. I'm as stumped as a . . . blank. When I was a girl, I left my bag of bobby-dazzlers in the classroom, or maybe the playground, but when I looked it was gone and I never found it again – I'd lost my marbles. Did that happen? Did I happen? Am I currently happening?

Sadie runs off again, plays with another puppy, sniffs its backside. Dogs have anal sacs located either side of the anus at four and eight o'clock, foul-smelling glands, or nasal nirvana if you're Sadie.

'We could plant a new tree for Grandma in our garden,' Ewan says.

'I suppose we could,' Rachel says. 'What kind of tree would be good, do you think?'

'You don't even remember Grandma,' William says to Ewan.

'How do you know?' Ewan asks.

'You were a baby. You still are. Baby. Baby. Baby.'

'William, enough,' Gem says.

What's got into him? I'd have bashed the girls' heads together if they behaved like that. No – I never hit them, Henry either. But Rachel, from twelve to twenty, even older, there were so many times I'd have loved to box her ears. It's an unfulfilled (and unfulfillable) ambition of mine to punch someone, to know what that feels like. It looks so satisfying in films, the noise it makes . . . They're not really making contact,

242

of course, and the sound effects are mostly violent acts against vegetables and animal matter. A bone snap – celery. A human cheek – flank steak. A stab – a chicken being knifed. Henry and I came out of the cinema once to find two men brawling on Union Street, their sleeves rolled up, their arms poised like pugilists. They were going to town but their wallops sounded watered down.

Still, I wish I'd done it, just once, to someone, anyone, who deserved it. Even if they didn't – what does it matter in the long run? *Kapow! Kablam!* You apparently had to be careful not to break your fingers and thumb, sprain your wrist.

Ewan is tying a knot in Sadie's lead that the others either don't notice or don't care about. 'The thing I don't understand about life is, what's the mission?'

'That's a good question,' Gem says.

'I don't know any good answers,' Rachel says. 'What do you think, mate?'

'I don't know,' Ewan says.

'Because you're a baby,' William says,

'Well, what do *you* think?' Rachel asks William. 'Come on then, smarty pants. What's the point of life?'

'To call Ewan a baby.'

That's just rude. What's got into him?

'Do you remember those stories I used to tell you, with Alyosha and Ilya?' Rachel asks.

'Maybe,' William says.

'I do,' Ewan says. 'The Angry Tree.'

'Wasn't it the Augury Tree?' Gem says, laughing.

'Do you remember what the moral was?'

'They had to win stuff,' Ewan says. 'Lollies, medals . . .'

'They were stories for babies,' William says.

I'm in the back of an ambulance with Eva and a man in a bottle-green uniform. Green, how I want you green . . . one of Eva's favourite poems, by Federico García Lorca. It's called 'Romance Sonámbulo' and she can recite it off by heart in Spanish and English. *Verde* . . . That's the word for green, apparently. *Green flesh, green hair, with eyes of cold silver.* He's called Leo, the paramedic, and he has sexy stubble, white teeth, a cracking accent.

I'm lying on a stretcher bed (Leo insisted) and they're in swivel chairs next to cupboards and monitors, IV equipment, oxygen tanks. It's roomier inside than you might think when you see ambulances flashing by. There's no siren, though – it's not that serious. Just a run-of-the-mill dying woman with a mask on her chest in case she needs some air, but she doesn't, I don't, right now. How would that look to Rachel?

The phone trills three times, four.

'Hey, Mum, what's up?' Her image takes longer to materialise than her voice, but I can see her now, and she me. 'Where are you?'

'We're just on our way to the hospital,' I say. 'They thought it was best that I come in. I've been a wee bit short of breath.'

'You're going to the hospital?' she asks. 'Is that an ambulance?' She sounds fretful, looks uneasy. It's night-time there, must be. She's in her bedroom, but dressed, wasn't sleeping. Where's Gem? She might be with the boys.

'It's just a precaution,' I say. 'But I wanted to let you know.'

'Will they keep you in overnight?'

'I don't know, dearie. Your sister thought it was best to call the hospital, just in case.' I turn my head, smile at Eva, who grins. She and Leo have been exchanging furtive glances and might get married and have children, or at least enjoy a tryst behind Juan's back before she returns to Spain and Leo's swept forth in an endless sludge of bites, broken bones, burns and lacerations. *Your white shirt staining, three hundred dark roses blooming.* No, they won't share physical intimacy, as far as I know. I don't know everything; I don't know anything. I'm knowing less as I go – have you noticed that? Who even are you?

Silence, stasis – Rachel's screen might have stuck. Some movement. More silence. Is she buffeting?

If you'd seen my buffeting – once upon, I mean. Is that what it's called – buffeting?

'I'm worried about you, Mum.'

'Oh, I'm OK, love. For now, I mean, I'm fine.' Silence. I don't know where we are in relation to the hospital.

'So, I'll be able to call you there?' Rachel asks. 'I'll be able to talk to you?'

'Yeah, I think so, love. Eva will have my phone if I'm sleeping or anything.'

She looks upset – it's my tone, I can't help it. I'm trying to be reassuring but for Christ's sake I'm in the back of an ambulance, looking and sounding like I'm on my last legs, or on my last puny shoulders and withered bum muscles, my heavy legs up on a stretcher bed. She knows it's imminent. Intuition's unnecessary now, even though, looking back, I wish mine had been stronger. I don't sense this will be the last time we talk – I'd be genuinely surprised.

The gypsy girl was swinging
above the water tank.
Green flesh, green hair . . .

'Mum. I . . . I'm worried about you. Mum . . .'

'Don't worry about me, dearie. I love you. I'll call you when I'm settled in, or Eva will. Don't bother your dad with it. If you were planning to phone him, I mean. He's still in Cornhill, he'd only fret.'

'Mum, I . . .'

'Hey, I'll give you a laugh. You'll never believe this, but Leo, our paramedic, is from New Zealand. We thought that was a funny coincidence.'

'I just want you to be comfortable, Mum.'

'I'm perfectly comfortable,' I say, turning to smile at Eva and Leo, spinning the phone round so Rachel can see them.

'Oh, um, hello,' Leo says. *Green wind*. He's bashful. I don't mind that in a man. *Green branches*. 'Your mum said you live in Australia, hey. That's cool.'

'Yeah,' Rachel says. 'So . . . what part of New Zealand are you from?'

2015

It's nice to see Henry walking. The electro-therapy has obviously worked – he's galvanised. But how did he get here? He must have bussed or walked all the way from Torry. He's brushed his hair, his fleece jumper looks clean, his jeans are pressed, bless him.

He carries a bouquet of white carnations towards and into the Gramps. We're of a similar mind, it seems. He wants to get away from everything and I do too. We're both, right now, where we want to be, although I'd rather be alive.

The early morning light – it's summer and the sky is clear, that's something. Neither of us says anything. It's a shame we can't talk, but that was never our strong suit anyway.

I hope he's safe. A man of his age, walking in the Gramps with only his invisible wife for company. He'll be fine, I'm sure. But if anyone leaps out, a couple of crazed youths, say, who have spent the night on the hillside shooting up heroin and now need money for breakfast and more smack, or just want to rough up Henry because he's confused and weak, all of them in a dissociative state . . . Giraffes often die thanks to ageing joints that stop them fleeing beasts of prey. The thought of Henry trying to run, falling onto his hands and knees, hyenas and lions tearing strips from him, it doesn't bear thinking about. The beech trees – I'll contemplate those instead. The gorse and ferns. The willow scrub. Scots pine, larch, oak, alder, birch. The crunch and pop of stones under Henry's cut-price loafers.

He's not walking quickly, by any stretch. But it's faster than I've seen him move in years. It's amazing what a bit of electricity can do.

He reaches the end of one path, joins another, the bushes almost as tall as him, dodders eastward and . . . I know exactly where he's going and, for the first time since dying, I feel genuine excitement.

I told the girls I wanted my ashes dispersed at the lookout spot – I have so many good memories there, with them, with Sam, with Champ, with Henry, but particularly, I have to say, on my own. The view and the solitude – it was my place for reflective repose when flying solo was still something I chose. If they could scatter me there, I said – scatterbrained as I was, as I am – that would be lovely. My final resting place in the event of the university knocking back my generous offer to let first-year anatomy students dissect me or forensic scientists club and maim me, leaving me out in the elements to observe my state and rate of decay. I still can't believe they didn't want me. Rachel told me they wouldn't even entertain taking her cadaver in Australia because she'd lived in the UK during mad cow disease, her deceased meat potentially compromised by diseased meat. Just scatter me, I told the girls. If they snub me, just tip me out by the picnic bench, that'll be fine, no need for one of the little commemorative headstones – they look a bit naff.

I didn't know they'd done it, that they'd been able. Not Rachel – she would have been back in Australia by then, running off – again – when it mattered most. But Eva, it must have been her. Bless you, Eva. Or even Barb – she was proving herself quite the pal post-mortem.

Henry turns into the picnic area. Birds squawk and fly away. Something stirs in the bushes, through the pines, a dog, two dogs – hey Champ, hey Sam. Come here, boys. It's probably a squirrel, a doe, a hedgehog, I don't know.

Henry stops and I stop too, by his shoulder, feeling . . . happy – I can relax, finally. He takes in the view. It all looks flatter somehow. Greener. *How I want you, green*. Greyer. The curving coastline, the city, our city. We look north-east, can see all the way to Peterhead, north-west towards the Cairngorms and Aviemore. The spreadeagled sky. The wide water, oil rigs on the horizon. Norway, we can see that from here. Only joking. Siberia – you can't see that either, but you can feel its damp gulag chill if you have a functioning body.

Breathe it in, Henry. You're a widower, but you're free. And no. No, don't cry, Henry. Henry. No widow, no cry.

He wipes his eyes with his free hand, looks at me, through me, behind, as if someone might be there, someone with a camera who's been hiding in the bushes camouflaged for days in the hope of catching the lesser spotted *Henricus homosapiens lacrimabundus* sobbing at the memory of his wife of forty-odd years. Henry, cry as much as you want, there's no shame in it. Please cry, I'm sorry. He starts again, sniffles, coughs, tears.

Another rustle in the bushes. Sam, here boy. Sam!

Henry straightens the paper cone holding the white carnations, shuffles over to the little headstones. They didn't get one for me, did they, against my dying wishes?

'I miss you and I'm sorry,' he says, struggling to get down on his knees in front of a stone that says

blood pooling at my feet (no feet)

before a headstone that says—

my heart

I have no heart, don't want one

it hurts

a stone

Chapter 20

2014

I saw no stone, no stone no, but if I did, I would fashion it into a large disc and roll it across the entrance of a tomb. If three women came upon it early in the morning with anointing spices, they'd find no stone, tomb or body because I saw none of those things and they don't exist, so help me god.

My eyes are closed and will stay that way, no question. Champ is sleeping under the footrest of my big brown hospital chair. Rachel's lying back on the sofa, her head immobile but, somehow, still vibrating high-frequency disapproval. She doesn't want to hear what's coming from Eva. Neither of us do.

That's not strictly true. I'm listening because I enjoy hearing the girls hold forth. But I also don't want to, because it might make Rachel feel bad about herself, and that's something at which Eva unintentionally excels. I'm sure her students in Spain don't see her as supercilious. But she's probably more relaxed around them, lets the context do the talking – she's a teacher, of course she's a know-it-all, she's supposed to be. When she talks to Rachel, there's a self-defensiveness that thickens her delivery, clots her tongue, makes it hard for her to hold.

I could change the topic. The weather, it's been nice, still is – that glorious late evening light wending through the front window, the long shadows, the fleecy golden clouds, the last green ray of sunset still ahead of us. Or the open bottle of tempranillo by the sofa, we could have more of that. And hey, that's right, my biological functions are slowing to an irreversible halt – let's chew over that. Not that I want to, really – I'd rather die.

Rachel's book is splayed like a tent on her stomach. She seems to be summoning goodwill from imperceptible gods in the rafters.

'So, yes, Robert's in love with Victor,' Eva says. 'Victor's fed him a fishy story and he's gobbled it down, bones and all. Poor Robert's starving, that's why. So, of course, when Victor's corpse is laid out in a cabin, Robert's going to see the monster there, standing over it, in its *loathsome, yet appalling hideousness*. Or think he sees it. It's grief. It makes us delusional. Drives us out of our minds. Robert writes as much, doesn't he? *My tears flow; my mind is overshadowed by a cloud of disappointment.* And then, what, two seconds later, the monster's somehow on the ship?'

Rachel coughs slightly, and here it comes, the snidey remark, she can't help herself . . . but no, she was just clearing her throat.

'The monster can't stay for long, though, and nobody else on the ship will see it. It just wants to say a few unrealistically eloquent words to Robert and bid farewell to its father-creator. After which, it'll leap from the ship and slide off across the frozen sea in its ice-buggy. To do what? To throw itself on a funeral pyre, no less, where it will *exult in the agony of the torturing flames.*'

With that, she pauses and sips some wine en route to further pontificating, I mean expounding. It's a pointless line of enquiry in the grand scheme of things, even the smallest scheme, there is no scheme, but that's OK.

'So, here's something I don't get,' Rachel says. 'I'm fine with the idea that the monster doesn't exist, or even that Victor doesn't. But that's clearly not what Mary Shelley intended. She writes about it in the introduction. Hang on . . .' She thumbs through the pages, is looking it up. 'Yeah, so, she's just talked about Victor, says *he's kneeling beside the thing he had put together.* And then, talking about the monster: *I saw the hideous phantasm of a man stretched out, and then on the working of some powerful engine, show signs of life, and stir with an uneasy, half-vital motion.* So the monster must be real. I mean, unless I'm misreading it, that's definitely what Mary's saying.'

I could respond but won't. The three Marys at Jesus's tomb in Jerusalem . . . did anyone believe what they were saying? That they went with myrrh but there was no body? The three Marys at Calvary – was it Jesus on the cross, for sure, and not a doppelganger or his brother James? The three weird sisters in Macbeth – was it true that fair was foul and foul was fair? My best chance at playing the honest broker is to pretend I'm unconscious, which – even watching myself now – I might be. I'm no longer sure I'm feigning it.

'You can't believe everything an author claims,' Eva says, and she's off again, will keep going with alternate readings and theories, wheedling and needlessly needling at Rachel.

Of course there are different ways of seeing stories. Of course.

A sixteen-ton Lancaster bomber falls through the night sky with six tons of unexploded ordnance, its released human masters plummeting, trying to activate their parachutes. For me, Würzburg is primarily where my Grandad Duncan drowned in a lake or became a twenty-eight-year-old water-baby who had to earn redemption through a series of moral adventures. He was lost to us all, but to Nana Jean and my mother in particular, his remains creating endless ripples, or not even – a splash, just one, but then snagged by his chute cords under the surface of our lives.

I don't know how far he and his crewmates were from Würzburg when they leapt but I do know theirs was one of more than two hundred planes that night, almost all of which held formation and blanketed the city with thousands of incendiary bombs, its hospitals, suburbs and medieval town centre obliterated in an apocalyptic firestorm. Those who could, ran in flames to the river, jumped in and drowned. Firefighters tried, and failed, to flood the streets. Children and adults took shelter in the cathedral and churches only for the very stone to liquefy around them. The objective of the raid was to break the spirit of the German people, and it did. Nobody exulted in the agony of those torturing flames. It was a monstrous affront to humanity.

'Plausibility's a pliable entity,' Eva says. 'But you don't want to believe Mary Shelley, of all people. I mean, the author's dead in every sense of the word. I don't know if you've read any Barthes?'

Champ whimpers, must be dreaming. Me too, or sleeping at least. My head is lolling, mouth open, my denture plate hanging loose.

2017

'No, you do it, honey,' Gem says. 'If you don't mind.'

I love Gem. Have I mentioned that? Her hair has grown thicker and longer, like William's and Ewan's limbs. William is seven, maybe eight. Ewan is five, maybe six. All four of them are sitting on beautiful shiny cushions, the boys in their pyjamas, Gem and Rachel in leggings and T-shirts. Gem's extension to the house is done, or appears that way from the living room. It may have been completed for years already. I can see some of it through the hallway, past the kitchen, opening like a tulip, soft and exquisite. The boys must have their own rooms now. I'd like to see the pictures on their walls, their teeny bedspreads, tuck them in like little Baby Bears. Eat them. Will you show Grandma your rooms, boys?

I'd have loved a house like theirs but in Scotland or Spain. Australia didn't do it for me, or maybe that was circumstantial. When I think about it, the people I met there, Tash and Pete, Colin the Transylvanian doctor and a dozen or so other medical staff, they were exceptionally nice, and I wish them all well. It's just hard to cross the threshold when everyone says you're at death's door.

I've been gone for at least a couple of years. The little family's grieving days are over for now, but they'll return, they always do, as sad as a rental property with its furniture removed.

They're focusing on life, as they should. You can spend your whole life thinking about death, and then, like me, your whole death thinking about life. Hopefully not – I still pine for peace, feel confused, all out of puff. This is not the afterlife we were promised. Bring on the entropy . . .

'OK,' Rachel says. 'So Ilya and Alyosha had to swim across a big lake in the Fantastic Forest. But it was less like their normal swimming competitions and more like a three-legged race in the water.'

'What's that?' Ewan asks.

'Oh, you know, mate. Remember that time at Kinder when you and Archie tied your legs together and the teacher needed to cut the string?'

'Not really,' he says.

William snuggles into Gem, lays his head on her chest, looks like he might suck his thumb. His skin, it looks so clean, Ewan's too. Not because they've washed, although I'm sure they've had their faces wiped. It's just young skin, so fresh, so moist. You don't notice it at the time but it's practically dripping. Ewan's eyes are already half-closed, William's are heading that way too. Ewan backs his cushion further into the bay of Rachel's legs. The floor lamp casts a warm glow, a lighthouse in the distance, and, oh, I could fall asleep too. Can I do that? Can I rest now, please?

'They knew there was gold at the other side of the lake, and that they could take as long as they wanted. Hours. Days even.'

'How far is it to the gold?' William asks.

'Like the Brunswick Baths,' Rachel says. 'But ten times longer than that.'

'Woah, that's a big lake,' Gem says.

They're in a good place, she and Rachel, I can see it.

'Do they have armbands?' Ewan asks.

'No armbands,' Rachel says. 'They were banned after Lizaveta the lumberjack's daughter used hers as boxing gloves.'

'Alyosha and Ilya just had to help each other as best they could. They tied a thick elastic band around Ilya's right ankle and Alyosha's left, counted to three, and jumped in.'

'Was it cold?' Ewan asks, rubbing the tops of his arms as if he's in the water.

'Icy cold,' Rachel says, curving an arm round his belly. 'But they swam quickly and soon felt much warmer. Plus, their minds were on the gold and making their mummies happy.

'When Alyosha kicked his left leg, Ilya had to kick his right. But they managed – you know why?'

'They were seals?'

'No . . . I mean, yes, that's right, Will, they were becoming seals. They didn't notice at first. But then Ilya said, *Hey Alyosha, your face looks a bit flat, like you have a snout.* Alyosha said, *Oh? Yours too, Ilya. I didn't know you had whiskers.*

'They looked over their shoulders and saw that their legs had joined together for real. The elastic was gone and they only had three legs between them, but not for long – you know why?'

'One of their legs falls off,' Ewan says, nodding.

'Ew,' Gem says. 'This is getting a bit dark, isn't it, love?'

Rachel laughs. 'Their legs were no longer legs but had become flippers to propel them through the water. They were separate now – blubber brothers with short fur where their skin used to be. They had little claws on their front flippers, pointy teeth and their ears were just holes without a flap.'

'How do they hear things?' William asks.

'They just could,' Rachel says. 'But the only things they needed to hear were the little roars and honks they made as their bodies glided through the lake.

'Until, there it was, on the embankment – the gold! *Grab it*, Ilya said. *Take it in your mouth, Alyosha.* But it didn't sound like words, it sounded like–'

'Tweet, tweet, tweet,' Ewan says.

All four of them laugh. Me too. Hahaha, I have no mouth, no diaphragm, am consumed by the one thing I can't face up to even though I've seen the stone and will leave no stone unturned in my quest to convince myself otherwise.

'*Honk, honk*,' Rachel says. 'But they understood each other because they were both seals now. Alyosha took the gold in his mouth and they turned and started swimming back the way they came. Their mummies would be so proud of them.'

'Like you are of us,' William says.

'Exactly,' Rachel says.

'We're so proud of you both,' Gem says, kissing William's head, patting at the dinosaur on his pyjama top.

'Ilya was able to go faster because he wasn't carrying the gold, but then he heard something . . .'

'Honk, honk,' Ewan says.

'Exactly. *Honk, henk, help.* Alyosha had turned back into a boy and the gold was too heavy for him. He was struggling to stay afloat. What should Ilya do? Try to rescue him or run off to find an adult who could help?'

'It's getting late, love,' Gem says, smiling and rubbing Rachel's leg. 'Shall we wrap this one up for now?'

Rachel winks – the boys are still calmly attentive. 'Alyosha shouted to Ilya: *Help. Help. We should have stayed tied together. I'm sinking, Ilya. Help me.*'

'Honk, honk,' William says.

Gem looks concerned and I don't blame her. What a terrible story – it's awful, Rachel, make it stop.

2014

Rachel is sitting on the edge of her bed in Melbourne, crying, William and Ewan kneeling on the mattress either side of her. It might not be the day I die, but it's not long after. I'm guessing a week, estimating a day, a fortnight, that Ewan is three and William five.

But I'm fairly certain I've departed recently and that's why Rachel's sad. She wanted to be there for me in Aberdeen when the lights went out and wasn't – but she was there when it mattered most. If I could tell her that, just whisper it in her ear. I didn't need you at the final curtain, Rachel, but was happy you dropped in for most of the last act. You have your own family to worry about and I don't blame you completely for ruining most of my life but hold you and your father equally responsible – how could you both? I blame

blast fudging fudge

A static shock sending electrons from surface to hand – it feels like that but much stronger, a current passing through my body (no body).

I'm

all out of lily pad

have no puff, only

Ewan's little face. He's sad for his mum, of course he is. He wants her to be happy. William too, he's holding Rachel's hand so tenderly. My two, the girls, when they were William's age or older.

When they were twelve, sloppy and brackish

the summer of the Piper Alpha disaster, all of us shedding tears in separate rooms – me, Henry, Rachel. Eva.

'It's normal that Mummy's feeling upset,' Rachel says. 'I loved my mum, and she really loved you boys.'

'It's a shame she couldn't stay for longer in Melbourne,' William says.

'I love Ramma,' Ewan says.

The sweetheart. He's forgetting me already, they both are. The photo of William craning to kiss me on his third birthday – they have that one printed out, as does Henry, as do I. That's where I'll live for William, in that one picture, looking grey and prone to further fading. There's one of me with Ewan too – there must be. I feel so connected to Ewan, to both boys.

Rachel is sobbing, her head down. *You'll look after her, Ewan. I know you will.*

'I'll look after you, Mummy,' he says.

'We could go to the park later, if you're still alive,' William says.

'Thanks, darling,' Rachel says, wiping her nose.

Love your mummies, boys. Love them always.

'Love you, Mummy,' Ewan says.

'Love you too, Mummy,' William says.

2014

Rachel's in the air, on her way to see me in the country of eternal light.

'Ladies and gentlemen, we'll shortly be starting our descent into Aberdeen, where the weather's a respectable twenty-one degrees Celsius, seventy degrees Fahrenheit. The cabin crew will be coming through shortly to clear away any rubbish or unwanted items. Please be ready for them and thanks again for flying with us today.'

The short skip from London comes after a long jump from Dubai, another from Kuala Lumpur, another from Melbourne. She has her hoodie pulled up, her earphones in, is staring at an unwanted sausage and greasy bacon.

She's a little squished in her window seat, her legs – like Eva's – longer than the optimal length for economy flying. She looks wiped out, poor thing, props an elbow on the oblong windowsill.

Congealed egg has fallen from her fork into her copy of *Frankenstein*, greasing the pages:

if I could banish (egg-stain) *from the human frame, and render man invulnerable to any but a violent* (egg-stain).

She'll land soon. Champ and I must be waiting in my car behind the main airport carpark, listening to the helicopters.

I'm sleepy, could sleep, can't sleep.

Champ will be lying with his head on his front paws on the back seat and I'll have a bowl on my lap. On the radio, quiet under the hiss of the helipad with its workers going to and from the rigs, a man and woman will be discussing the referendum, saying it's only three months away. Independence – I like the idea, won't live to see the reality, more's the pity.

I felt delighted then, delighted now. To smell her, to feel her, the flesh of my flesh.

1987

I'm in stitches, only joking . . .

I'm with Barb, poor Michael, Barb's Michael, a handsome lad – his mother a great beauty, his father a fine-looking man.

We stand in her lobby for the longest time, holding and crying. The tears trickle and tickle, the dark smell of her skin, my hand on the back of her head. There's nothing you can say, not really. It's just about being there, bearing witness, or at least not running away.

I drive us down to the beach in Henry's van, on a whim – it's good to change the scenery, add some shells and seaweed. I'd have brought Sam if I'd known but he's at home with Henry and the girls – it's a Saturday, still early.

It's not warm, we could hardly go swimming. The tide's been in but is leaving now, chasing the moon. We walk along the wettest sand because it's firmer there, but there's still plenty of yield. We're heading towards Footdee – we'd be, what, thirty-seven, thirty-eight. Our hair . . . in our defence, it was the eighties.

Barb's cheeks are begonia red, her eyes watery, as they've been now for days, drawing tides from bad tidings. She waxed into motherhood before me, is waning earlier too. An orange tanker ship on the horizon, two distant oil rigs, the vast body of water clawing at the sand by our feet, its frothy fingers trying to pull it, pull us

to somewhere, or close by

the lighthouse, after which we'll go for an insipid instant coffee and say very little, not needing to, but this sensation, now, I mean, not then

of going under, legs kicking at

Those red and white circular lifebuoys on the barnacled wooden fence, their colours popping brightly from the greys, browns and greens – they'd come in handy if you ever needed them. Here, hold on to this – oops, let me try that again, keep treading water, mind that cresting wave, hold on to . . . Oops, I'll try again . . .

Our tracks diverge as we dodge the death rattles of worn-out waves. That poem Rachel had on a postcard during her brief religious phase, where two sets of footprints became one.

Have you abandoned me, spirit of dark and lonely water?
Don't be a fool, I was carrying you, precious child.

I was the fool, the unwary, had abandoned, not deliberately

. . . our groins crossing the groynes. 'Is that a jellyfish?' Barb asks.

'I think so,' I say. A blob of transparent mucus, the size and shape of a pancake. It's tempting to pick up the seagull feather lying next to it, poke the nib into the body . . . Do they feel pain? They have no heart, no brain, no bones, no lungs. They're like me, in other words, although

I'm hurting, right now

as if I've been dunked and can't get my breath back

I wasn't there

but

'Your hands look cold,' Barb says, and she's right – they have purple blotches, orange patches – I think it's my circulation. 'Give them here.' She stands directly in front of me, puts them together as if I'm praying, rubs on them, both hands at once, her breath steaming. Her eyes, Barb's eyes.

'I should be comforting you,' I say.

'You are,' she says. 'You always do.'

It feels so nice but I'm

in Aviemore, or close by, the green Scots pine, the golden hour, no

Barb cups one of my hands in one of hers, takes it carefully into her jacket pocket like a bird or a mouse.

Taking me . . .

Don't make me, I don't want to

Keep walking, we keep going, hand in hand, like a mouse, little mouse, my little Mousey.

Chapter 21

I'm in Aviemore, or close by, can see the Cairngorms through the Scots pine, so green, the hills a heathery purple. A summer evening sky – it's the golden hour, the silver hour, there's plenty more gloaming to go. It's June, maybe early July, I don't know. Birds, I can't hear any, no breeze either, just the water, deep water, *ummm*.

There's no sign of Living Margaret but I must be here because the girls are in the River Spey having the time of their lives – or Eva is, at least. Rachel must be just round the bend, floating merrily, merrily downstream. Can they touch the bottom? I doubt it. It looks cold, always does. The North Sea, this isn't the North Sea, but still – in the North Sea, the rig workers are told they'll have a matter of minutes after falling into the water before starting to feel the effects of hypothermia – or not feel them, that's the thing. The body conducts cold through a symphony of symptoms: confusion – what's happening? – clumsiness – why won't my arms work? – slurred speech, assuming you have anyone to speak to or can be bothered while several shades of sleepiness cast their aggressively somnolent shade, the heart still marking time but sluggishly, the respiratory system stifled.

The Piper Alpha – it's the same summer, isn't it? The summer it happens, but just before, maybe a week before – those poor men. I cried rivers that summer, couldn't stop – it hit me so hard. They erected a memorial at Hazlehead Park near the maze – three verdigrised men in boiler suits and helmets, the gold-leaf names of all 167 victims.

I'd prefer that Eva was on a float of some sort, or one of those rubber tyres. Or in a wetsuit. She's in her lime all-in-one swimsuit, her arms under the surface, doggy paddling, not even, just letting the water carry her, its silver sheen, her silky skin. And Henry – where's Henry? Why is Eva on her own? She's having fun, though. Is she having fun? My sense of smell has partially returned, is cutting in and out.

Living Margaret's not here because

because

Living Margaret's not here

because

she's had a fight, not a fight, an argument

no

a minor disagreement with Henry in which

I haven't come

I should and could have, right up to the last minute. I didn't even wave them off. Imagine that – no cheerio. I helped load the caravan, though . . . Did I? Is that what happened?

Said I'd be back in five with the last of our things.

The last I saw of them, of her

It was easier to pack every year – the first trip was a pain, but for the second and third there was a routine. The Tupperware, all the things we knew we'd need, others we'd almost certainly want. But there was a disagreement – was there? – with Henry, that's why I'm not

I wasn't here.

I am now. The smell of the pine needles on the grass, severed branches, wet mud and algae.

Eva – she's within touching distance of the embankment, that's good. Just hold on to a branch, any branch, and wait for Rachel – can you do that? She's travelling at speed and I'm moving with her, there's that, at least – I float quite well for someone with no surface area, there's little in the way of hydrodynamic drag. She's being carried, supported in a way, and it's picturesque, the trees, so green, the sky.

Henry had been critical of me, that's why. Not even all that critical – and not deserving of this. My arms, it was something about my arms. That I was putting on weight, or that they looked bigger. It wasn't the first time he'd said something of that sort. My behind – well, it was normal after kids, just little things like that, expressing his dissatisfaction. Was it even dissatisfaction? He was just pointing out that my arms were getting bigger, the tops of them. Maybe that was a good thing. It might have been muscle. I was no strongwoman, but I was toned that year, my biceps bulging. The running, you see. I'd been running – OK, jogging, let's call a spade a sharp-edged, long-handled implement primarily used for digging. My legs. My quads, you could see those muscles too, they had definition, more than before. They were strong, strong enough, I loved my legs.

Why won't you swim, Eva? Get closer to the side, at least.

Open your eyes, Eva.

A green branch, a fallen trunk. She grabs it, her lips blue – no, not a grab, but it catches her by the underarm, holds her in place and, thank god, she'll be fine. From here she can climb onto the embankment. It looks slippery, it's not ideal, but this is her chance and she should take it. Take your chance, Eva. Come on, Eva, take it. Hold on to the branch, use your biceps, your flexors, your hands. The roots run deep, they're secure, pull yourself up by the branch. But she's resting, that's how it looks, content to let the current cartwheel her body, her legs now pointing downstream, a leaf on her head, from the water, an early autumn leaf turned red with anthocyanins – no, there's blood coming from your head. Have you bashed your head, Eva? Ouch.

'I don't give a fig if the girls are upset' – that's what I said to Henry. I did care, of course, but I wanted Henry to know he'd crossed me, make him squint into the light emanating from me, his avenging angel.

'You take them, Henry. Use it as bonding time, father and daughters – how does that sound? Look, I've even made you some egg sandwiches for the journey.'

'Margaret.'

'Just bloody go, Henry. I'm not coming, I'm sick of being run down by you.'

Henry looking at his feet, unsure what to say next. 'What will you do?'

'I'll stay here. Four days of peace and quiet – I think I'll be fine with that. I can maybe use the time to work on my arms, try to make them a little less hideous.'

'Marg, that's not what I meant.'

She's on the move again – Eva, your chance, you may not get another, her eyes closing, to stop the water getting in, the silver water, cold skin reflecting the green surrounds.

'What am I supposed to tell the girls, Marg?'

'Tell them what you want, Henry. That I have a headache. That I'm dying. I don't care.'

'Marg.'

'Just go, Henry. And you look after them in that water. Don't take your eyes off them for a second.'

I have no eyes, take them off Eva only long enough to look down the river and it's really not ideal because the current is

268

robust, you can see it – not rapids, that would be an exaggeration, but surface dimples like cellulite, white caps signalling speed, maybe rocks and an undertow. Eva, wake up, Eva.

Eva, come on.

Funny thing is, I didn't think Henry would go without me. I thought he'd just keep apologising until I changed my mind, or have to cancel the trip and shoulder the burden of that, not this.

I haven't seen this, not even in my imagination or nightmares, haven't ever let myself. I locked it away. Locked me away.

I wasn't there.

We're moving faster now, Eva, wake up. There are rocks ahead, the river narrowing, its scope for treachery widening. Where's your sister? What's she doing? Sunning herself on the bank further upstream. Happily treading water, no concern for your wellbeing. No, she's running. They told me that, I think they did.

Rachel's running, sprinting even, from the river to the caravan site. She saw it – Eva jumping from a tree limb overhanging the water. She didn't make her do it – it wasn't a dare, they both wanted to. At worst, they'd sprain an ankle, get a bruise, but probably not, probably not, because the water ran deep there – they'd held their noses and ducked under to check the depth, on this trip, on previous, and it was deep, deep enough.

Henry told me, no, he didn't. He tried to but it wasn't true, I didn't want it to be, and not listening stopped it from ever happening – that's how it worked, two parts opacity, zero parts veracity. I didn't want to know, still don't. It can't be

Eva.

Green flesh, green hair,
Dreaming in the bitter sea.

Henry, I'm imagining this because I didn't ask, not even once in all this time, but I can picture him with sleepy eyes at the caravan door in shorts and a polo shirt asking Rachel to slow down, tell him again what's happened. And Rachel gasping, crying, saying, I've told you, Dad, I've told you. Eva slipped, I think she hurt her head. She's still in the river, the water's taking her away. Dad, come on, Dad, hurry.

And Henry, unable to think, his brain rattling between fight and flight. Why wasn't he with them? What the hell was he thinking, letting them go down to the river on their own, two twelve-year-old girls? What did he think would happen? No, it's not really so young, twelve, it's not, and yes, they were good swimmers thanks to him, but, yes, he should have been with them and, no, he didn't deserve forgiveness or redemption, then or now. I can picture him setting off at a clip, stopping, turning, eyes stricken. You wait here, Rachel. No, listen. Go to the phone at reception. Tell Fiona you need to call an ambulance, or the coastguard, I don't know. Just tell her you need help. Hurry. I'll get your sister.

Henry, running towards the river – does he? Is that what he does? It barely matters. I'm the faster runner in this era, would have never thought that possible when we were younger, and even I would have stood little chance.

Her head goes under, back out. Her skin, she's still warm, under the skin, I can feel it, she's still alive.

Green.

The water, green-brown and silver.

I didn't want to be here but now I am, smelling fish scales and rotting moss, plants and pine, rust, water, iron. The reporters, I don't care about reporters. The helicopter. I remember now, a chopper comes – whoop-de-do. But not yet. It's just me and Eva, lovely Eva, wake up, Eva, wake up.

Her eyes – they open, shut . . . Wake up, Eva, sweetheart, wake up. You have so much life ahead of you. You'll move to Spain, become a teacher, just like you always wanted. You'll be a champion debater, get a First Class Honours, have a partner called Thom and another called Juan. You'll be loved, Eva, I'll love you, you'll love me. Your sister, she'll love you, she always has. We'll be warm, Eva, the two of us. You'll be with me when I die, hold my hand. You're the best thing I ever created – you and Rachel. I love you both so much. Eva. Eva, wake up.

It's slowing, the water, the river wider, an eddy, some more rocks. Another chance, she has one here. If I could lift her – what use is being here if I can't help? The current carries her towards the bank again. This is it, Eva, open your eyes.

They're open. She reaches out for a rock, grabs it with one hand, two, good girl, Eva, good girl, pulls herself against it, her shoulders out of the water, vomits on the lichen, that's good. A deer, is that a deer in the woods, watching us? Who cares? Vomit, Eva, get it out. There's some food – it looks and smells like macaroni and cheese, a Henry speciality, but there's water too, seaweedy spew.

Her head – yes, that's right, she's bashed her head, the blood running crimson through her hair, the white of her scalp.

Your dad must be coming, I say. *He'll be here soon. I wish I could hold you, Eva. You look so cold.*

'That's OK,' she says, violet lips, shivering, skin almost translucent. 'Mum, it's fine.'

She's

Can you see me, sweetheart?

'I can see you, Mum – course I can. I've hurt my head, though. I smacked it on something. I slipped as I was jumping from a tree. It's sore, Mum.'

She holds her head, her other arm still round the rock, hugging tight, sees scarlet goo on her fingers, skin green, eyes silver.

'I'm bleeding,' she says. 'Mum, am I going to be OK?'

I don't know. Honestly, love, I don't know. If your dad can get here. He's trying, love. I know he is. He'll be running as fast as he can. We'll probably hear him calling your name any second.

'We snuck out,' she says. 'Dad fell asleep on the sofa. He didn't know we were going to the river. I'm going to get it, aren't I?'

He won't care about that, I say. *I don't either, it doesn't matter. I'm so sorry I didn't come.*

'You're here now,' she says.

I'm here now, I say.

'Love you, Mum.'

Love you too, I say. *So much. Can you just climb out of the water, pet? Your skin's a funny colour. I can't give you my hand, but you can hang on, just here, see, just over here, pull yourself from one rock to another, but hold on tight. Can you do that, Eva, can you?*

'I might just snooze for a second,' she says. 'Can you wake me when Dad gets here?'

You can't sleep, Eva. You can't. Come on. Wake up.

Her hand, I want to take it, but

it slips from the rock, one arm, then the other, and she's borne towards the centre of the river.

'Eva. Eva.'

A voice – Henry's. He's not nearby, still far away, but maybe . . .

Henry, I shout. *Down here. Henry. We're down here, hurry.*

The river has widened, the water, it's not stagnant, but it's tamer. Eva's head ducks under, shoots back out – she coughs, splutters. She's swimming, she's trying to, but clumsily.

272

Kick your legs, I say. *Try treading water.*

'OK, Mum.'

She's trying, good girl, she's trying

A 12-year-old girl has died after getting into difficulty in water at a beauty spot near Aviemore, where she was swimming with her sister.

No.

No, no, no.

Keep going, love, that's it, you're doing so well. She is. She's doing well. Henry's getting closer and I can hear – what's that? A distant helicopter, I think, its rotor system rending the sky.

You're doing great.

'Eva,' Henry cries. 'Eva.'

He's getting closer.

Emergency crews raced to the river after the alarm was raised at 8.45 p.m.

Can you still hear me, love?

'Yeah, my arms are tired, Mum, my head's sore.'

Just a little longer, dearie, can you manage that?

'I think so. Rachel's going to have conniptions. It was my idea, Mum, not hers.'

'Eva.' Henry's voice – he sounds desperate, hoarse. 'Eva.'

Can you try something, love? Take my hand. Can you try that? I reach out my hand (have no hands) and she takes it, her fingertips furrowed.

Green flesh, green hair
With eyes of cold silver.

'Eva.' Henry's voice.

273

I can't take the weight of her (feel no weight). She goes under, comes back up, startled, her legs kicking.

'Your hand feels nice,' she says. 'If I rest for a minute, will you be angry?'

Of course not, darling. But can you keep trying? They're coming, Eva – can you hear the chopper?

She was taken by helicopter to Aberdeen Royal Infirmary but passed away a short time later.

Her head cranes back, her face out of the water. 'I'm glad you're here, Mum, so I'm not on my own.'

Me too, love. Me too.

Chapter 22

1988 . . .

A sapling stripped of bark, that's how I feel – my underwood exposed to the elements. Take an axe to me, I promise to burn blue, would do it myself if I could.

Why am I still compos mentis, compost – I can't believe Eva's gone.

I can. I can believe it.

I can now.

I knew. I must have. My brain: a casket with an airtight gasket.

I knew and I didn't. Both are true, maybe neither.

I've been to the funeral now, to pay my regrets. I stood by the side wall in the crematorium, unseen, bawling without tear ducts – wanted golden brooches to stab out my eyes (no eyes). If there was a rock, I'd have dropped to my knees and slammed my open mouth into it, bashing my teeth (no teeth) again, again, again . . .

Henry and Rachel with their heads down, and me not there, a Marg-shaped hole, the Tale of the Missing Mum. I couldn't, I just

My father standing next to them, still sprightly at nearly sixty, looking dashing in his black suit, a cotton handkerchief dabbing at his eyes. My mother with one arm through his, in her dark fur coat, even though it's summertime, ashen with compassion, mascara webs on her cheeks. Others, Eva's teachers, Mrs Robertson – or Lauren – Miss Falconer, Mr Whatshisname. Rachel's friend Barry and his parents, other young people starting out.

The lanky, pink-faced minister: *Let the little children come to me and–*

I couldn't listen, didn't want to, it was hard enough watching. Barb and Des, of course. My Barb.

And Eva in a white box with a gold trim that

I couldn't

was smaller than an adult crate

Eva.

In her best dress, no doubt, the one she wore to The Corries with the green and white stripes, if it still fitted. I didn't know, don't know – what was she . . .

They'd have done her hair, slapped on more make-up than I'd have allowed at that age, my beautiful dancer in her music box, not rotating, heading head-first into the fire.

I've roared, torn my throat (no throat), ravaged myself.

Entire days, they're not days, yelling, *Let her live, let her love.*

Years, not years, dragging invisible nails through my fictive flesh, howling, *Let me leave, how could you, you bloody*

Decades, that's how it feels, bawling, squealing, falling

Apart

But I'm calmer now, however long it's been – I'm all screamed out and quietly jittering.

My girl is dead. I am dead.

So, please, I'm asking nicely, just let me go.

I don't know this park but the trees are river red gums and they're common in Melbourne – Rachel showed me some near her house when Henry and I visited. She had a book that explained how to identify them, their creamy barks wrapping wood that would look blood-red if you were to saw into it, the chemicals creating a natural antibiotic when combined with air – but they shouldn't be cut unless you really had to, and even then, probably not as a settler. Like the rest of the country, they belonged – if that was the right word – to someone else. I like their white flowers, their leaves a pale green that, to be honest, I wasn't particularly drawn to when we were there. The plants, trees and grass seemed like they needed a polish, maybe a bit more water, but now, I don't know . . . I'm seeing things differently.

I like that they're eucalypts – that's got to be healthy, a country steeped in essential, if highly flammable, oils, an open-air sanatorium. That's why it smells so good. I remember thinking that as soon as we left the airport, even as I clutched at my abdomen. And shade – the red gums provide plenty of that.

Pete, Gem's dad, has his back against a trunk, bites into a red apple. He has to eat well now, no choice, but he doesn't have to enjoy it and is exercising that right. Tash is sitting cross-legged.

She looks well, her skin healthy, lots of life in her eyes. Her grey roots are showing, but that's OK. There's nothing wrong with roots. Without them, no trees, without them, no teeth, without them, no connection to the land and other people. *Every nature, every form, every creature exists in and with each other, but they'll dissolve again into their own roots.* That was Mary Magdalene . . .

Rachel's and Gem's hair, too, I didn't notice it before – an inch of grey, the colour leached. But that's fine. They look healthy, that's what counts. The face masks – there are some on the picnic blanket, and one on Gem's wrist like a scrunchie. Ewan doesn't have one in front of him, of course. Sadie sniffs at the blanket, her front paws out ahead of her, tail wagging, good girl.

William – *hello, darling* – is scraping some hummus with a cracker that, oops, yes, breaks in half, they always do. They're not strong enough for shop-bought hummus, it's always too thick with coagulants. The humus in the earth isn't much better – crackers don't stand a chance.

Ewan hasn't had a haircut for quite some time, by the looks of it. William's frizzes and curls like Gem's, so it doesn't look as long, but Ewan's is down past his shoulders.

'Someone thought he was a girl the other day,' Rachel says. 'At the coffee shop. They were like, *Would your daughter like anything?*'

'Oh, you don't want that, Ewan,' Pete says.

'Dad,' Gem says.

'You're being sexist,' William says.

'Oh, am I now? OK, OK.' Pete raises his hands, his half-murdered apple in one.

'I'm fine being a girl or a boy,' Ewan says. 'I don't really mind.'

'That's right,' Rachel says. 'You be whatever and whoever you want, mate. Don't let anyone tell you otherwise.'

'It's so nice to see you all,' Tash says, swiping at a fly, reaching for an olive. 'To be together again like this.'

'To be allowed,' Gem says. 'We've really missed you both.'

I don't understand what's going on, only that they haven't seen each other in the flesh for ages, even though they live in the same city. It's very strange. Their protective masks – they

278

don't seem to need them permanently now but some of the people walking past are still sporting theirs. I don't know why, and probably don't need to.

'That's a gorgeous locket,' Tash says to Rachel. 'Is that new, darling?'

'No, it's actually really old,' she says, holding it up from her chest and looking at it. 'It was my mum's but I've only just started wearing it. I've been missing her more than usual, I guess.' She lifts the gold chain – hers, not mine – over her head, opens the locket before passing it to Tash. Inside, a picture of the girls as babies, no

would you believe

a photo of me, I remember it, taken by Rachel near the Gramps when we were out walking Champ, my bobbled blue cardigan, sun in my eyes, smiling.

'And this design,' Tash says, tracing a finger across the eternity knot. 'Do you . . . Oh, darling, are you OK?'

Rachel's face falls into her hands. Tash rubs one shoulder, Gem the other. The boys and Pete look concerned but not embarrassed – good: it's just Mummy having a cry in public. That's not like her, though. If I could comfort her, I would.

'Come help me get something from the car, love,' Gem says. I follow them, watch them sit on the edge of the open boot, out of sight. Rachel has a scrunched napkin in her hand, dabs her eyes.

'We can go up to the Dandenongs, to your mum's tree, if you want,' Gem says. 'It's not too far from here.'

'That could be nice,' Rachel says. 'Let's see how the boys are, though. This is the most socialising they've done in ages.' More tears, her face clenching, settling. 'I don't know why it's worse at the moment. I think it's just everything, you know. I miss her, miss both . . .'

They sit in silence, no pretence of getting anything from the car.

'You know, I'm proud of you,' Gem says. 'The way you were with your mum, never pulling her up on the Eva stuff.'

Me too, I have to say, now that I can see it all. Bloody good job, Rachel.

'It wasn't always easy,' Rachel says, searching for a clean bit of napkin and wiping her nose. 'I just told myself it was really hard on her. And on my dad.'

'And on you.'

Thank you, Gem, for being there for her, thank you thank

'Yeah, I suppose,' Rachel says.

'I feel I know her,' Gem says after a while.

'My mum? I mean, you did . . .'

'No, your sister. I feel I've known her all this time, since I've known you. That I'm still getting to know both of you.'

'She'd have adored you.'

'Same, I'm sure.'

'And made you laugh.'

'You make me laugh.'

'Eva would've too.'

She would have, that's right. I miss her laughter so much, Rachel, and yours, the way it was before. I'm so sorry, darling. I really am. I'm sorry.

'Shall we?' Rachel says.

They stand. Gem grabs a blanket before slamming the boot. And then they embrace, not romantically – the kind I could join if I was physically present, squishing in between them like the girls used to when Henry and I hugged in front of them, life force crackling from body to body to body.

I follow them back through the park, strolling (no legs).

'We were just saying how much the boys have grown,'

280

Tash says, smiling at Rachel, her expression open and warm. 'Can you believe it's been five months?'

'Let's just hope it stays this way,' Gem says. 'No more locky Ds.'

'We need to make up for lost time, don't we,' Tash says. She squeezes William's leg. 'Have you missed Nana?'

'I guess,' he says.

'And all that home-schooling,' Pete says. 'Mummy tells me you did really well, Ewan. You too, William.'

The boys shrug but seem happy. They all do, in a way. A bit tired, that's all, as if they've not seen much daylight. I suppose I'm the same, can feel sleep finally coming on.

'They're talking about opening the borders again soon,' Tash says.

'Any plans for a holiday?' Pete asks, grimacing at his apple core, laying it on the blanket.

'I don't even know where we'd go,' Gem says. 'The world seems so different now.'

'Maybe Scotland?' William says.

'Yeah, Scotland,' Ewan says.

'Och aye the noo!' Pete says.

Jesus, that's a blast from the past.

'Jesus, that's an old one,' Rachel says, and they all laugh.

I don't think they'll be going to Scotland any time soon, but that's OK. *You stay there, dearie. Your roots are strong. I love you.*

2020

It's hard to mark Hogmanay without thinking of the people and times that have passed. I never liked those nights, but this one might be different. Although that's why I don't like them – the

281

idea the year that's about to start will be different. I mean, they are, they're all different, but the implication is that they'll be better. And maybe they will be. You can always hope. Always.

Nana Jean – I remember drinking sherry with her on Hogmanay. Do people even drink sherry anymore? Do they still make it? With my parents, so many Hogmanays when they were young but seemed old, when they were old but seemed young. It's a topsy-turvy time of year, that's just how it is. With the girls, with Henry. Those early years – the only years with Eva, my darling girl.

Henry's watching TV – of course he is. The programme's called *Hogmanay 2020*, which means we're heading into 2021. Or Henry is. I'm not heading anywhere, haven't had a head for some time. I've departed, will soon be gone for good, an old acquaintance to be forgot.

A woman called Amy Macdonald with quite incredible eye shadow and a sparkly silver top is playing the guitar and singing a song that keeps asking where we're going to sleep tonight. It's a good question and a catchy song. I assume she's famous.

I put my feet up (have none) on the chair next to Henry's. We could hold hands, that'd be nice, but this is nice too, just watching TV together. Even better, from where I'm sitting, I can see the harbour. That view – have I mentioned the view? The lights on the water, the city stretched out, granite draped in darkness and obscured by the lights from ships and boats. Their crews, I can see some, little people, they're not with their loved ones, unless their loved ones are on the ships too. Maybe they'll call, or send a text, at least. *Happy New Year*, or whatever the equivalent is in their language. *Feliz Año Nuevo* – that's what they said in Spain, Eva taught us all that one Hogmanay when the girls were eight or nine.

She was a prodigy, I suppose, really would have gone to live in Spain, done great things. Or normal things. It's OK to do normal things.

'You have to say it like *anyo* and not *ano*,' she said to my mother. '*Ano* means . . . I can't say it. You know what it means, don't you, Granda?'

My father laughing. 'Yes, I know, pet.'

Rachel asking, 'What does it mean?'

'Bumhole,' Eva said. 'It means bumhole.' She covered her mouth and all of us laughed – Henry, me, my parents, the girls. Why was bumhole so funny? Is it the fact there's a hole in your bum, or is it more about what comes out of it?

'Happy new bumhole,' Rachel said, raising her glass of Ribena, and we all laughed again.

You could change the channel, Henry, see what else is on. He's not listening, can't hear me. There's a muscle twitching in his forearm – or a vein pulsing, I'm not sure which, but I hope that's not the speed his heart's beating because it's very fast. He doesn't look stressed, though, doesn't look much of anything. He's just watching the telly, me too – from the window now. I'm standing, sort of.

There was a conga line when we were young that started in Henry's parents' house and snaked outside, through the snow, picking up neighbours and friends until there were lots of us singing and dancing in the street and wishing each other a happy new year.

He's not drinking this Hogmanay. He can't. He has a physical and emotional dependence on something he can no longer depend on. I'm sorry about that, for all those years, glad he's sober now. His seven-day pill dispenser should keep him busy enough – I've no idea what's in its little compartments, shudder to think.

According to the TV there are only a couple of minutes to go before the new year. 'And what a year it's been,' the presenter says, laughing. It's a strange laugh, like she doesn't mean it in a good way. 'There's plenty to reflect on as we prepare to first-foot the nation.'

I can't first-foot anyone, but Henry could first-foot the other people in the residence, the woman – what's her name? Cath. I've seen them chatting at seated yoga – she looks rough, truth be told, but they seem to get on OK, could offer each other company, console each other. Why not? It would be better than sitting like a sad sack on his own.

'And now, let's join our lone piper on the ramparts of Edinburgh Castle.'

The TV cuts to a kilted piper playing his bagpipes in front of flames, two black tassels on his long white sporran and all sorts of military insignia on the arms of his jacket. 'Rest, Gallant Soldier' – that's what he's playing. It's good seeing him like this. The piper was so far away when I went to the Tattoo with . . . when I went there on my own. I'd have really loved to go to the Tattoo with Eva, or Rachel, even Henry.

He's in a dwam, unable to have a dram.

The countdown is on. 'Thirty seconds . . . twenty . . . ten . . .'

That's it. Bells are ringing on the TV, fireworks exploding over . . . is that Stirling Castle? It would be good if they told you. There are fireworks outside too, exploding over the harbour, the reflections making it hard to tell sky and water apart, a blaze of colour and noise, whistling, banging, bells pealing and ship horns sounding, so many of them, their plaintive drones like whales singing songs of home. I wish them well, the crews.

The girls always enjoyed watching the fireworks from our old house, would have loved the view from here. Looking out, in their pyjamas, awake later than on any other night of the year, wonder in their faces, in mine. Rachel at seventeen, we had a good Hogmanay that year too, I remember. It felt like she'd turned a corner, or that she could, that the corner was in sight and she was sizing it up. She missed her sister. I missed her too. I struggled to say that to Rachel, but she knew. Did she know? I'm sure she did.

Sam and Champ, both of them, years and houses apart, running around and barking during the fireworks – it's OK, boys, you'll be fine.

Henry's up at his window now, watching, standing next to me.

On the TV there are fiddle players and a singer with the most beautiful red hair. They'll perform 'Auld Lang Syne', as they always do. It sounds wonderful, the piano, the voice, the fiddle players waiting patiently for their moment to shine. Even above the noise from the harbour – greens, reds, yellows – it still sounds good.

And there's a hand, my trusty fiere!
And gie's a hand o' thine!
And we'll tak a right gude-willy-waught,
For auld lang syne

I never understood the lyrics but feel the sentiment. On the TV, they keep cutting to people on what looks like a computer screen – maybe fifty rectangular boxes in people's living rooms, kitchens – I don't understand, but it looks good. Some people have dressed up for the occasion, some have lights wrapped round their heads and shoulders, some are dancing on their own next to their furniture, others are crossing arms, getting ready for the quick bit.

The fiddles have started and now they're speeding up, the piano, the singer, the people in the boxes holding hands, smiling, clapping.

We'll tak a cup o' kindness yet
For auld lang syne

The water, it's ablaze, Henry's face illuminated. He's crying. Cry, Henry, you cry, my love, it's good for you. You cry. I put my hand on his shoulder, draw deep on his comforting scent, hold him close.

I can hear the music still, the lingering hangover from Hogmanay, the lone piper playing 'Rest, Gallant Soldier'.

The bathwater is just right, its temperature, its depth, but what were the words to that song?

> *In the soft meadow*
> > *they're a-sleeping*
> > > *While the*
> > > > *trees sing their lullabies*

They're not simply sleeping, you see, those soldiers – they're a-sleeping. A-sleeping and no longer a-marching because they're no longer a-live. They fell, I seem to recall, in their hour of glory. Not to worry – it was just a-falling over onto their sides in the cool grass, those who aren't quite a-sleeping takkin a cup o' kindness, bearing witness.

Just like Frankenstein's monster, clambering aboard the ship, seeing its creator's cadaver a-sleeping and Robert Walton a-weeping before, like a lord, a-leaping from the window. So what if he was a figment of their imagination? So what?

Farewell! I leave you, and in you the last of humankind whom these eyes will ever behold. Farewell! Fare

well, I'd dearly love to yawn and it feels like I might, any second now . . . I lie back (have no back) but

leaning on my scarred elbows, willing tension into those mandibles, the jaw constraining, straining until

Yes

The maw finally opening, sending blood and spinal fluid –

Keep going, love, that's it, you're doing so well

– from the brain, down into the body, the sudden intake of air, water, air . . .

My heart rate is rising, my eyelids – let's just imagine – flickering. A figment or not, I was there with my daughter – the last of humankind she beheld with those green eyes, their hint of cold silver. I was there, and I am thankful

I am relieved

I am forgiving

Of everyone and also, or almost, the hardest one

Myself

Oh

I'm so

tired

I hear the hum of a vacuum cleaner, the womb I once inhabited, they sound the same to me

or similar

not the same

and, shh, look

Henry is snoozing, Rachel is snoring, Gem is slumbering, William is dreaming, Ewan is drifting, Eva is a-sleeping, and me

The water mellow bellow morphine

I'm sinking into the land of eternal darkness

Goodnight all, goodnight

Goodnight.

Acknowledgements

Thanks to Polygon editor Alison Rae – I couldn't have hoped for a better publisher and supporter. Thanks to Martin Shaw for your help, steadfastness and encouragement. Thanks to everyone at Polygon for championing this book and many excellent others.

Thanks to June and Jean Dalgarno for being my closest allies and greatest teachers growing up, and similarly to Alexander Forman and Donald Cunningham, my fallen heroes.

Thanks to Kate Mulqueen for believing, and having the best belly laughs. And to Stuart Wilson for being a valued friend over the years.

This is the third book I've published since moving to Australia in 2010 but the first to be published in my home country, which feels like a beautiful return.